"Mind if I sit do...
It was a long, tiring drive.

"Go ahead," Marina said coldly.

Ignoring the rudeness, Stephen smiled and said, "Thanks."

He sat down then, leaning well back in the comfortable chair.

"I knew you'd be mad. That's why I didn't call. I thought you'd probably hang up on me."

"Yes, I would have. But first I would have told you exactly what I think of you."

"Oh, but you did a pretty thorough job of that the last time we were together. As I remember, you said I make rotten movies and was undoubtedly going to ruin your story."

She was caught off guard by the frank way he spoke.

He looked at her intently. "Is it your story?"

She was caught by surprise. "What do you mean? Of course, it's my story."

"Is *Casey* autobiographical?"

Dear Reader,

Spellbinders! That's what we're striving for. The editors at Silhouette are determined to capture your imagination and win your heart with every single book we publish. Each month, six Special Editions are chosen with *you* in mind.

Our authors are our inspiration. Writers such as Nora Roberts, Tracy Sinclair, Kathleen Eagle, Carole Halston and Linda Howard—to name but a few—are masters at creating endearing characters and heart-rending love stories. Their characters are everyday people—just like you and me—whose lives have been touched by love, whose dream and desire suddenly comes true!

So find a cozy, quiet place to read, and create your own special moment with a Silhouette Special Edition.

Sincerely,

Rosalind Noonan
Senior Editor
SILHOUETTE BOOKS

PAMELA WALLACE
Forever and a Day

Silhouette Special Edition

Published by Silhouette Books New York

America's Publisher of Contemporary Romance

To very special twins, Aaron and Erica Aldridge,
with love.

SILHOUETTE BOOKS
300 East 42nd St., New York, N.Y. 10017

ISBN: 0-373-09334-9

First Silhouette Books printing September 1986

America's Publisher of Contemporary Romance

Printed in the U.S.A.

Books by Pamela Wallace

Silhouette Special Edition

Love with a Perfect Stranger #63
Dreams Lost, Dreams Found #102
Tears in the Rain #255
All My Love Forever #312
Forever and a Day #334

Silhouette Desire

Come Back, My Love #13

Silhouette Intimate Moments

Fantasies #24
Cry for the Moon #48
Promises in the Dark #58
Scoundrel #83

PAMELA WALLACE

is a professional writer who has written for TV and magazines, as well as having published numerous works of fiction. Her spirited characters come alive in every page as she weaves a thought-provoking story of true-to-life romance. Ms. Wallace lives in Fresno, California.

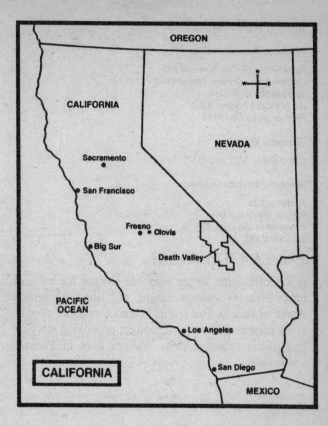

Prologue

Marina Turner sat in her rather battered, white Volkswagen Beetle convertible and stared at the Church of the Wayfarer. On this August Saturday afternoon the quaint village of Carmel on the central California coast was packed with tourists. Many of them stopped to admire the church, to walk in the sunken terraced garden next to it and to take photos.

The church was lovely. Built of white stucco in the style of old Spanish architecture, it was trimmed in blue-green wood. Normally the wide double wooden doors were open invitingly. Today they were closed and a small sign discreetly informed passersby that a wedding was in progress.

Marina's gaze had been fixed on that sign for half an hour now. She was oblivious to everything else—the passing tourists and the church itself. She was torn by conflicting emotions. Should she go in or not?

While making the one-hour drive up Pacific Coast Highway from her home in Big Sur, she had argued back and forth with herself. She didn't want to attend this wedding. But if she didn't, she knew it would deeply hurt the person she loved the most in the world.

A cool breeze from the ocean only a half mile away blew a wavy strand of her short, tousled hair across her cheek. Irritably she brushed it back. Her wide, full mouth turned down at the corners in a frown, and her gray eyes, so startlingly pale in contrast to her glossy black hair, shone with unshed tears.

Nagging at her was something her mother, Caroline, had said once. "The most important thing is to do what has to be done when it's the hardest to do. The worst thing that can be said about anyone is that he was at his best only when the going was easy."

At the time Marina had thought she understood. But she hadn't. Only now did the full meaning of those words come home to her. Because now she was faced with the hardest thing she'd ever had to do.

Glancing at her wristwatch, she saw that it was one minute to two o'clock. The wedding would begin at two. She had no more time to put off making a decision. Either she walked into that church right then, or she turned her car around and headed back down the coast.

With characteristic impulsiveness she stopped trying to make a decision and simply acted. She opened the car door and got out, slammed the door behind her and hurriedly crossed the narrow street. Quietly she opened one of the double doors of the church and slipped into the vestibule.

The pews were mostly empty. Only a few people had been invited to the wedding.

At the far end of the small church a minister stood at an altar. From opposite sides a man and a woman entered and met in front of the altar. Marina felt her stomach constrict in a tight knot and she had to force herself to exhibit a composure she didn't feel.

The man was darkly handsome in an elegantly cut blue suit. His coloring—black hair flecked with gray at the temples and an olive complexion—hinted at a Latin heritage. Despite his conservative attire and air of restraint, a flash of silver in his gray eyes suggested he had a passionate Latin temperament as well.

Those eyes were surprisingly pale in his dark face—and awfully like Marina's.

The woman, like the man, wasn't young. Fine lines barely discernible at the corners of her eyes and mouth revealed she was past forty. But she was as beautiful as all brides long to be. Her glistening blond hair shone with white-gold highlights and was pulled back in a sleek chignon. Her milky complexion was as fair as Marina's. In the pale oval of her face, her brown eyes were dark and haunting.

A simple dress of cream-colored silk came just to midcalf, and she carried a tiny bouquet of white baby's breath surrounding one yellow rose.

For an instant the man and woman had eyes only for each other. Then, as if sharing the same thought, each turned slightly to cast a quick glance at the wedding guests.

Intense disappointment was etched in their expressions. Then, when they saw Marina standing at the very back of the church, the disappointment turned to relief.

The woman flashed Marina a quick, tentative smile. Instinctively Marina started to respond, then stopped.

She ignored the man completely.

The ceremony was brief and to the point. Only once did it veer from the strictly traditional. That was when they vowed to trust their love for each other and to let nothing come between them ever again.

Marina knew why this couple had written those words. So did everyone else there, for there wasn't a dry eye in the church.

Then the man slid a plain gold band onto the woman's finger. There was something fiercely possessive in the way he held her hand, as if he was afraid that someone might try to tear them apart.

The woman looked up at him, her brown eyes locked with his gray ones, her face transfixed with a tenderness as compelling as his fierce possessiveness. And as the minister said, "I declare you man and wife," the bride smiled exultantly, as if she had cheated fate itself.

When the bride and groom kissed, there was something magnificent in the way they claimed each other. Marina felt a sharp tug at her heart and wondered if she would ever know the kind of transcendent joy this man and woman had found in each other.

Then, just as they drew apart, Marina turned and fled— out of the church, back to her car, away from Carmel and down the coast highway. She couldn't bear to see them one moment longer, to talk to them, to congratulate them. They had found each other, but in the process she had lost herself. And she had absolutely no idea what to do now.

Marina carefully maneuvered her car into the small lean-to at one side of the cabin where she lived. As she got out she felt strangely reluctant to go into that silent, empty house. Instead, she turned and walked toward an old ranch house a half mile away. There, she knew, she would find companionship and comfort.

The cabin and the ranch house were in a small valley surrounded by low hills browned to an Indian summer gold. The unfenced, grassy fields would be emerald green in the spring, but now they were parched. A nearly dry creek ran through the middle of the valley.

And yet, though it wasn't green and verdant right now, it was nevertheless lovely; utterly quiet and peaceful, cut off from the hustle and bustle of the rest of the world. That was why Marina had rented the cabin originally—because she thought the isolation would be conducive to writing the novel she'd wanted to do for so long. And because it was cheap. On her salary as a waitress, she couldn't afford much.

It had worked out as she'd hoped. She'd written her novel and it had sold recently. It would be published in the spring. But besides writing her book, there had been an unexpected bonus in living here.

Rosie.

Rosie was Marina's landlady. Her family had homesteaded the small ranch a hundred years earlier. She rented out what used to be the bunkhouse more for companionship than money. Despite the fact that she lived far from most neighbors, she wasn't at all a hermit. In fact, she had a reputation as being the friendliest person in Big Sur. She never refused a handout or a hand, and her shoulder was always available to cry on.

So Marina naturally headed toward Rosie now as she had done when her world had come crashing around her a month earlier.

The small wooden house was immaculately kept. Painted white with yellow shutters, it had a small front porch with a table and two chairs. That was where Rosie entertained visitors on days when the weather was nice. Many, many times Marina had sat out there, sipping homemade lemonade and eating cookies fresh from the oven, and talking to Rosie about her book. Rosie was the perfect listener—interested, intelligent, caring. And unfailingly supportive.

When Marina had come racing over with the news that her book had sold, Rosie had responded matter-of-factly, "Course it did. I knew it would. It was too good to be rejected."

Now, Marina stopped at the screen door and called through the open doorway, "Anyone home?"

"Damn and blast!" The words rang out furiously. Then, in a milder tone, the speaker went on, "I'm out in the kitchen!"

As soon as Marina reached the kitchen at the rear of the house, she realized what the swearing was all about. Rosie was a small, thin woman with enough energy and spirit for someone twice her size. Dressed in faded jeans and a short-sleeved madras shirt, her curly gray hair cut very short, she looked like the farm woman she was.

At the moment she stood staring angrily down at her dog. An empty cookie sheet sitting on a low table, a guilty-looking dog, and an angry Rosie all pointed inescapably to one conclusion.

"Homer ate some cookies again, I take it."

"Not some cookies, *all* the cookies. And it was a new recipe I was trying out for the first time. I was only gone for a minute and when I got back I found the cookie sheet on the floor and Homer licking crumbs off his whiskers."

Homer was a pathetic-looking little mongrel, all wiry black hair and brown eyes, as woebegone as Emmett Kelly's sad clown. Rosie had taken him in as she took in all helpless, needy beings.

"Just look at that fat little stomach!" Rosie went on irately.

Marina couldn't help it. She burst into laughter. In a moment Rosie joined in good-naturedly, and Homer relaxed visibly. Once more, he'd gotten away with murder.

"All right, you little thief, outside with you." Rosie held open the back door and Homer waddled out as quickly as he could on a very full stomach.

Turning back to Marina, Rosie put her hands on her hips and gave her a long, penetrating look. Then she said, "You're back awful quick."

"I didn't want to stay," Marina answered defensively.

Rosie's plain, heavily lined face softened with compassion and understanding. "Well, you went. That's the main thing. It would've hurt them a lot if you'd stayed away. Want some iced tea?"

Marina nodded, then helped Rosie put the pitcher of tea and two glasses onto a tray. She carried it outside onto the front porch. As they sat down, Rosie said, "We would've had cookies to go with this if Homer hadn't been so greedy. Damn ungrateful hound."

But there was no bite to her words now, and Marina knew she was over being angry.

After a moment, Rosie asked with her usual forthrightness, "So, how was it?"

"Okay, I guess."

"Just okay?"

"I don't have anything to compare it to. I've never watched my... my parents get married before."

Rosie leaned forward and her hazel eyes were warm with concern. "Don't be bitter, Marina. Bitterness is the most self-destructive emotion there is."

"I'm not bitter!" she snapped. Then, feeling guilty, she added, "I'm sorry. I'm not mad at you."

"No, you're mad at your mother and father. But you shouldn't be."

"Why shouldn't I be? They turned my whole life upside down. After spending my whole life thinking one man was my father, now I'm supposed to accept that another man actually is."

"Well, it's the truth. Hard as it may seem, you can't fight it."

"Well, I don't have to accept it. He comes waltzing into my life when I'm twenty-four years old and expects me to welcome him. It's a little late!"

"From what you told me, it wasn't his fault. He didn't even know about you until a month ago."

Marina couldn't argue with that. But she wasn't about to admit that Rosie was right. Instead, she sat there in unhappy silence, thinking about her parents.

It had all happened so fast. She'd grown up amidst financial and emotional security, thinking she was part of the ideal family, with happily married parents. Then, seemingly overnight, everything had changed. Her father's business failed. He left her mother, Caroline, for another woman. There was a divorce.

Though Marina and her father weren't close, she was fond of him. It meant a lot to her that they were a strong unit, a family, and when he had walked out it hurt her almost as much as it hurt her mother.

Then Caroline had moved back to her hometown of Clovis, California, and there met a man she hadn't seen in twenty-five years. The man she now said was Marina's real father. Rafael Marin.

Marin—Marina. It was no accident, of course, that their names were so similar. And they looked so much alike. Seeing him today for only the third time in her life, Marina was struck again by how much they resembled each other.

It wasn't that she doubted the truth of her mother's words. Obviously, Rafael Marin was her father. It was just that she couldn't accept the explanation behind it all.

They had been high school sweethearts, Caroline had told Marina. When she became pregnant, her parents were furious. Rafe's family was poor, his heritage Mexican-American. His own parents weren't happy about Rafe's involvement with a girl out of his culture and his class.

Both sets of parents conspired to separate them, and it worked. Rafe thought Caroline had given up their child for adoption, and Caroline thought Rafe wanted nothing to do with her or their child. Caroline married someone else and never told Marina the truth about her parentage. Until a month ago, when she and Rafe finally resolved the terrible misunderstanding from the past and decided to get married.

Looking at Rosie now, Marina said haltingly, "You don't understand how it feels to learn that your whole identity—your whole life—has been a lie."

"That's not true. You're still the same person you always were."

Marina shook her head. "No . . . I don't know who I am. I don't know how I feel about my mother anymore. The only thing I'm sure of is that I'll never accept that . . . that *stranger* as a father!"

"Marina, your mother was always there for you. And your father would have been if he could."

"I don't believe that. Oh, Rosie, I just don't know what to believe anymore. Who do I trust? The people I trusted most lied to me."

"I know it's a lame excuse, but it was in your best interests. At least, that's probably what your mother believed."

"I know. But—"

"Yes—*but*." Rosie looked out at the fields stretching up to the hills. Sighing, she said, almost to herself, "The things we do in someone's best interests . . ."

Then, looking back at Marina, she went on, "So what happens now?"

"Nothing."

"You're not going to give your father a chance?"

Marina shook her head stubbornly. "And I'd rather not hear any advice about it, if you don't mind."

"Now, I'm not one to give out unwanted advice," Rosie insisted.

This was so patently untrue that Marina couldn't resist a smile.

Rosie returned the smile. "That's better. Smiles suit you better than frowns. By the way, what happened to that cute young man who was hanging around?"

"I told him I didn't want to see him anymore." At Rosie's disapproving look, Marina continued defensively, "We weren't at all right for each other. He's a conservative attorney and I'm a crazy writer."

"Maybe so, but eligible bachelors don't grow on trees nowadays, young lady."

"I don't care."

Rosie's expression was thoughtful. "I'm afraid you mean that." Then she went on, "So what are you going to do now?"

"Throw myself into my work. Enjoy the peace and quiet here."

"In other words, run away."

Marina didn't respond. Instead, she finished the last of her tea, then rose. "I've got to get back to work. I don't want to be a flash in the pan, someone who only had one book in her."

"No way. You're going to be rich and famous, and I'm going to double your rent."

Laughing, Marina retorted, "Let's hope so." The pall that had hung over her all day seemed to have lifted. "By the way, thanks for the tea...and sympathy."

"Anytime. There's just one last thing I have to say, and you can take it or leave it. You can't run away from life, Marina. It has a habit of catching up with you in the most unexpected ways."

Marina met Rosie's level look, but didn't speak. As she turned and walked back to the cabin, she had a nagging feeling Rosie was right.

Chapter One

Marina sat at an ancient oak desk, typing away at an old-fashioned manual typewriter. It was hardly the latest in high-tech writing equipment, but it suited her. Besides, her cabin had neither electricity nor a telephone. It was truly rustic and she loved it. She cooked on an oil stove, read by the light of a kerosene lamp and warmed the one-room cabin with a crackling fire in the stone fireplace.

She drew the line at doing laundry by hand, however, and instead used Rosie's washing machine and dryer once a week. She also used Rosie's telephone. Now, as she glanced out the window, she saw Rosie's old pickup pulling up outside. She knew that Rosie had probably come to tell her about a phone call, because that was the only reason why Rosie would interrupt her when she was writing.

She hurried outside and Rosie leaned out the window. "Phone call. Your agent. I told her you were working, but she said it was urgent. Hop in."

"I wonder what it could be?" Marina mused aloud as the pickup bounced along the deeply rutted dirt road that led from the cabin to the main house.

"Well, maybe it's more money for your book. That would be nice," Rosie responded pragmatically.

"I doubt it, unfortunately. They've already sent my advance and it's too early for royalties to start coming in."

"Well, here we are," Rosie said as she pulled to a stop in front of her house. "I've got to run into town, so I'll just drop you off. Hope your agent didn't mind waiting."

Marina grinned. "Liz hates waiting. She always acts like she's about to rush off to an urgent meeting with Sidney Sheldon or Swifty Lazar."

She jumped out of the truck and gave a quick wave as Rosie drove off. Then she hurried inside Rosie's rather shabby, but warmly inviting, living room and picked up the phone. "Hi, Liz, how are you?"

"When are you going to get a phone? Do you know how long I've been waiting?"

"About two or three minutes at the outside."

"Marina, darling, this is no way to live. Quaint is one thing, but you're wallowing in an absolutely Spartan lifestyle."

Liz's voice was tinged with an upper-crust English accent. Since she'd been born and raised in Manhattan, Marina had no idea where the accent came from. But she assumed it was affected to help Liz get what she wanted out of life—money, power and status. She was as much into those things as Marina was into the simple life.

Yet, despite glaring differences in personality, somehow they got along. Beneath that determinedly sophisticated exterior, Liz was actually much more caring than she'd ever admit. She'd taken on Marina as a client when Marina was a scared, novice writer without a single credit. Despite numerous rejections, she'd kept pushing Marina's first novel until a publisher finally bought it a year later.

"Now, listen, darling," Liz went on, "I've got *big* news. You are shortly going to be rich whether you care to be or not. A producer is interested in optioning *Casey*. In return for a substantial down-payment, he'll have exclusive rights to it for the next year. If he doesn't get it produced during that time, the rights revert to you. If he does, you get even more money."

Marina was stunned. Liz had never even discussed the possibility of a movie sale with her. It hadn't occurred to Marina that any studio would be interested in her simple coming-of-age story.

"But why would any studio want my book? It doesn't have sex or violence or anything remotely commercial."

"I know that, dear, but I'm not going to point out those things to Stephen Kramer."

"Kramer! *He's* the one who wants it?"

"For heaven's sakes, Marina, you sound insulted. Kramer's the hottest producer in Hollywood right now, a real boy wonder."

"He's also known for making movies that are absolute trash."

"No movie that grosses over a hundred million can be called trash. Commercial, maybe, even escapist, but . . ."

"Liz, his movies are the worst kind of teenage tripe. He wouldn't recognize quality if it walked up and hit him."

"Apparently he would," Liz purred, "because he wants to option your book."

"Why? So he can turn it into more tripe?"

"Marina, you're obviously naive. Do you think every novel gets optioned, especially by a top producer like Kramer?"

"No, but I'm not sure I want *Casey* made into a movie at all. And certainly not by a . . . a schlock merchant."

Liz gave her patented long-suffering sigh that Marina suspected was reserved for recalcitrant writers who didn't fully appreciate Liz's efforts on their behalf.

"Now, listen, darling. I'll explain it in words of one syllable that even a very talented but very misguided writer can understand. First novels, especially a serious one by a young, unknown author, rarely make it to the best-seller lists. You're not going to make much money from *Casey*."

"I know that. I didn't do it for the money—hard as that may be for you to understand."

"Don't get snappish. It doesn't suit anyone who looks as young and innocent as you do. I'm aware you didn't write it for the money and I admire that. Dedication and self-sacrifice are wonderful—in moderation."

Marina couldn't repress a smile. Liz *was* funny in her own way.

"Liz, it isn't that I want to starve in a garret for my art...."

"Good, I'm glad to hear it. It's the first sensible thing you've said during this entire conversation. Look, Kramer's offering fifty thousand for the movie rights."

"Fifty thousand dollars?" Marina gasped.

"It ain't pesos. Of course, there's the usual catch that you only get a small percentage up front, and the rest if the movie gets produced."

For a moment Marina was silent, her mind working furiously. Fifty thousand dollars would free her from her part-time job as a waitress and let her devote herself entirely to her next book ... and the one after that.

As if reading her mind, Liz went on, "That kind of money buys a lot of freedom."

Still, Marina reflected, she'd poured her heart and soul into that book. It was largely autobiographical. She couldn't bear to see her deepest emotions turned into cheap titillation just so Stephen Kramer could make another hundred million dollars.

"Liz, I can't. I'm sorry. I know you don't understand. And believe me, it isn't easy to turn down that kind of money. But I just can't see my book turned into something unrecognizable.''

"Marina, take some time to think about it. Believe me, you'll regret this decision for the rest of your life."

Marina stood there silently, thinking about what Liz was saying. She didn't want to continue working as a waitress, writing only in her spare time. But there was too much of her in *Casey* to simply sell it to the highest bidder without regard to its integrity.

Suddenly, she had an idea. It was crazy, she knew, but just maybe... just maybe...

"Liz, what if I write the screenplay?"

"But you've never written a screenplay before."

"So? I can learn. How hard can it be?"

There was an awkward silence and Marina sensed that Liz was trying to think of a polite way to discourage this insane notion.

"Marina, darling, it doesn't work that way. Kramer will want to hire an experienced screenwriter...."

"Then he won't get my book. It's that simple. Either I do the screenplay or I don't sell him the rights."

"You realize you're making it very difficult for me to bring fame and fortune into your rustic little life."

Marina laughed. "I have nothing against fame and fortune. I just want to keep a little integrity, as well."

"Won't you reconsider?"

"Nope."

There was another long sigh, one that Marina knew could probably be heard all the way from Manhattan to the Hamptons. "Why didn't I marry a nice doctor like my mother wanted, instead of dealing with crazy writers? Ah, well, easy come, easy go."

"Thanks for understanding, Liz."

"I don't understand at all. But I will tell Stephen Kramer you want to do the screenplay. You realize that will probably blow the deal?"

"Yes, I realize that."

"Very well. Ciao, *bella*."

Marina was a little confused by the Italian endearment until she remembered Liz had just returned from a vacation in Italy. As she replaced the receiver, she smiled indulgently. Liz was quite a character.

She locked Rosie's front door and walked back to her cabin, wondering what Kramer's response to her ultimatum would be.

The next morning she got an answer. She was having breakfast with Rosie when the phone rang. It was Liz.

"Well, I talked to Kramer just now."

"And?"

"He was furious, to put it mildly. He said you're being difficult, that apparently you don't realize he's the only producer interested in your book, and you're lucky he's even considering it."

"I'm lucky? He's lucky I'm even considering selling him the rights, under any circumstances!"

"That's exactly what I told him."

Marina was taken aback. "You did?"

"Of course, darling. I am your agent, remember. Even when you're being totally wrongheaded I have to stand behind you."

"Thanks... I think."

"He said there was no way he would hire someone who didn't know the first thing about screenwriting to do the script. And I said in that case we had nothing further to talk about."

Marina was surprised by the jolt of disappointment that went through her. She had known it probably wouldn't work out. Yet somehow she had hoped it would. "So, that's it, then?" Her voice was small and lost.

"Of course not. You don't understand haggling, dear. He made various disparaging remarks about egotistical writers in general and you in particular—"

"Egotistical!"

Liz continued, ignoring the interruption, "And I simply listened patiently until his anger had run its course. Then I made the deal for you to write the screenplay."

"Oh, Liz, you're marvelous!"

"Yes, I am."

In the background, Rosie, who had been listening unashamedly to the conversation, asked in a whisper, "Did you get it?"

Marina nodded enthusiastically and a huge grin completely erased the anger that had been written all over her face a moment earlier.

Liz continued, "Of course, the deal is only for guild minimum and there's a cutoff after first draft."

Marina's head was swimming with mingled relief and confusion. "What's guild minimum?"

"That's Hollywoodese. You'd better start learning it if you're going to be a screenwriter. The guild is the Writers Guild. All television and film writers *must* belong to it. As soon as you get your first check for this project, you will become a dues-paying member. Also, all studios and independent producers must sign agreements with the guild or else they can't hire guild members as writers. The guild contract, with the studios and independents, establishes minimum payments for writers in all categories—half-hour television, feature films, etc."

"What did you say about a cutoff?"

"You are innocent, aren't you? Marina, are you sure you want to do this? I feel that I'm sending a lamb into a pack of wolves."

"I'm sure. Now what's a cutoff?"

"Screenwriters get paid in increments—for the treatment, which is more Hollywoodese for outline, then for the first draft of the script, and finally for the second draft. There was no way Kramer would accept a deal where you were guaranteed to be paid all the way through the second draft. You'll be paid guild minimum, fifteen thousand dollars, for the treatment. But if he doesn't like what you've done, you can be cut off at that point."

"But that's no problem," Marina replied confidently. "I wrote the book. Of course I can write an outline of it."

There was a pause, then Liz went on slowly, "Marina, the film business is nothing like publishing. It's a cutthroat industry in many ways. You've got a lot to learn about it."

"Then I'll learn it."

"You are nothing if not confident. I just wish . . . well, never mind. By the way, you'll have to meet with Kramer as soon as possible."

"Why?"

Exasperation crept into Liz's voice. "Because that's how they do things in Hollywood. They have meetings. Endlessly. Be a pet and just do it."

Marina had absolutely no desire to meet Stephen Kramer, whom she had already decided was a jerk. But she knew she'd given Liz enough problems already and it was time to be conciliatory. "All right."

"He's available next Monday at ten. Can you make it down to L.A. then?"

"Yes, the restaurant's closed on Mondays."

"Marina, you can quit working as a waitress now, you realize."

"I realize that. But I've got to give them two weeks notice. It wouldn't be fair to just walk out."

"You are a nauseatingly nice child. Now, show up at National Studios in Culver City on Monday at ten. The guard at the front gate will direct you to Kramer's office. And, darling, be polite to Kramer."

Marina grinned slyly. "Of course. You just said I'm nice, remember?"

"You're nice to people who don't count and unbelievably difficult with those who do. It's a bad habit you must break if you want to be a success. Now, I must run, I have a million things to do. Call me after the meeting."

"Okay. Thanks for everything, Liz."

"You can thank me by not telling Kramer his movies are tripe. Bye, love."

The instant Marina hung up the phone, Rosie asked impatiently, "Let's not beat around the bush—how much are you getting to do the movie?"

Marina laughed happily. "Fifteen thousand lovely dollars."

"On top of the fifty thousand for the movie rights?"

"Well, I only get ten percent of that 'up front' as Liz says. The rest comes when, and if, they make the movie."

"Course they'll make it," Rosie insisted. "You're going to be rich and famous and I'll be able to brag to everyone that I know you."

"I'm not rich yet, but I'm solvent, which is nice for a change. I can actually get my car fixed now. If I got the dents pounded out and painted it..."

"To heck with your car, tell me about Kramer."

"There's not much to tell. He didn't want me to do the screenplay, of course, but he had no choice. Do you know he actually said I was lucky he wanted to make my book into a movie?"

Remembering that, Marina grew angry again. "Of all the egotistical—which reminds me, he said *I'm* egotistical! Can you believe it? He probably isn't aware there's another ego in the world besides his own inflated one."

"I saw him on some talk show on TV once," Rosie interrupted musingly. "Quite a charmer. Like a young Robert Redford, I'd say. Or maybe Jeff Bridges."

"He sounds like the blond beachboy type," Marina replied sarcastically.

"Well, if he is, it's a beachboy with a brain. The man was definitely sharp. I wonder if he's married?"

"Rosie! Whether or not he's married is beside the point."

Rosie gave her a level look. "Marina Turner, you're far too young and pretty to be uninterested in an attractive man's availability."

"I doubt that I'll find Stephen Kramer attractive."

"Then you're dead from the waist down."

"Rosie!"

Rosie smiled wickedly. "Oh, for heaven's sakes, don't look so shocked. I thought you young people were supposed to be outspoken and us older folks were supposed to be uptight."

Marina gave her a disapproving look. "It isn't just Kramer, is it? You're trying to tell me, in your not very subtle way, to get out and mingle."

"It beats spending all your time with that old typewriter and me."

Marina felt a stab of guilt. "Am I being a pest?"

"Course not! Don't be ridiculous. Fact is, it was pretty lonely out here before you came. It's just that I don't want you to let all this business with your parents turn you against men."

Marina didn't respond. Actually she *was* feeling very wary where men were concerned. But she wasn't going to think about that now. Right now all that mattered was getting this meeting with Kramer over with and turning her book into a good film.

At a quarter after ten o'clock on Monday morning, Marina pulled her car to a stop at the front gate of National Studios. She'd never been to L.A. before and had gotten lost trying to find the studio. Being late increased the nervousness she was already feeling about the meeting. And, as usual, being nervous made her defensive.

As she gave the guard her name and waited for it to be checked off on his list of approved visitors, her nervousness grew. Her fingers drummed impatiently on the steering wheel and she kept glancing at her wristwatch every few seconds.

With exasperating slowness, the guard scanned the list. Finally he said, "All right, miss. The visitors' parking lot is full, so you'll have to turn around and park on the street. When you come back, just walk onto the lot. Mr. Kramer's in Building H just down this main street here."

Great, Marina thought irritably. Another delay. Just what she needed.

As if a malevolent fate was controlling her day, the street was packed with cars, and it took her several minutes to find a parking place. By the time she walked back onto the lot it was ten-thirty. She'd never been on a movie lot before and would have loved to take time to look around. But she was so late that she barely had time to glance curiously at the rows of massive gray soundstages that she hurried past on her way to Building H.

Telling herself that Kramer probably would have kept her waiting anyway, she squared her shoulders and marched into his suite of offices. She tried not to look as upset as she felt.

A young secretary with a curly mop of red hair, freckles and a friendly smile, sat at a desk just inside the door. Marina was glad to see she was wearing jeans and a black and white T-shirt emblazoned with the logo of Kramer's last movie, *Rebels.* Marina herself was in her usual jeans, which she'd dressed up with a new gray silk shirt she'd splurged on recently.

"May I help you?" the secretary asked politely.

"Yes. I'm Marina Turner, I had an appointment with Mr. Kramer at ten. I'm afraid I'm a little late."

Immediately the secretary's friendly smile evaporated. "Yes...Miss Turner. Mr. Kramer had another appointment and couldn't wait. He isn't here."

"What time was his other appointment?" Marina asked suspiciously.

The secretary hesitated, clearly surprised by the challenging tone of Marina's question. Finally she answered reluctantly, "Ten-fifteen."

Anger surged through Marina. So, he'd planned on giving her all of fifteen minutes to discuss turning *Casey* into a movie. The guilt she'd felt at being so late evaporated instantly and was replaced with indignation. Obviously Stephen Kramer felt she didn't rate much of his valuable time. That her own time might be as valuable wouldn't have occurred to him, of course.

She'd spent eight hours driving down to L.A. from Big Sur and had spent the night in a motel as uncomfortable as it was expensive. And for what? For fifteen lousy minutes.

Liz had said Kramer was furious at Marina's insistence on being the one to write the screenplay. Clearly, his attitude hadn't changed. She'd been wary about working with him and now she realized her wariness was justified.

Marina's first inclination was to turn around and leave. But she quickly decided that she wasn't going to let him off the hook that easily. Looking at the secretary, she asked, "When will he be back?"

The young woman was obviously surprised by the question. "Well, I'm not sure...."

Marina doubted that was true. His own secretary must know his schedule, she reasoned. But the woman clearly felt that Marina had blown her chance for a meeting with the boss and couldn't expect to be given another chance.

Sitting down in a nearby chair, Marina said firmly. "Then I'll wait."

"But ... he may be quite a while."

"I'll wait," Marina repeated obstinately.

She had a stubborn streak, as everyone from her mother to Liz had commented on at various times. Right now she was stubbornly prepared to wait for Kramer if it took all day.

The hours passed slowly. By one o'clock Marina's stomach was growling and her back hurt from sitting in the low, hard chair. Still, her pride wouldn't let her give up. Every time the secretary glanced at her, she returned the look defiantly.

Fortunately, there were some interesting people to watch. As a novelist, Marina was interested in anyone and everyone. The fact that these were movie people, a breed she'd never had the opportunity to observe before, made them all the more fascinating.

They were surprisingly alike. Men and women both wore jeans and a harried look. In the large reception area were three other desks manned by secretaries who came and went casually. Behind each desk was a large bulletin board filled with notices, scrawled notes and production schedules. Phones rang constantly and there was an air of controlled chaos.

Several smaller offices opened off the reception area. Most of the doors to these offices were open and people ambled in and out, sometimes to ask a hurried question, other times to put their feet up on the desk and chat.

Marina realized early on that casting was taking place. One actress after another, each seemingly more beautiful than the last, came in, gave her name to one of the secretaries, waited for a while, then was ushered into a closed office. After about two minutes the actress would come out again, leave an eight by ten glossy photo on the secretary's desk, then leave.

Each actress was immaculately groomed and expertly made-up. Their clothes were the latest in L.A. chic, and one or two wore dazzling jewelry.

Marina herself rarely wore makeup. And as for her clothes... well, even her jeans were a bit too faded to be considered stylish. With her fresh-scrubbed face and wind-blown hairstyle, she began to feel distinctly at a loss.

At one point there were four actresses sitting in the reception area, waiting to be interviewed. Marina noticed that they avoided speaking to each other. But they surreptitiously glanced at one another, sizing up the competition. As they did so, their perfect faces were marred by a hint of insecurity.

Marina asked an actress sitting next to her what she was being interviewed for.

"Don't you know?" the young woman, a stunning brunette, shot back guardedly.

"Oh...I'm not an actress," Marina explained, surprised that she would have been taken for one.

The young woman appraised her shrewdly, then said, "Of course not. Well, the part's just a walk-on. A girl sitting at a bar. No lines."

A walk-on. No lines. Marina couldn't believe it. All these gorgeous women were being interviewed for the most minor of roles. And even though there were no lines, they were so desperate to get it that they eyed the competition jealously. They couldn't even allow themselves the luxury of commiserating with each other, being supportive of each other, because they were in such fierce competition. There were so many beautiful girls, and so few roles....

My God, Marina thought sadly. What a life. She could well imagine what it must do to them after a while. The intense competitiveness, the rejection, the insecurity. And when they weren't quite so young or beautiful...what then?

She remembered what Liz had said. "It's a cutthroat business." Oh, how right she was. And men like Stephen Kramer ran it. He probably enjoyed wielding such power over women, Marina decided, disliking him even more now.

At that moment the door swung open and two men entered. One was short and slim, dark haired and dark eyed, with an engaging grin. He was overshadowed, however, by the other man, a blue-eyed blonde with the muscular build of a college wrestler or gymnast.

The blonde wasn't tall. He was no taller than Marina, who was five feet, eight inches in her bare feet. But there was something compelling about him, an aura of barely leashed power. His entire body seemed to pulse with it, as if at any moment he might explode.

That power was completely unexpected in a man who was otherwise conventionally attractive. It transformed his even features—a strong nose and firm mouth—so that instead of being merely handsome he was a great deal more. He was interesting.

"Damn it, Marty, he's a month late as it is! Tell his agent if he doesn't have the final draft in by Friday we'll declare him in breach of contract and hire someone else!"

Marty seemed used to the other man's temper for he didn't look at all concerned. He replied with a touch of humor. "He'll file an arbitration with the guild."

"To hell with the guild! He can't hide behind it this time. His laziness is throwing a twenty-million-dollar picture behind schedule."

"It isn't laziness, Stephen. He just married some girl half his age and she's running him ragged."

Stephen. It had to be Stephen Kramer, of course, Marina realized. She rose and marshaled all her composure so she could tell him who she was and what she thought of him.

But as she stood up, he noticed her and stopped dead in his tracks. "This is more like it. At least this one looks fresh."

Fresh! Marina opened her mouth to angrily retort that she wasn't a piece of meat. But before she could speak, Kramer reached out and she felt his hand roughly turn her chin toward him so that their eyes met evenly. For an instant she stared into that disconcertingly attractive face and took in every aspect of it. A lock of dark-blond hair fell boyishly over a wide, deeply tanned forehead. His brows were straight and strongly marked. His mouth seemed almost harsh and utterly without humor.

But it was his eyes that were so arresting. They weren't the pale blue that normally accompanied blond hair. Instead, they were a deep royal-blue, so dark they almost looked black. It was impossible to read the expression in those dark eyes, which lent an air of reserve, almost of mystery to Kramer.

She had told Rosie he sounded like a beachboy, but this man was no vapid, innocuous pretty-boy with nothing more on his mind than surf and sex. In fact, despite his blond good looks, there was an intensity about him that was just a little bit frightening.

He went on, "She's too tall, but since she'll be sitting at the bar the whole time, it won't matter."

Gritting her teeth, Marina pulled back. Her voice shook with anger as she shot back, "I'm not an actress, Mr. Kramer. My name's Marina Turner. And I've been waiting to see you for quite a while. We had an appointment, remember?"

The dark blue eyes opened wide in surprise for just a moment, before narrowing again. They flicked from the toes of her flat gray leather shoes all the way up to her tousled hair. If he liked what he saw, he didn't let it show. His expression was cold and hard.

"I remember, Miss Turner. I waited for you. I wasn't about to wait all day."

Marina seethed with irritation at his high-handed manner. "You waited fifteen minutes. That's all the time you were prepared to give me."

Marty and the secretary looked startled by her blunt words. Probably, she realized, Stephen Kramer was used to being deferred to.

He said tightly, "That was all the time I could afford to give you." It wasn't an apology or even an explanation, but a bald statement of fact. And his cool tone clearly suggested she could take it or leave it, it didn't matter to him.

Something snapped inside Marina. Her tone was deceptively calm as she responded, ''In that case, Mr. Kramer, you obviously don't place a very high priority on my book. Since no contracts have been signed, it will be easy to cancel the deal.''

And with that, she turned on her heel and strode out, leaving Marty and the secretary watching in amazement.

Chapter Two

Marina had to fight back angry tears as she strode down the same street she'd come in on earlier that morning. It was over, she thought. Finished, before it had even begun.

She told herself it was for the best, disappointing though it might be. Stephen Kramer was an even bigger jerk than she'd expected him to be. Fresh, indeed! If this was how people were in the film industry, then she wanted nothing to do with it. She'd written her first book in her spare time while working as a waitress, she could do the same with the second.

"Miss Turner! Wait!"

Looking back over her shoulder, Marina saw Marty hurrying toward ner. She waited until he caught up with her.

He was out of breatn and spoke haltingly. "I'm sorry...Stephen really isn't as much of an ass as he seemed...and this project means a lot to him."

"That's hard to believe."

By then Marty had caught his breath, and he went on, "I know. I don't blame you for being mad."

A wry smile softened his face and she realized he was younger than she'd first thought; no more than thirty at the outside.

He continued, "I must say, it was fun seeing Stephen get a dose of his own medicine for a change. Most people kiss up to him. They sure don't stand up to him the way you did."

"I appreciate the apology, Mr...."

"Stein. Marty Stein. I'm Stephen's production manager."

"Well, Mr. Stein..."

"Marty, please..."

"I think your boss should do his own apologizing, Marty."

He grinned impudently. "The idea of Stephen apologizing is certainly interesting, but I wouldn't want to hold my breath waiting for it to happen. Even when he first started out and didn't have two nickels to rub together, he had more pride than was good for him. He got thrown out of a lot of offices for not toadying to some bigwig."

"That sounds like arrogance, not pride."

"Well, he does love to tell people how to do things. Which would be thoroughly irritating except that he's usually right. His talent makes his arrogance bearable."

"I didn't find it bearable. He was rude, overbearing, inconsiderate...."

"Etc., etc.," Marty finished for her. "Seriously, I realize it must have seemed like that to you, but you just don't know him."

"I don't *want* to know him."

Marty's expression grew serious and his dark eyes watched Marina intently. "The fact is, Stephen is anxious to do this project. It means a lot to him. He'd never admit it to you, but believe me, it's true."

He gave Marina a long, appraising look. "I'm sure it must mean a lot to you, too."

When she didn't argue, he went on persuasively, "He's over at the commissary now. Come back and meet with him over lunch."

"No, I . . . I couldn't do that."

"Because he isn't here asking you himself?"

"Yes," she admitted.

Marty shook his head. "You're as stubborn as he is. Miss Turner, I told him I was going to bring you over to the commissary. He wants to see you. Please, give him a second chance."

Marina felt herself unbending just a little under Marty's earnest entreaty. Sensing this, Marty urged gently, "Come on, what do you have to lose? You'll get a free lunch and you can still walk out when it's over."

He smiled broadly. "Now *that* would be something to see. Someone walking out on Stephen Kramer twice in the same day."

Now that she was more or less calm again, Marina realized just how much she didn't want to blow the deal. Marty was offering a second chance to make it work, after all. She took it.

"How's the food at the commissary?" she asked with a hint of a smile.

"It's great!" Taking her arm, he turned her around and led her toward a low, square building. "Just great! But don't order the chili."

The commissary turned out to be a huge, high-ceilinged room partitioned off into smaller dining areas by a judicious use of tall planters and lush foliage. On the walls were giant posters of many of National Studios' biggest hits, including Stephen Kramer's first movie. A low-budget teen romance, it had earned more than seventy-five million dollars. His second and third films had been even more successful, Marina knew. But despite the huge grosses, none of his movies was well received by critics.

As Marty guided Marina through the maze of tables, she saw several film and television actors she recognized. A surge of excitement, like a rush of adrenaline, raced through her. For the first time since her belated arrival on the lot that morning, it really hit her that she was in the middle of a movie factory. These people took the stuff that dreams are made of and turned it into reality—at least on celluloid.

Casey might be part of that. It might become a movie that millions of people would see and relate to and enjoy. She remembered the movies that had touched her in a profound way—*Gone with the Wind*, *The Way We Were*, *The Elephant Man*. The thought that she might write a movie that would touch audiences in the same way was so heady that Marina almost felt dizzy with excitement.

She gave a silent, but heartfelt thank-you to Marty for not letting her walk out on that possibility.

Kramer was sitting alone at a small round table in a corner. When Marty and Marina reached the table, Kramer stood up and nodded politely toward her. His expression was no longer angry, but guarded. Once more Marina was struck by the contrast between what one would expect from his blond good looks, and the unexpected compelling, complex personality behind them.

A white-coated waiter handed Marina a menu, and before she could peruse it Kramer suggested firmly, "The sole is always good."

But she wasn't willing to give in to him, even on so small an issue as fillet of sole, which she loved. Ignoring Kramer, she looked up at the waiter and said sweetly, "I'll have the chef salad, please."

"You're too skinny to be dieting," Kramer commented matter-of-factly.

Marina opened her mouth to retort, but Marty stepped in and nipped the argument in the bud. "Would you like wine, Marina? By the way, do you mind if I call you Marina?"

She shook her head, then added, "And I don't care for any wine, thank you."

The waiter looked at Kramer, but Kramer dismissed him with a brief, "No wine, then."

Marty continued easily, "Now, then, let's get down to business. Everyone in the office just loved *Casey*. I understand it's your first novel."

"Yes. I was writing short stories and getting nothing but rejection slips, when I decided to try a novel. It went very well and I was pleased with the way it turned out. My agent, Liz James, was able to find a publisher after a year of trying."

"A year?" Marty responded in surprise. "I don't know why it wasn't snatched up by the first publisher who saw it."

Marina flashed him a grateful smile. "Thanks. But Liz says first novels by unknown authors are hard to sell."

Kramer interjected, "Did she also explain to you that those same inexperienced authors usually aren't given the option of adapting their novels into screenplays?"

Marina turned to face him and forced herself to meet his hard look without flinching. "Yes, she did, as a matter of fact. And I believe she explained to you that I wasn't willing to sell the rights to my book under any other conditions."

On the other side of her, she heard Marty cough into his cupped hand. It sounded suspiciously as if he was trying to smother a chuckle.

Kramer went on, "You've never written a treatment, let alone a screenplay. Is that right?"

Marina nodded.

"Then why don't you let an experienced screenwriter, someone who knows the medium, adapt your book?"

"I may not know the medium, Mr. Kramer, but I know my own book better than any other writer possibly could. That story, those characters, were born within me. I understand them, feel for them, in a way that no one else can."

"She has a point, Stephen," Marty said.

But Kramer wasn't about to give in so easily. "Do you know the first thing about writing a treatment?"

"I'll learn." The words were clipped almost to the point of rudeness.

It was going to be impossible, Marina decided, for them to carry on a civil conversation.

Fortunately, at that moment the waiter returned with their food. The chef salad looked delicious, but Marina was too nervous to have much appetite. Kramer, she noticed, was eating the sole, while Marty attacked a big, juicy hamburger.

By unspoken agreement, they didn't discuss business while they ate. Marina had never enjoyed a meal less. She toyed with her salad, forcing herself to eat some of it. But every bite seemed to stick in her throat.

It was a mistake to let Marty talk her into coming back, she decided. Kramer was impossible. He had judged her to be difficult before he'd even met her. And now that they had met, things were even worse.

But she was damned if she was going to let him intimidate her. Assuming a nonchalance she didn't feel, she turned to Marty and asked some questions about the studio. He happily answered her questions, and the friendly dialogue they kept up prevented the atmosphere at the table from degenerating into a tense silence.

Every few minutes someone would stop by the table to say hello to Kramer. Sometimes Kramer seemed genuinely glad to see the people, and at those times he showed a pleasant side to his normally brusque personality. But at other times he didn't bother to hide the fact that he was irritated about being approached.

At one point, an elderly actor whom Marina recognized from watching innumerable movies on the late show on TV, stopped by. He wore a loud checked suit and a jaunty tam-o'-shanter that seemed out of place among the laid-back attire of most of the other diners.

"Stephen, my lad, it's good to see you!"

For once, Kramer's expression was almost warm. Setting down his fork, he took the older man's hand and shook it vigorously. "Ben, how's it going?"

"Fine, couldn't be better. I'm up for all sorts of things. Frankly, I don't know which to choose."

"Good, glad to hear it. I hope you'll keep enough free time to do a cameo in my next picture. You'd be doing me a favor."

Ben scratched his chin thoughtfully. "Cameo, you say? I might be able to make time. Only for you, though."

"Good. I'll give your agent a call."

"See you later then, lad. Take care."

When he was gone, Marty shot Kramer a rueful look. "Now, Stephen..."

"Don't say a word, Marty."

"You know that was all hype he was giving you. He hasn't worked in a year."

Kramer's dark eyes flashed warningly. "I said not a word."

Marty sighed. "Okay, okay."

Just then someone else stopped by, a middle-aged woman with "studio executive" written all over her. She had the aura of a chic barracuda, from her designer suit to her Gucci accessories. Kramer didn't show her any of the warmth he'd just shown the elderly actor.

"Stephen, I'm glad I ran into you. I got your memo on *Rebels*. Surely you didn't mean—"

"I always mean what I say, Sheila."

"But if you don't compromise we'll have all sorts of problems making a sale to cable—"

"And I don't compromise," Kramer added, interrupting her once more.

Frowning, she said, "Well, I'll have to take it up with Chuck."

"Do that," he snapped.

Sheila hesitated for just a fraction of a second. Then with a toss of her platinum-streaked brown mane she spun around on her stiletto heels and hurried away.

At that point the waiter came to clear away their plates and Kramer faced Marina once more. He didn't mince words. "There are any number of good screenwriters, women among them, who would do a damn good job of adapting your book. They wouldn't butcher it, if that's what you're afraid of."

"I'm not afraid of anything," she retorted. "I'll adapt it myself or I won't sell the movie rights. It's that simple."

For one long, drawn-out moment their eyes locked. To Marina's chagrin, she was the first to lower her gaze. Then she quickly looked back up at him again, refusing to buckle under the challenge in those deep blue eyes. Kramer could be as difficult as he chose, he could argue with her forever. She wasn't going to give in.

As if realizing this, he leaned back in his chair and said curtly, "Fine. According to the deal I worked out with your agent, your treatment's due November first."

"You'll have it well before then."

"I'd better, or you'll be in breach of contract."

And on that inauspicious note, Marina's first lunch in a studio commissary ended.

Marina returned to Big Sur and began writing the treatment, which Liz had told her should be between twenty and thirty pages long. She thought it would be easy to write an outline of the book she knew so well, but as she got into it Marina discovered that it was hard to compress everything into thirty pages or less.

The story was a relatively simple one. Casey, the protagonist, turned eighteen, fell in love for the first time—with an older married man—and eventually broke up with him when she realized she couldn't build her happiness on someone else's unhappiness. In the process she went from being a naive, self-centered girl to a woman who has experienced pain and loss, but has developed the capacity to care for others.

There wasn't a lot of action in the story, which took place in Big Sur. But there was a great deal of emotional development, and she didn't want to leave out any of it in the treatment. Her first draft ran over fifty pages. The second was forty-five. With some judicious cutting she managed to get it down to forty pages by the middle of October.

That, she decided, would just have to do. And she mailed it off to Liz to send on to Stephen Kramer. Then she got back to work on her second novel, which she was having a great deal of trouble with.

Early in November, on a cold, overcast day, she received a letter from her mother. Before she even opened it, she knew what it would say. Sitting down in a rocking chair by a bright, crackling fire, she slowly opened the envelope and took out the single sheet of pale blue paper.

For a moment she simply held it, reluctant to unfold it and begin reading. Finally, she forced herself to do so. The letter was brief.

Marina,

I realized you needed time to think, so I didn't contact you before now. I want to tell you how happy it made your father and me that you came to our wedding. I know what it took for you to do that and we will be forever grateful.

You're angry and confused—I understand. You have every right to be. There was so much pain in the past for your father and me. Despite all my efforts, it seems inevitable that you will experience some of that pain, too. Your father and I made a decision to put the past behind us and to live in the present. We hope you will be able to do the same. Finally, we have a chance to be the family we always should have been—the family we would have been if our love for each other had been allowed to flourish.

I know it's difficult for you to accept a stranger as your father. It will take time for a relationship to develop between you. Believe me, your father doesn't expect more than you are able to give now. All he asks is the chance for you to get to know each other. I know if you will give him that chance you will eventually come to love him as much as I do. He's a good man, darling. He wasn't responsible for the events that tore us apart.

We both ask you to join us at Thanksgiving. Please.

Mother

After she'd read it, Marina continued staring at the letter for long seconds. Then she carefully folded it, hesitated for a moment, then threw it into the fire. Her soft gray eyes shone with tears as she watched the blue paper turn dark at the edges, curl and burn.

"So, are you going?" Rosie asked the next morning as she and Marina baked cookies together. Rosie's kitchen was warm and smelled of cinnamon and sugar and other delicious things.

Marina shook her head, avoiding Rosie's gaze. "No, I don't think so."

She put the last round ball of cookie dough onto the baking sheet, then bent to slide it into the oven. When she straightened she found Rosie facing her, hands on hips, her narrow, lined face troubled.

"Now, Marina, Thanksgiving is a time for families to be together. You should go."

"If it was just Mom, of course I'd go," Marina responded defensively. "But I don't want to be around him."

"He has a name, you know. It's Rafael Marin. Rafe, I think your mother calls him. If you can't bring yourself to call him Father, at least you can call him by his right name."

"He comes waltzing into my life when I'm twenty-four years old and I'm supposed to call him *Father*? No way!"

"I swear, child, you're as stubborn as I am, and that's sayin' a lot. What am I gonna do with you?"

Smiling tentatively, Marina said, "Invite me over for Thanksgiving?"

"And if I don't, will you go to your parents' house?"

"No."

"All right," Rosie said with a sigh. "Consider yourself invited. But if you come to your senses at the last minute, I won't be insulted if you go there instead of here."

"I won't."

Rosie flashed a wry grin. "No, I don't imagine you will. So, how's the new book comin'?"

Marina sat down heavily at the round oak kitchen table. "Not good. Actually, it's awful. Nothing's going right. The story's confused and the characters aren't at all sympathetic. *Casey* was easy to write compared to this. You'd think it would be easier the second time around. I don't know what's wrong with me."

Rosie sat down opposite her and poured both of them a cup of hot black coffee from a pot on the table. "I do. I'm no writer, but I understand that writing has a lot to do with your emotions. And right now your emotions are all jumbled. You don't know whether you're comin' or goin', and it shows in your writing."

"Maybe you're right. But I've just got to get over it. There's so much to do—this book, maybe the screenplay for

Casey. I don't have time to indulge in emotional upheaval, and that's that," she finished determinedly.

Rosie set down her cup of coffee and gave Marina a long, thoughtful look. "That's that, huh? It isn't that easy to ignore our feelings, Marina. You can try real hard, but it just doesn't work. It's better to face them, no matter how much it hurts. Believe me, I know."

Marina had the impression, as she often had had in the past, that there was something very painful in Rosie's history that she preferred not to talk about. It was on the tip of her tongue to ask Rosie about it, when the phone rang shrilly, shattering the intimacy of the moment.

After answering it, Rosie handed the receiver to Marina. "It's your agent."

"Hi, Liz, how's it going?" Marina asked brightly, trying to dispel the depression that had settled over her.

"Not very well. Bad news, Marina. I just heard from Stephen Kramer. He's cutting you off and hiring another writer to do *Casey.*"

"What?" Marina was stunned. She and Kramer certainly hadn't gotten along, but she had been confident her treatment was good enough to persuade him she should do the adaptation.

"I'm very sorry. But I warned you it could happen."

"Did he say what the problem was with my treatment?"

"To be perfectly honest, I'm not even sure he read it. When I tried to get at what was wrong, he was noncommittal. I think he wanted to hire an experienced screenwriter all along and he was just getting this obstacle out of the way so he could go ahead and do it."

Of course. The certainty that Liz was right hit Marina like a splash of ice-cold water on a winter morning. Kramer never had any intention of seriously considering her to do the screenplay. That was why he'd set aside so little time for their meeting...why he hadn't seemed particularly interested in talking with her, aside from trying to persuade her to let someone else write the screenplay.

She'd made the trip down there for nothing. And she'd been so excited at the prospect of turning *Casey* into a really good movie that would reach an even greater audience than the book would do.

Kramer had played her for a fool, she realized, manipulating her so that she would agree to sell him the rights, then discarding her at the earliest opportunity.

"Damn!"

"My feelings exactly," Liz responded with a heavy sigh.

"Isn't there anything I can do?" Marina asked desperately. "Any way I can get back the movie rights?"

"I'm afraid not, love."

"I'll return the money."

"It won't do any good. Kramer wouldn't accept it, I'm sure. For whatever reason, he really wants to do this movie. He's already in negotiation with one of the top screenwriters in the business."

"Damn it, Liz, it isn't fair!"

"I know. I won't stoop to banality and point out that life isn't fair. Ah, well. It's all a learning experience, you know. And remember, you'll get a great deal of money if they make this movie. With Kramer pushing it, it'll probably get made."

"The money doesn't matter if he ruins my story."

"I do understand how you feel, Marina. You're not the first author this has happened to. The fortunate ones simply take the money and run. I know you're not made that way. If there was anything I could do, I would, even if it meant losing money—God forbid. But believe me, there's nothing. So just put it behind you and go on to the next project."

"Liz, I've got to go. I'll talk to you later."

"Right, love. Bye."

When she hung up, Marina's expression was one of barely controlled fury. *Put it behind you,* Liz had said. That was just what her mother had asked her to do. It seemed she was being asked to put a lot of bad things behind her.

"What is it?" Rosie finally asked when it became apparent that Marina was lost in thought.

Briefly, Marina explained what had happened.

"Oh, dear, I'm sorry. I know how excited you were about doing the adaptation. It's a shame there's nothing that can be done about it."

There was no way she could simply lie down and take it, Marina decided suddenly. "Maybe there isn't any way of stopping Kramer. But I can sure as hell let him know what I think of him!"

She rose and strode toward the front door.

"Where are you going?" Rosie asked anxiously.

"To L.A.," Marina flung back over her shoulder, then slammed the door behind her.

She didn't even bother to pack a bag. She simply got in her car and headed south.

Eight hours later she was in Los Angeles. It was dark, a cool, clear evening with a light breeze and nary a hint of smog. On either side of the San Diego Freeway the myriad lights of the city twinkled brightly. In the distance, to the east, the tall skyscrapers of downtown L.A. were well-lit spires piercing the inky sky.

But Marina was oblivious to the city pulsing around her with its own special excitement. When she reached the Culver City area, she concentrated intently on finding the right turnoff. A few minutes later she pulled up at the front gate of National Studios. To the right the visitors' parking lot was nearly empty. It was late and few people were left on the lot. Marina prayed that Kramer hadn't left yet.

"Marina Turner to see Stephen Kramer," she said to the guard.

He scanned the list of people approved to enter the lot, then looked up at her. "Afraid there's no pass for you, miss. Is he expecting you?"

"No." She fumbled for the right words. "I . . . I had a meeting with him here recently and I need to speak to him about it."

"I'll have to call his office. Wait just a minute, please."

Anxiety gripped Marina, twisting her stomach into knots. Would Kramer refuse to see her? It wouldn't surprise her in the least. If he did refuse to see her, she had no idea what she would do. She only knew that she was going to tell him what she thought, one way or another.

The guard was on the phone in his cubicle for only a moment before hanging up, then turning back to Marina. "Sorry, miss, he's gone home for the night. If you'd like to leave a message, I can give it to him in the morning."

Marina didn't know if Kramer had really left or if he was simply avoiding her. She sat there in her car, unsure what to do next. The guard looked impatient and she knew she'd have to say something.

Suddenly there was another car behind her and the guard looked even more impatient. "Well, miss?"

"I'll just pull over to the side and write a note to leave for Mr. Kramer," Marina finally responded.

"Fine." The curt response indicated the guard didn't care what she did as long as she stopped blocking the entrance gate.

As Marina pulled her Volkswagen over to the side of the wide entrance lane, she saw someone leaving through the exit on the other side. Through his open car window she caught a glimpse of Marty's dark head.

Leaning out her own open window, she called out, "Marty!"

He braked his car to a sudden halt and looked back.

Marina got out of her car and hurried over to him. As she bent down to speak to him through the window, she saw that he had the grace to look embarrassed.

"Marina, what on earth are you doing here? Did you have an appointment with Stephen?"

"Not exactly."

The tone of her words dispelled any doubt he might have had about her unexpected appearance. "Now, Marina, I think I know why you're here."

"It was all a ruse, wasn't it? He never intended to let me do the adaptation."

"I wouldn't say that—"

Marina interrupted furiously, "You wouldn't say it, but it's still true!"

"The writer Stephen wants to use is wonderful. Just keep an open mind and I think you'll be very pleased with his work."

Marina hadn't thought it was possible to get even more angry than she'd been, but now she exploded. "*His* work! He wants to hire a *man* to write a female coming-of-age story?"

"Now, Marina, just listen for a minute."

"Don't 'now, Marina' me, damn it! I trusted you when you asked me to give him another chance. Despite everything, I trusted *him*."

Her voice broke and she knew that at any moment she'd burst into tears. She hated herself for being so weak at a moment when she wanted to be strong. But she simply couldn't help it.

The only good thing about the situation was that Marty looked as guilty as a child caught with his hand in a cookie jar. "God, I'm so sorry," he repeated. "If there's anything I can do..." Sincerity shone in his dark brown eyes.

Pulling herself together, Marina responded, "You can tell me where Stephen Kramer is. I want to tell him exactly what I think of him."

A rueful look transformed Marty's woebegone expression. "It won't do any good. There's no way he'll change his mind."

"I don't care. I just want the satisfaction of facing him."

Marty hesitated, then sighed heavily. "What the hell. I guess he has it coming. He's at home—1142 Gull Drive, just off Pacific Coast Highway in Trancas. Don't tell him who gave you the address."

Marina's smile was warm. "I won't. Thanks."

"Sure. Go get him, kid."

Marina got back in her car, took out a map of Los Angeles County, found Trancas, then headed in that direction. She drove for more than an hour before finally reaching Gull Drive, a narrow road that branched off to the left on the ocean side of the highway. Beach houses lined the road and it took a few minutes for Marina to find 1142. It was at the end of the road, apart from the other houses. A two-story structure built of redwood and glass, it was completely dark. There wasn't even a light shining over the door.

Marina knocked on the door, but without much hope. She wasn't surprised when no one answered. No one was home. For a moment she was afraid Marty might have lied to her. Then she noticed "S. Kramer" on the mailbox, and decided that Kramer simply hadn't arrived home yet. He was probably having dinner somewhere.

Although Marina hadn't eaten since breakfast, ten hours earlier, she wasn't hungry. She was too upset to even think about food.

A cold wind blowing in from the ocean, only fifty yards away, made her shiver. She decided to wait in her car for Kramer. He had to come home sometime, and when he did, she would have the satisfaction of telling him exactly what she thought of him.

In her car, she sat bolt upright, waiting expectantly for a few minutes. But she was absolutely exhausted. It had been

a long drive from Big Sur. The trip and the emotional upheaval she'd been through began to take their toll.

Leaning her head back against the headrest, she told herself she would close her eyes for a minute . . . just for a minute. . . .

But the moment her lids closed she felt her mind begin to
wander as she drifted off. And the last thing she was conscious of was a mental image of a man whose eyes were as
deep and dark and unfathomable as the ocean. . . .

Chapter Three

As Stephen Kramer turned onto Gull Drive, he had a sense of intense relief. He'd thought that damn dinner would go on forever. When eleven o'clock came and went, he'd finally told Chuck Weymouth he had an early-morning meeting and had to get to bed.

Chuck, the head of production at National Studios, was a hard man to get away from when he was trying to get something from someone. And he was definitely trying to get something from Stephen—concessions that would make the sale of *Rebels* to cable more profitable for the studio.

But Stephen had no intention of lowering his profits so National Studios could make even more money than it had already made from *Rebels*. He had a pretty shrewd suspicion about exactly how much money the studio had short-changed him with its creative accounting practices. And that didn't put him in a mood to be amenable.

He knew Chuck was angry, but it didn't matter. Chuck would contain his anger because he needed Stephen. That was how things worked in the film industry. Of course, if the day ever came when Stephen's movies weren't profitable for the studio, then Chuck would feel free to treat him like dirt. That was also how things worked.

Stephen's mouth curved upward in a smile that was totally humorless. It was a vicious business in many ways. But it was also the most exciting game around. He'd fought and clawed his way into the game and he intended to remain in it for a long, long time.

As he pulled into the driveway of his home, he remembered something an old-time director had told him when he was first starting out. The crusty old director was known as much for his legendary battles with studios as he was for his magnificent films. He'd taken a swig of Jack Daniels straight from the bottle, fixed Stephen with a beady eye and bellowed, ''There's nothing to be scared of, kid. They can kill you, but they can't eat you.''

From that moment on, Stephen had refused to be intimidated by the people he dealt with.

Stephen pushed a button on his automatic garage door opener and waited for the door to slowly rise. As it did so, the light from inside the garage illuminated a Volkswagen parked nearby. Stephen had been too tired and too preoccupied to notice the car before. Now, he wondered what it was doing next to his house.

He drove his black jeep into the garage and turned off the engine, but he didn't lower the garage door. Instead, he left it up and walked over to the Volkswagen. There was someone inside, he could tell, someone who looked asleep.

Bending down, he peered inside the closed window and was dumbfounded to see Marina Turner. What on earth was she doing here? he wondered. And how had she managed to get his address?

He didn't have to wonder why she'd come to see him. That much was all too obvious. Her agent must have informed her that she was being cut off from the screenplay for *Casey*. And being the stubborn, argumentative young woman she was, she'd come to raise hell with him.

This, on top of a wasted evening with Chuck, combined to make him thoroughly angry. He should leave her out here, he thought. It would serve her right. She'd been nothing but trouble from the start and he wasn't inclined to go out of his way to take pity on her.

But a nagging conscience told him it was very late, very dark and very cold outside. It wasn't safe for a young woman to spend the night outside in her car alone. And it sure wasn't comfortable.

Then he saw that she hadn't even bothered to lock the car doors. "The little fool," he muttered under his breath. Was she stupid enough to think Trancas was immune to crimes like rape and robbery just because it was a wealthy area?

Anyway, that did it. He couldn't leave her out here, he decided, easy prey for a prowling criminal looking for some house or car to break into. He opened the door, but to his surprise she didn't wake up. She lay slumped in the seat, sleeping as soundly as a child and looking about as innocent and helpless. Moonlight shed a golden glow on her pale skin. Her dark, tousled hair framed her oval face in stark contrast. A fringe of thick, dark lashes curved upward at the top of high cheeks.

In a glance, he took in her faded jeans tucked into worn tan leather boots, and a bulky black sweater. In his business he was used to seeing women expertly made up and dressed in the latest styles. It was quite a change seeing one who was completely natural. A refreshing change.

His irritation with her was softening, and he didn't want that to happen. She was a problem, he reminded himself. She had been from the first. And the sooner he got rid of her, the better.

The question was, how to get rid of her? Reaching out, he touched her hand with the idea of shaking her enough to wake her up. To his surprise, her hand was ice-cold. She'd been waiting for a while, he realized. Then he gently touched her soft cheek and found it was ice-cold as well.

That did it. He couldn't just wake her up abruptly and send her on her way. If he didn't warm her up fast, he told himself, she might get pneumonia.

He hurried back to his front door, unlocked it, then left it open as he returned to the car. Tenderly, he picked Marina up in his arms, taking care not to wake her. He wasn't sure why he was being so careful with her. He wasn't sure he wanted to know.

As he picked her up, she stirred but didn't wake. Her head lay cradled against his chest. Through the thin cotton of his white V-neck sweater, Stephen felt the smooth curve of her cheek. Something was touched within him that hadn't been touched in a long, long time—protectiveness. He was filled with an overwhelming urge to protect her.

A powerful sense of déjà vu jolted him as he carried her inside. Suddenly he realized what it was. The way she felt in his arms, so helpless and in need of his strength and protection, reminded him of how his little sister had felt when she'd fallen asleep in front of the TV and he had carried her to bed.

That was so long ago, another time, another place—another life. A life filled with hardships and unhappiness. He'd worked hard to put it behind him, and he thought he'd done so. Until this moment, when those bittersweet memories came rushing back with all the force of water bursting through a broken dam.

Suddenly he felt like a fool, standing there holding a sleeping woman, and indulging in unprofitable reverie. This wasn't at all like him. From the time he'd left home at sixteen, he'd focused on the future with a ruthless intensity. What lay ahead was all that mattered—not what had come before.

He closed the car door with his shoulder and strode inside the house.

He carried Marina effortlessly, for she didn't weigh much. Too skinny for his tastes, he thought with casual arrogance. He liked women with lush curves. This one had a rather coltish figure, all long legs, slender hips and small breasts. Even though she was tall—nearly as tall as he was, in fact—she felt tiny, for her bone structure was delicate and fine.

Gently he laid her down on the brown leather sofa, then reached over to turn on a nearby lamp. At one end of the sofa was a thick white wool afghan. He spread it over Marina, from her feet to her chin. But she needed more than that to warm her, he realized. Bending down, he turned on the gas jet in the gray-tiled fireplace in front of the sofa. In a moment a brisk fire was warming the cold room.

Then he sat down in a chair flanking the sofa and looked at Marina Turner. He grudgingly had to admit that she was pretty. Especially when she was asleep. The firm, round chin didn't look quite so stubborn, and the eyes that could blaze quicksilver when she was angry were hidden.

They were unusual eyes, he remembered. Dove-gray. Not what one would expect with such dark hair. That pale skin was unexpected, too. It was the color of rich, thick cream. Where curling tendrils of blue-black hair fell across her cheeks and forehead, the effect was striking. Stephen wondered idly what physical combination of parents had produced this young woman.

Reaching out, he touched her cheek. The chill had left her skin and it was warm now. She would be fine, thanks to him. She was just lucky that he'd come home tonight, he thought arrogantly, instead of spending the night at Laura's Santa Monica apartment.

Suddenly it occurred to him that Laura would be jealous if she learned that a young woman had been here alone with him. But she had no reason to be jealous. Aside from the fact that he wasn't sexually attracted to Marina Turner, he also wasn't given to playing the field. He preferred to stick to one woman at a time, and right now that woman was Laura Bufano, a very smart, very beautiful fashion designer.

It was a moot point anyway, he told himself, because Laura would never hear of this. Marina Turner would be gone shortly and he would never see her again. That would certainly be a relief, he thought. Writers were often a pain to deal with, and novelists who fancied themselves screenwriters were the worst.

The question was, how to deal with Marina? Should he wake her up, get the inevitable angry confrontation over with, and send her on her way? he wondered. It was one o'clock in the morning, though, hardly a good time to send a young woman alone out into the night.

He yawned and slumped lower in the chair. It was beginning to hit him just how exhausted he was. It had been a long, long day. And even though the next day was Saturday, there was a great deal to do: an early meeting with Marty, a 10:00 A.M. conference call with an English actor and his agent, lunch with the screenwriter whom he was trying to persuade to adapt *Casey*, then an afternoon full of financial discussions.

His eyes were heavy and he realized he needed to get to bed immediately or he'd be a wreck in the morning.

To hell with it, he decided abruptly. He'd leave her here on the sofa and he'd go to bed. She looked so out of it, he doubted she'd wake before morning.

He stood up and stretched tiredly. Then he heard high-pitched mewing and a faint, but determined scratching sound. Glancing at a sliding glass door, he saw a familiar sight—a mangy gray tomcat peering in, an expectant expression on his narrow, whiskered face.

"Well, hello there," Stephen whispered out loud. He walked into the kitchen, took a small bowl from a cupboard, filled it with dry cat food, then went back into the living room. After sliding open the glass door, he set down the bowl on a redwood deck, then stood for a moment watching the cat eat.

He had no idea where the cat came from or where it lived. It looked so unkempt, he doubted it belonged to anyone. It had begun showing up outside his window a few months earlier, and once he began to feed it, it kept coming back. He and the cat had developed a ritual of sorts. It waited patiently out on the deck until Stephen got home at night. On nights like this one, when Stephen neglected to feed it immediately, it scratched on the window to remind him.

While the gray tom took advantage of Stephen's generosity, it seemed to have no inclination to become friendly. At first Stephen had attempted to pick it up, or at least to pet it. But his overtures were coolly rebuffed. Respecting the cat's independent nature, he didn't press the issue.

Now, Stephen watched while the cat ate. Noticing a slightly torn ear, he whispered, "Been fighting again, huh? Well, it is a pretty rough world out there. I'll bet you gave as good as you got."

The cat gave him a quick, furtive look, then went back to eating.

"I know," Stephen went on. "It's none of my business. Okay."

The cat finished eating, then paused to clean his face, which wasn't something he ordinarily did. Usually he trotted off, slightly crooked tail held high in the air, as soon as he licked the bowl clean.

Stephen smiled, and for once there was real humor in his expression. "Got a hot date? She must be pretty special for you to be so concerned about your appearance. Don't worry, you cut quite a dashing figure. Not strictly handsome, perhaps, but definitely interesting looking. A Humphrey Bogart among cats."

The cat finished his toilette. With nary a backward glance at Stephen, he trotted off.

"Good luck, my friend," Stephen whispered. Then in a voice tinged with more raw emotion than he normally revealed, he finished, "Maybe now you won't be quite so alone."

After closing and locking the window, Stephen turned and looked back at Marina. She lay curled on her side in a fetal position, her head resting on her hands. What a funny kid she was in some ways, he mused. Driving that pathetic car. Wearing jeans all the time, and not even designer ones at that. Sporting a hairstyle that could charitably be described as "casual."

And yet she'd written a book about an upper-middle-class girl who had everything money could buy, except happiness. She'd seemed to have a real feeling for that particular class that could only come from familiarity. For the first time he felt a stirring of curiosity about her. Where did she come from? Was she an eighties version of a hippie, trading the materialistic life she'd grown up with for a simpler one?

He shook his head tiredly. It didn't matter. *She* didn't matter. All that mattered was making *Casey* as well as it could be made so that finally the critics and his peers would stop dismissing him as a producer of junk-food movies.

He'd always wanted to do films he could be proud of, films that would say something—films that would earn him respect as well as money. But no one would give him a chance to do so when he first started out. So he made movies that earned so much money he finally got the clout he needed to attempt something better.

He wasn't going to let Marina Turner spoil it by writing a bad script in the process of indulging her ego. In the morning, he would send her packing. And then he could get on with the business of making one hell of a picture that would stand this industry on its ears.

But before heading toward his bedroom, he reached down and pulled the afghan just a little closer to her chin.

Marina stirred. Deep in her half-conscious mind, she realized she was cold, and she pulled the blanket a little tighter around her. Then, through the fog of sleepiness, she began to remember...she'd been in her car and there was no blanket.

Her eyes flew open. It was no blanket, she saw, but an afghan covering her. She lay on a long leather sofa. In front of her a small fire burned in a stunning gray-tiled fireplace.

Where am I? she wondered anxiously.

Sitting up, she looked around. She was in a living room. It was huge and high ceilinged. Dark, heavy beams contrasted sharply with the stark white of the walls, which were almost blindingly bright from the morning sun. One entire wall was floor-to-ceiling windows. Through those windows, Marina could see a broad, sandy beach and the ocean.

Kramer's house. It had to be.

But it was odd—aside from the sofa, a matching chair, a low table and one lamp, the room was empty. There was no other furniture, no paintings or other decorations on the walls. No personal mementos of any kind. Nothing to reveal what kind of person lived here. Maybe Kramer had just moved in, she decided. Anyway, it wasn't important. The question was how had she got in here? And where was Kramer?

The latter question was answered almost immediately. Through the windows she saw a familiar figure wearing bathing trunks, with a large towel flung over his shoulder, coming up the beach toward the house.

Hurriedly, Marina ran her fingers through her hair to brush it back off her face, and straightened her rumpled sweater. She felt nervous and gauche. She hadn't planned to confront Kramer this way—tired, disheveled, having spent the night in his house. But she had no choice. Angry at him, and at herself for putting herself in such a ridiculous position, she waited for him to come.

He crossed the redwood deck that ran along the back of the house. The briefest of blue bathing trunks revealed a muscular body and a broad, smooth chest. His body, tanned to a golden sheen, dripped water. His blond hair was plastered wetly against his head.

Her breath caught as it suddenly hit her how totally masculine he was. She felt an unexpected pulse of physical attraction begin to grow deep within her as she looked at those hard, corded muscles, that broad chest. Yes, he was very much a man, all right. And he had carried her into his house where she had spent the night. He had held her against him, and she hadn't even been aware of it.

The thought shook her profoundly. She swallowed hard and forced herself to regain control of her errant emotions. A moment later he entered the room.

He looked younger, less hard and intimidating than when she had met him before. For an instant, Marina felt her defenses relax. But as soon as he fixed her with a decidedly cool look, her defenses came right back up again, stronger than ever.

"So you're up." The words were curt and unencouraging.

"Yes. I—" Marina stopped, suddenly tongue-tied.

Kramer went on, "I'll be right back," and headed toward a hallway opening off the living room. He flung back over his shoulder, "There's a bathroom off the kitchen," then disappeared into the hallway. A moment later Marina heard a door open and close.

She continued standing there, unsure what to do next. Finally, she decided to go in search of the bathroom. She found it easily, on the other side of a large, immaculate kitchen that looked as if it was rarely used.

Staring into the small mirror over the sink, she was dismayed at her appearance. She looked like a vagrant, her hair a mess, her sweater wrinkled, her face creased from resting on her hands.

She would have given anything for a comb, a toothbrush and a change of clothes. But she didn't even have those things in her car, let alone here. So she settled for washing her face and hands and running her fingers through her hair to roughly style it.

When she walked back into the kitchen, she found Kramer standing by the counter, setting out two brown earthenware mugs. Next to him, an electric coffee maker was on, and the rich aroma of brewing coffee was beginning to fill the air. Kramer had dressed in tan gabardine slacks and a matching shirt, open at the throat, but minus the gold chains Marina thought all Hollywood producers wore.

"Coffee?" he asked, his tone still curt.

She nodded. Normally she preferred tea, but she didn't feel up to asking for it.

"Cream or sugar?" he went on.

"No...thank you." She wished her voice sounded more confident and self-assured. But his brisk, no-nonsense attitude made her feel completely at a loss. And the knowledge that he must have been the one to bring her in last night and cover her up, only made things worse.

He poured coffee for both of them. As he handed her a cup, their eyes met. For a moment she stared intently into his eyes, trying to read them. But as usual it was impossible. She had no idea what was at the bottom of those dark blue depths.

Without saying a word, Kramer took his coffee and walked into the living room. Marina followed, feeling rather like a puppy being obedience trained, who isn't sure yet of the drill.

Kramer stood in front of the fireplace, his hands wrapped around the warm mug. Marina would have liked to sit down, but she didn't want to put herself at a physical disadvantage with him. She already felt she was at an emotional one. So she stood facing him, sipping the hot black coffee and wondering how to begin.

It was a relief when he began the dialogue, though the tone of his words was anything but encouraging. "I assume you came here last night to talk to me about being cut off from *Casey*."

She took a quick, final sip of coffee, then set the mug down on the table in front of the sofa. Straightening, she faced Kramer and marshaled all her resolve. "Yes, I came to talk to you about it. My agent told me you want to hire someone else to do the screenplay."

"That's right. I intend to hire someone else."

The difference between *want* and *intend* wasn't lost on Marina. The anger that had sent her on the precipitate journey from Big Sur to L.A. returned now in full force.

"I gave you a treatment that faithfully reflected my book. There's no reason why you shouldn't let me do the screenplay."

"That wasn't a treatment, it was an outline of a novel," he said sharply.

"You're splitting hairs," Marina insisted. "Treatment, outline, what's the difference?"

His expression was maddeningly condescending. "They're two entirely different things. But you wouldn't understand that because you don't know the first thing about writing a screenplay."

He didn't bother to keep the sarcasm from his tone.

Marina felt her anger deepen, fueled by a nagging suspicion that he might be right.

She shot back, "I*f* they're so different, tell me how."

Putting his coffee cup on the table, he focused intently on her. "I'll be glad to give you a beginner's lesson in screenwriting. You can use it."

She stared at him sullenly. Even *if* he was right that she'd made some mistakes in the treatment, that was no excuse for his treating her as if she were a not-very-bright student and he a teacher.

He went on matter-of-factly, "Moving pictures are just that—pictures that move. A screenplay is action and dialogue. Period. Nothing more."

"I understand that," Marina responded defensively.

"Apparently not, because you filled your version of a treatment with a lot of internalization. You can do that in a novel, but you can't do it in a screenplay. *Action is character* is the basic tenet of screenwriting. You have to *show* not tell."

With a sickening sense of being wrong, Marina realized she'd done exactly what he was accusing her of having done. She'd simply lifted portions of her novel and put them into the treatment without stopping to consider if they would work in a movie.

Kramer went on relentlessly. "And the length—my God, do you realize you put in every major scene that was in the book?"

This, at least, was one criticism that Marina felt was unwarranted. She said confidently, "Presumably you bought my book because you liked it. You can't turn it into a movie and leave out the most important things in it. In that case, why bother?"

"I bought your book because I thought it would translate well to the screen."

Marina noticed that he didn't say he bought it because it was well written. Or even because it was a compelling story. Obviously, the man couldn't bring himself to say one complimentary thing about her. Even if he was right in his criticism of her, that didn't excuse his rudeness toward her.

Throwing caution to the wind, she confessed, "I didn't want to sell the movie rights to you because I knew what you'd do to the story."

Anger shone in his eyes and his tone was deceptively calm. "Is that right? What exactly did you think I'd do to your precious novel?"

"Ruin it! Take out everything that matters in it, and throw in some jiggle and cheap humor. Just to make sure it will appeal to the lowest common denominator."

It was a harsh accusation. Such harshness wasn't like her, but Marina was too wounded to care.

She was surprised to see him smile, then realized that the smile didn't reach his eyes. "I take it you're not a fan of my movies. Fortunately, a lot of people are."

"A lot of people like crude jokes about sex and simplistic characterizations. That's not what my book is all about. My treatment reflected my book."

Kramer's cold anger turned to impatience. He seemed to be trying to figure out how to explain something to her that she couldn't begin to understand. He spoke slowly, carefully. "Look, Miss Turner, if you'd gone on to do a screenplay based on your treatment, it would have been two hundred pages long. Do you have any idea what that would have meant in movie length?"

"Two hundred pages doesn't sound all that long," she argued. "My book was over four hundred."

"Well, a one hundred-twenty-page script is a two-hour movie. And two hours is all we've got. We're not shooting a major epic here that can go three or four hours."

"Then you're talking about cutting out a lot of my novel," she replied, irate at the thought that her carefully constructed story would be slashed to the bone.

"Exactly. We use the high points, and that's it."

Marina stood there, absorbing everything he'd said. Her mind reeled with the realization that on many counts he was right. It was humiliating to accept. With her fierce pride, humiliation wasn't something she handled well.

It was especially hard to take because it was coming from a man. Recently her feelings about men had become confused and fraught with bitterness. Under the best of circumstances, she found it difficult to deal with men. And this wasn't the best of circumstances, it was close to the worst.

Kramer watched her and something like pity softened his harsh expression. When he finished, his tone was less accusatory and more gentle. "Anyway, as I said, novels and screenplays are two different forms. Just because you can write one, doesn't mean you can write the other."

Slowly, Marina said, "It sounds as if you don't believe anyone can write both."

A hint of a smile curved Kramer's firm mouth. "Well, William Goldman has managed to do it, but there aren't many writers like him. Novelists can't look at their work objectively and cut what has to be cut for a movie."

The mention of a male screenwriter reminded Marina of a major source of her anger. She said accusingly, "You want a *man* to adapt my book."

"Yes," he admitted readily. "A man who happens to have won an Oscar for adapting a screenplay from a book."

"But don't you understand, this is a female coming-of-age story! No man could possibly understand it."

He smiled again, condescendingly. "That's rather a sexist philosophy, don't you think? What if I suggested the opposite—that no woman could write about men?"

Marina fairly shook with frustration and helpless rage. "It isn't the same thing, and you know it!"

"It's exactly the same thing. A good writer can write about anything. Sex has nothing to do with it."

With a sickening feeling, Marina realized that she wasn't going to win. There was no way she could persuade him to let her adapt her book. He'd made up his mind—probably from the very beginning.

She whispered helplessly, "I never had a chance, did I? It didn't matter how well I did the treatment, you never intended to let me do the screenplay. You had this man in mind all along."

The truth of the accusation seemed to have some force, for Kramer had the grace to look less self-assured.

"I know now it won't do any good to try to talk to you, Mr. Kramer. But there's one last thing I want to say. *Casey* is my story. It came from my heart. I understand it, feel for it, in a way that no other writer, man or woman, could possibly do. So hire your Oscar-winning screenwriter. Maybe he'll give you the kind of movie you want, a financially successful one. Who knows, if he's really a good writer, maybe he'll even give you a good movie. But it will never be his story. He'll never love those characters like I do. And in some way that will show through."

By the end of her impassioned speech, tears were streaming down Marina's face. She would have given anything to stop them, to appear strong and controlled. But she couldn't. This meant too much to her.

Without waiting for his response, she spun on her heel and left.

In her car she found her purse and car keys. She started the engine, quickly wiped her eyes, then turned the car around and headed back up Gull Drive. She felt drained of all emotion. All she wanted to do was go home.

Inside the house, Stephen was rooted to the spot where he'd stood during the entire argument. Marina Turner was emotional and immature, he told himself. Everything he'd said about her treatment was accurate. She didn't know the first thing about screenwriting. This project would be a lot better off in the hands of an experienced professional who would know how to turn her delicate novel into a satisfying film.

So if all that was true, he asked himself, why did he feel like a monster? It wasn't the fact that they'd argued vehemently. He did that nearly every day, with a wide variety of people, men and women, and it rarely bothered him. He knew he was right, and that was all that mattered.

Only this time it wasn't all that mattered. He'd deeply hurt that surprisingly vulnerable young woman. And it bothered him more than he ever would have expected.

Chapter Four

Stephen sat at a table next to a window in a restaurant on the beach in Malibu. Through the glass he watched the ocean glistening darkly on this clear, starry night. There was no wind and the water was smooth as glass. Small waves broke in a gentle froth on the sand, and small birds scurried about on long, skinny legs.

"Stephen... hey, Earth calling Stephen."

Startled, he looked at Marty sitting across the table.

"You haven't heard a word I've said."

A rueful grin softened Stephen's face. "No, I haven't. Sorry."

Marty shrugged good-naturedly. "It's okay. I wasn't saying anything too important anyway." He hesitated, then went on, "You've been pretty preoccupied lately. Something wrong?"

"No, of course not. Just... just business stuff. You know."

"Sure?"

"Sure."

Marty's dark brown eyes watched him intently. "Hey, this is good old Marty, remember? If there is something wrong, you can tell me."

"There's nothing wrong, okay? By the way, I think I've just about persuaded Simon Ryland to adapt *Casey*."

"I thought he wasn't interested in it."

"He's not. But he's interested in money. And I'm willing to meet his price. Three hundred thousand and a no-cut deal."

"But Stephen, if he's not too thrilled with the story maybe it's not wise to hire him."

"He'll do a good job. He's a professional. He's never done anything that wasn't exceptional."

"Okay, if you're sure..."

But Stephen wasn't listening again. He stared out the window, remembering....

A waiter stopped to refill their coffee cups and Stephen turned back to Marty. He said abruptly, "Marina Turner came to see me last week."

He noticed Marty's look of chagrin, but thought nothing of it. Marty was too nice for his own good, and Stephen assumed he was simply feeling sorry for the girl.

"Oh, really?" Marty responded, not quite meeting his look. "You didn't say anything about it."

"There wasn't anything to say."

There was an awkward silence, then Marty asked with studied casualness, "So what happened?"

"She was mad about being fired, of course."

"Of course."

Stephen shot Marty an irritated look. "I know you liked her, but that's beside the point. This is business, not a popularity contest. She just couldn't cut it."

"Hey, am I arguing?" Marty protested.

"No, but your silence on this subject has been eloquent."

"I just think you should've given the kid more of a chance. She wrote a great book."

"I know it's a great book. That's why I bought it," Stephen snapped. "And I gave her a chance, didn't I?"

"In a manner of speaking. You and I both know that you more or less bought her off with the deal to do the treatment. You wanted Ryland all along."

"Damn it, Marty, she blew it. She did a rotten job on the treatment. Anyone could see that."

"I know. But if you'd worked with her on it—"

"Worked with her! What was I supposed to do, take her through the process step by step? I'm not teaching a course in Screenwriting 1A here. This is the real world where there are budgets to stick to and deadlines to meet. Ryland will do a good job, he'll do it fast and there won't be any headaches."

"Well, I admit there'd probably be a lot of headaches with her."

"You're right about that. Marina Turner is a walking headache. She's been a pain in the neck from the first minute I laid eyes on her."

Marty eyed Stephen curiously. "She really gets to you, huh?"

"She sure as hell does! She—" He stopped, suddenly realizing what he was saying. He backtracked. "She irritates me more than just about any woman I can remember."

"Yeah, she's as stubborn as—" Marty looked at Stephen and finished with a wry grin "—as you."

Stephen grinned in return. "All right, enough about her. How'd we get on the subject of Marina Turner, anyway?"

"You brought it up."

"Oh. Well, anyway, there's no point in talking about it because if she can't even write a treatment, she sure can't write a screenplay."

"You're right. She doesn't know the craft. Of course," Marty added diffidently, "she'd probably bring a lot of passion and commitment to the story. And unlike craft, that isn't something you can buy.''

"That's what she said," Stephen responded thoughtfully.

As Marty slowly sipped his coffee, he watched Stephen.

The latter abruptly said, "Let's change the subject. By the way, why didn't Amy come with you tonight?"

To Stephen's surprise, Marty's cheerful countenance grew sober.

"She's visiting her mother."

The words were clipped and the tone clearly discouraged further questions. It was entirely unlike Marty. Suddenly Stephen became aware of what he'd been too preoccupied to notice earlier—Marty hadn't been his usual outgoing, joking self all evening. In fact, he'd been quiet and thoughtful. And physically, he looked tired and drawn, instead of bursting with energy and enthusiasm as he usually was.

Marty was his closest friend. They'd known each other since high school, and Stephen understood him well enough to sense when something was wrong. Tonight something was very wrong.

When he spoke there was a caring note in Stephen's voice that would have surprised anyone but his few really close friends. "What is it, buddy?"

Marty stared intently into his nearly empty cup of coffee. "We separated."

Stephen was stunned. Marty and Amy had been high school sweethearts. They'd married at twenty and recently celebrated their tenth wedding anniversary. To Stephen they were the ideal couple, devoted, supportive, as tight as a man and woman could ever hope to be. In a business where personal relationships seemed especially fragile, and divorce and infidelity were rampant, they were reassuring proof that some marriages did make it. If they could find that kind of happiness, then it encouraged Stephen to hope that maybe someday he would, too.

Now, he looked at Marty and wondered how he could have been so self-centered not to notice the devastation evident beneath the breezy facade.

"What happened?"

Marty hesitated. He looked more uncomfortable than Stephen could ever remember seeing him look. When he finally answered, his voice shook. "She...she had an affair."

Stephen simply couldn't believe it. If he didn't know that Marty wouldn't make a statement like that without being absolutely certain, he would have accused him of imagining things.

"If you'd rather not talk about it..."

"It's not that. If I don't talk to someone about it, I think I'll go crazy."

Stephen didn't say anything further. He didn't have to.

After a long pause, Marty went on, "She told me about it. Some friends found out and she was afraid I would find out, too. She didn't want me to hear it from someone else. She thought that would be harder somehow. Who knows, maybe she was right. And she was afraid I wouldn't hear the true story."

"What happened?"

"The guy's an actor she met on the lot one day."

At that point, Marty managed a disdainful smile.

Stephen smiled gently in return and shook his head. *"Actors."*

"Yeah. *Actors.* Amy was flattered that he was attracted to her. She said she'd been married for so long, she thought romance was something she'd never experience again. So...it happened."

Looking at his old friend, Stephen felt for him. He knew how hard Marty was taking it, though he was trying to be cool and composed.

"I take it that it's over," Stephen said slowly.

"Yeah. She said as soon as it happened she felt awful and realized it wasn't what she wanted at all. She apologized for hurting me."

"Did she want to separate?"

Marty shook his head. "No. She said she realizes now how much I mean to her and she wants another chance."

"But you don't know if you want to give it to her."

"Yeah. She decided to stay at her mother's while I think things through."

"Well, now that she's gone, how do you feel about her?"

The pain apparent in Marty's eyes softened. "I miss her. Every single minute. I can't believe how silent and empty the house is without her." He shrugged. "It's the little things, you know? The odor of food cooking when I get home at night. Hearing her laugh when she talks to friends on the phone. Reading something interesting in the paper and wanting to share it with her."

"But?"

"But I don't know if I can forgive and forget. I never cheated on her once. Not once."

"I know."

The two men were silent for a while. The waiter returned and filled their coffee cups again, but neither drank any more.

Finally, Stephen asked bluntly, "Do you just want sympathy or are you open to advice?"

A half smile played at the corners of Marty's mouth. "I know you're gonna tell me what you think whether I want to hear it or not. So go ahead. Get it over with."

Stephen crossed his arms on the table and leaned toward Marty. "Don't be a fool. Amy's the best thing that ever happened to you. So she made a mistake—one mistake. She isn't perfect. But neither are you. She deserves a second chance. Maybe you can't forget. But you can forgive. The alternative is the failure of your marriage. And that would be a tragedy.''

Marty didn't respond. He leaned back in his chair, looking thoughtful. Then, shooting a curious look at Stephen, he said, "Six months ago you told me you were going to ask Laura to marry you. But you haven't done it. If you're so high on marriage, why didn't you do it?"

Stephen was taken aback by the unexpected question. Any other time he would have refused to get into such a personal area, even with his best friend. Now, for some reason, he felt compelled to answer.

"I was going to ask her. I even bought a ring. I was waiting for the perfect moment—you know, the right time, the right place. So that for the rest of her life she would remember it as being absolutely perfect."

"What went wrong?"

"We were talking one night—Laura and another designer and I. Laura and this guy said that vows, promises, contracts, all that kind of thing, should be honored only while it's convenient."

"Situational ethics." Marty snorted disdainfully.

"Exactly. I couldn't believe what I was hearing. I asked her if she meant marriage vows. She said yes. After all, what seemed right at the time might not be right later. She said she would always want to feel free to explore other options, as she put it. In case something better came along."

"My God! What a way to begin a marriage."

"That's how I felt. So I returned the ring."

"But you still see her."

Stephen nodded. "Yes. And we have a pretty good relationship. It's just not quite good enough to last."

"You're a romantic at heart, my friend."

Stephen smiled sardonically. "Because I believe in marriage?"

"Because you believe in love. You really think it can last forever."

"I guess I do. At any rate, I intend to try to make it last forever. And I don't want a woman who is willing to settle for less."

Marty sighed. "Look at us. Sitting here getting maudlin over women. Hell, let's go."

"Okay."

Marty reached for the bill, but Stephen took it. "No, this one's on me. You can pay me back by inviting me over for dinner with you and Amy."

"You know," Marty said slowly, "she isn't all that good a cook."

"I know. But she stuck with you through thick and thin. When you didn't know where your next dime was coming from. And not once did she say, 'Stop trying to make movies and find a steady job.' So, how about that dinner?"

There was a pregnant pause. Stephen waited, saying nothing. He'd said all he could say. He only hoped his friend would come to the right decision.

Finally, Marty asked, "Is Friday okay?"

Stephen smiled broadly. "Friday's just fine."

Later, at home, Stephen sat on the sofa in front of a low fire. The sound of waves lapping the beach was soothing and peaceful, yet Stephen was anything but at peace. He thought about Marina Turner. Somehow, the knowledge that Marty almost let Amy walk out of his life made Stephen think twice about letting Marina walk out of his. Not that it was in any way the same thing, he insisted to himself.

He'd thought that all he wanted was to get rid of her and proceed with making *Casey*. Well, he'd gotten what he wanted. She was gone. She wasn't a nuisance anymore. He could concentrate totally on making the movie that meant so much to him.

Except he couldn't seem to concentrate on it. He kept remembering that night and the following morning—how she'd looked, what she'd said. The first time he'd met her, when she was late and then had the gall to get mad at him for going on with his other appointments, he'd thought she was willful and stubborn. But when she came to his house, he'd seen how vulnerable she was beneath that determined facade.

And she was so damn young and naive. How could anyone so young have written a novel that had such insight? he wondered. One thing was certain: she cared about that story. As Marty had said, she brought passion and commitment to the project, even if she did lack the necessary craft.

Craft could be taught, if one wanted to take the time to teach it. Passion couldn't.

The phone on the coffee table rang suddenly, shattering the silence and interrupting his thoughts. Reaching out, Stephen answered it tiredly. It had been a long day, and the evening had been emotionally exhausting.

"Hello?"

"Stephen, it's Laura." The familiar voice was soft and sexy and very confident. It was ironic, Stephen thought, that she should call when he'd been talking about her only a few minutes earlier.

She went on, "Sorry to call so late, but I tried earlier and you were out."

"Marty and I had dinner together. How are you?"

"Fine, love. Listen, about this weekend. I know we planned to go up to Lake Arrowhead, but I'm afraid something's come up and I'll have to cancel."

The weekend at Arrowhead was something they'd planned for weeks. Stephen rarely took off an entire weekend to relax, and he'd been looking forward to this. He felt a surge of disappointment and there was a sharp edge to his voice as he asked, "What happened?"

"Oh, nothing devastating. It's just work. There are some problems that have come up at the last minute, and I need to take care of them immediately."

"Are you saying we won't be able to get together at all this weekend?"

"Afraid so, darling. It's too bad, but there's nothing I can do about it. Businesses don't run themselves, as you well know."

"Yes, I know." His voice was flat and unemotional.

"I feel as disappointed about it as I know you must feel. If there was any way around it—"

"Don't worry, Laura," he interrupted. "I understand."

"Oh, I knew you would. Stephen, you're a dear. The perfect example of the New Man, so supportive of a woman and not expecting the world to revolve around you. Most men are so old-fashioned. Thank heavens, you're evolved."

"Is that what I am—evolved?"

There was a hint of sarcasm in his voice, but Laura chose to ignore it.

"Anyway, I won't keep you. By the way, don't bother calling, I'll be at the office all weekend. And I won't answer the phone there because I don't want to be interrupted."

"I'm sure you don't. Goodbye, Laura."

She hesitated, as the hard tone of his voice finally got through to her. When she finally responded, "Goodbye, love," there was slightly less confidence in her tone.

Stephen hung up, then went into the kitchen. If he'd been a drinking man, he'd have fixed himself a strong drink. But he'd seen enough of what alcohol could do when it destroyed his father, and he made a point of never touching liquor.

Instead, he took a soft drink from the refrigerator, popped the tab and drank it slowly.

He wasn't sure how he knew Laura was lying. But somehow he did know it. She'd never before canceled a weekend trip due to work, and he didn't believe that was why she was canceling this one. There was something in her voice; it was just a little too offhand, under the circumstances. And while she had tried to sound disappointed, she wasn't entirely convincing. The words were right, but beneath them lay a barely suppressed excitement.

She was going to spend the weekend with someone else. He was absolutely positive. That was why she didn't want him to try to reach her all weekend. He didn't for one moment believe that she was going to be in her office.

Finishing the last of the soft drink, he tossed it in the trash basket under the sink, then went into his bedroom. In the bathroom that opened off the bedroom, he stripped off his clothes and stepped into the large, glassed-in shower. As the first burst of hot water hit his chest, he realized that he wasn't nearly as upset about the situation as he should be. He was a little hurt, but not much.

More than anything else, he was angry at the dishonesty of the situation. If Laura had simply said she wanted to cancel their arrangements, and didn't care to go into the reasons why, he would have accepted that. He would have still felt rejected, and wouldn't have enjoyed that feeling, but he wouldn't feel as if he was being played for a fool.

That was the difference between Laura and Marty's wife, Amy, he decided. Amy had the courage to be honest, because, when all was said and done, she didn't want to put Marty in a position where he would feel like a fool. Stephen realized that was why he'd urged Marty to forgive her and give their marriage another chance. There was something there worth saving.

With Laura there wasn't.

It was odd, he thought, how quickly he had just decided that he didn't want to maintain his relationship with Laura. Why hadn't he come to that conclusion months earlier, when he realized they didn't place the same value on commitment? Why was tonight different from six months ago?

Because six months ago he hadn't met Marina Turner.

The unexpected thought struck him with all the force of the water beating on his chest.

That's stupid, he told himself irritably. Marina Turner didn't mean anything to him. She wasn't even his type.

He turned off the water, then stepped out of the shower and began toweling dry. What a night! he thought, shaking his head. First Marty's troubles, then Laura's little games. And now here he was actually paying careful consideration to the rudest, most troublesome young woman he'd met in quite a while.

After tossing the damp towel into a nearby hamper, he strode into the bedroom, still naked, and slipped between cool linen sheets. He reached over to turn out the bedside lamp, then lay there in the darkness, his mind racing. Grudgingly he faced a thought that had been at the back of his mind all week. He could give Marina a shot at doing the screenplay for *Casey*. Of course, there was no way she could do it on her own. She'd need help, and lots of it.

Logic told him that she was a damn good writer. Clearly, she'd learned how to write a novel. She could, presumably, learn how to write a screenplay if someone took the time to teach her. It would mean working closely with her, Stephen knew. He couldn't just send her on her way with a few basic lessons in screenwriting. In fact, he'd probably have to sit down and do it with her every step of the way.

Surprisingly, the thought wasn't all that unpleasant.

He knew that he was talking himself into doing something that he'd made a point of not doing. And he wasn't at all sure why he should change his mind now. There were a lot of compelling reasons why he shouldn't let Marina do the screenplay. And only one, rather doubtful one, why he should.

Maybe Laura was right in her opinion of him, he thought with dry humor. Maybe he was a fool. He was letting himself be swayed by emotion rather than reason—not the wisest course in a ruthless business like his. And not like him, at all.

If he did let Marina Turner tackle the script, instead of putting it in Simon Ryland's experienced hands, he was certainly making the whole process more difficult and time-consuming. By going one-on-one with Marina, who had made it clear she despised him, he was letting himself in for a whole lot of trouble.

But then, he'd never been afraid of trouble.

By late Saturday afternoon, Stephen had reached Rosie's house. He'd never have found it, he knew, if a gas station attendant in the village at Big Sur hadn't given him perfect directions. Like many Big Sur residents, the man was a friend of Rosie's, and knew the fastest way to her ranch.

Now Stephen got out of his car and smiled at the middle-aged woman sitting on the front porch. At her feet lay one of the ugliest, most useless-looking dogs Stephen had ever seen. "Afternoon, ma'am."

"Afternoon." The reply was noncommittal as she looked him up and down.

"Are you by any chance Rosie Delgado?"

"I am. Who are you?"

"My name's Stephen Kramer. I'm looking for Marina Turner. I understand she lives on your property."

The woman's expression went from mild curiosity to intense interest, tinged with disapproval, in an instant.

"She lives here. What do you want with Marina?"

"Mrs. Delgado, I'm a film producer and—"

"I know who you are, Mr. Kramer. And I know the sneaky, unfair way you've treated Marina. So I ask you again, what do you want with her?"

A slow smile spread across Stephen's face. "I take it you're a friend of hers, as well as her landlady."

"I am."

"You know that I'm making a movie from her book."

"I know you're not letting her write the screenplay."

"Well, I've changed my mind. I came to tell Marina that."

The woman looked startled, then wary. "This isn't some Hollywood trick, is it, Mr. Kramer?"

"I don't do tricks, ma'am. I leave that to the guys who do trick photography."

She eyed him thoughtfully. "No, I don't imagine you do. But I'll bet your killer grin charms the socks off every woman you meet."

Stephen laughed with genuine amusement. Then he commented frankly, "I didn't charm Marina."

"No, you sure didn't. You won't be welcome at her place."

"I expect not. But I want to see her anyway."

"Mr. Kramer, you don't strike me as the kind of young man who changes his mind on a whim. Why'd you do it now?"

"I wish I could tell you, Mrs. Delgado. But I'm not sure I understand it myself."

She hesitated, then asked, "You married?"

The question caught him by surprise. "No, ma'am."

She nodded to herself, as if to say, "I thought not." Aloud she said, "You can call me Rosie. And Marina's cabin is down this dirt road about a half mile. Good luck, Mr. Kramer."

"Thanks, Rosie. I'll probably need it."

Marina sat at her desk, working on her second novel. She wore her usual writing attire—her oldest jeans tucked into mid-calf-high moccasins, and an old college sweatshirt with U.C. Berkeley emblazoned in fading letters across the front. Her hair was even more messy than usual because she kept running her hands through it nervously.

She'd been working on the same chapter for the past week, and it wasn't going well. When she'd returned from that futile trip down to L.A., she'd decided that the only way to maintain her sanity was to put *Casey* behind her and get on with her new book. But each day it was the same thing. She began with the determination to concentrate on the story, but she ended up reliving that awful final argument with Stephen Kramer. With the virtue of hindsight, she thought of all sorts of telling rejoinders to his comments. She fantasized about how it would have gone if she'd remained cool and confident, instead of giving way to tears. If only she'd been strong instead of emotional, she thought bitterly.

She couldn't seem to help going over it again and again, even though she knew in her mind that it didn't matter what she'd said or done. He'd made up his mind and wasn't about to be swayed by her. As she faced that, all the frustration and anger and disappointment came back to the surface. There was something else, too, something she shied away from identifying. Something that had begun as she watched him walk up from the beach.

Put it behind you! she told herself for the hundredth time. Get on with it. Write.

In front of her the sheet of paper that was nestled in the typewriter remained as blank as it had been an hour earlier.

Marina swore under her breath, then began typing something, anything. As she was doing it, she knew it wasn't any good and would be thrown out later. But right now all that mattered was getting past her writer's block.

The sound of a car pulling up outside made her stop typing. It didn't sound like Rosie's old truck, but that didn't matter. Marina didn't care who it was. Right now, any visitor was welcome because it gave her an excuse not to write.

Pushing her chair back, she got up from her desk and gave a quick glance out the window before heading toward the door. She didn't recognize the jeep parked outside. That piqued her interest.

Then someone knocked at the door and she hurried over to it. When Marina opened it, she found Stephen Kramer standing on her doorstep.

"You!"

He smiled dryly. "Hello, Marina. May I come in?"

Chapter Five

Part of her mind registered the fact that he looked wonderful in white slacks and a royal-blue sweater that was nearly the same color as his eyes. Right now those eyes were lit by a warmth and humor that she never would have expected.

But she wasn't about to respond to that warmth. The memory of their last encounter came rushing back in vivid detail and she felt cold anger build within her.

She toyed with the idea of slamming the door in his face. Even though she knew that would be rude and childish, there would be a certain amount of satisfaction in it. But there would be even more satisfaction in talking to him and telling him exactly what she thought of him. At that point she was so angry, it didn't occur to her to wonder what he was doing there.

Without saying a word, she stepped back and held the door open. He walked across the threshold nonchalantly, his hands shoved casually in his pockets, his expression maddeningly calm. He stopped in the middle of the room and looked around curiously.

Watching the way his glance quickly took in everything, Marina seemed to see all the familiar things anew through his eyes—bright hooked rugs scattered over the wood floor, the old brass bed in the corner covered with a handmade red-and-blue quilt, an old oak rocking chair and a faded chintz armchair drawn up before the stone fireplace, a square oak trestle table with two rush-seated chairs in another corner and finally her desk.

She'd always thought her home was cozy and warm, with red-and-blue curtains at the windows to match the quilt, and a pottery jug filled with fresh wildflowers on the table. But now she wondered how Stephen Kramer saw it. It wouldn't be his style, of course. He would be used to luxury, the more modern the better. His house had certainly been decidedly modern, and while Marina had liked its proximity to the ocean, she hadn't liked the house itself.

Now her eyes met his, and there was a challenge in them as she silently dared him to betray any hint of condescension toward her home. His eyes glinted mischievously and she sensed that he knew exactly what she was thinking.

"Nice place," he said.

Whatever she had expected, it wasn't that. She didn't really believe he meant it, of course. But she didn't understand why he would bother to be polite about it. Nice manners certainly hadn't seemed to be one of his virtues before.

She forced herself to respond with equal politeness. "Thank you. I like it. Now, Mr. Kramer—"

"Stephen, please."

Her expression was obstinate. She went on, "Mr. Kramer, why—"

He interrupted again, "Mind if I sit down? It was a long, tiring drive."

He was playing with her, Marina thought irritably. Gesturing abruptly toward the easy chair, she said in a tone that was openly rude, "Go ahead."

Ignoring the rudeness, he smiled and said, "Thanks."

But he didn't sit down. Instead he hesitated, watching her expectantly. After a moment she realized he was waiting for her to sit down first. She wasn't sure she wanted to do that. Somehow she felt it would put her at a disadvantage. But she felt stupid standing there with his eyes on her. So she crossed the small room and sat down on the edge of the rocking chair.

He sat down then, leaning well back in the comfortable chair. He continued to look at her with a disconcerting expression that seemed to be mingled humor and interest. The expression, which she didn't for one moment understand, and his intent gaze, shook her rigid control.

But before she could speak, he did. "You're madder than hell at me, aren't you?"

"Of course I am!"

"I knew you would be. That's why I didn't call. I thought you'd probably hang up on me."

"Yes, I would have. But first I would have told you exactly what I think of you."

"Oh, but you did a pretty thorough job of that the last time we were together. As I remember, you said I make rotten movies and was undoubtedly going to ruin your story."

She was caught off guard by the frank way he spoke, seemingly without rancor. But she noticed that the humor was gone and he was quite serious now.

"You see, Marina—may I call you that?" He didn't wait for her to agree, but continued. "It's damn hard to make any movie, good, bad or indifferent. Nobody sets out to make a bad movie. I certainly didn't. But I did set out to make commercially successful movies. And in the present market, that meant pandering to certain tastes."

"Well, I don't want to see my story ruined in the process of pandering to those tastes!"

Leaning forward in the chair, he looked at her intently. "Is it your story?"

She was caught by surprise. "What do you mean? Of course, it's my story."

"Is *Casey* autobiographical?"

Marina hesitated, her lips parted slightly, her expression defensive. She had talked about the personal elements in her book with other people, especially Rosie and her mother. But she was extremely reluctant to do so with this man. In asking about it, he was probing in areas that were too intimate for an impersonal discussion. She had no intention of opening up to him that way.

She stammered, "It's a novel, not . . . not an autobiography."

"No? But I thought writers always put some of themselves into their fiction, whether they intend to or not."

"It's a question of imagination," Marina insisted, though she knew quite well that he was right. No writer could help but reveal something of himself, or herself, even if he was writing a very far-fetched story that on the surface bore no resemblance to his life. The facts might be different but the feelings were genuine and came from experience.

Kramer looked as if he didn't buy what she was saying. But instead of arguing as she half expected him to do, he simply asked, "So there's none of you in *Casey*?"

"Of course, there is some of me, but it's not the story of my life. It's . . . a novel, a work of fiction."

"That's not what you said the last time we talked," he shot back. "You said it was your story, and you said that with a great deal of passion."

Despite her determination not to let him get personal, he'd neatly circumvented her defenses, she realized with a sinking feeling. At least before when they'd argued, it had been about impersonal matters, especially her book. For some reason she couldn't begin to fathom, now he seemed interested in her.

She'd sensed something vaguely frightening about him the first time she'd seen him. She had that same feeling now, as if somehow he were a threat to her.

"Why are you here?" she asked in a whisper.

His gaze became even more intense. "I've decided you should do the screenplay after all."

"What?"

"Just what I said."

She was bewildered—and furious. "You've decided I should do the screenplay. Just like that."

"Not exactly. It took me a whole week to come around to the idea. Which was quite a while, since normally I make decisions quickly."

"What's wrong, wasn't the Oscar-winning screenwriter available?" she asked, gray eyes glinting quicksilver with anger.

"He was available, for a price."

She thought she understood now. "Oh, I see. You want to hire me because I'm cheaper. I don't have an Academy Award to hike my price."

He frowned. "Don't be ridiculous. Money has nothing to do with it. There are more than six thousand members of the Writers Guild. Most of them would be so eager to work on a major feature film that they'd be willing to work for guild minimum, like you. They are also a great deal more experienced."

This didn't make sense, Marina thought confusedly. Apparently he hadn't changed his mind about her abilities, only about hiring her. On top of that, even though he wanted her to do the screenplay, he wasn't in any way apologizing for his past rudeness. In fact, he was as insulting as ever.

She asked the obvious question. "Then why me?"

"That's a very good question. I thought about it all the way up here and wasn't able to come up with a satisfactory answer."

For an instant she thought he was teasing her—though the thought boggled her mind. Then, looking at him, she realized he was quite serious. And that was even more mind-boggling.

"Mr. Kramer..."

"Stephen, please. Surely two people who've fought as much as we have should be on a first-name basis."

Once more there was humor in his expression, but she refused to be drawn to it. "You told me in no uncertain terms what you think of the treatment I did. You said I couldn't possibly write a screenplay."

"You can't, without help."

"Whose help? Another writer? If you think I'm going to collaborate with some stranger, you're wrong. I don't work that way."

"Oh, you're not going to collaborate with anyone, and certainly not a stranger. But you are going to accept my help because you have a great deal to learn about screenwriting."

"Your help?"

"Yes. But don't worry, I'm not interested in sharing screen credit. You'll get sole credit, unless you just can't hack it. In which case, I'll have to hire someone else, after all. But with me helping you, showing you how to do it, I don't think it'll come to that."

Marina was thoroughly confused now. Not only was he offering her the chance to adapt *Casey* after all, he was apparently planning on working on it with her. She didn't understand what was going on. Was this the same man she'd argued with so bitterly only a week earlier? At times he seemed to be, when he was sharp or arrogant. And yet, something was different.

"Are you hesitating because you're still mad at me?" he asked bluntly.

She met his look. "I'm hesitating because it doesn't make sense. There's a trap somewhere."

He smiled. There was a surprising tenderness in the smile that made her heart do a funny flip-flop. Her breath caught, and for a moment the room seemed airless and stifling.

"There's no trap, Marina. I think it's just possible that you will bring something to this project that no other writer could."

She asked slowly, "And what is that?"

His eyes locked with hers. His voice was at once rough and gentle. "Passion."

For an instant everything was strange. The world around them seemed to fade, while Stephen's physical presence became sharper. With sudden clarity, Marina saw things she hadn't seen before: the tiny white scar at the corner of his mouth, slightly marring that otherwise perfect face; barely discernible lines at the corners of his eyes and across his forehead that hinted of stress and, perhaps, great unhappiness; the sensuous way his muscles were outlined against the thin silk of his shirt.

Then she blinked and everything went back to normal. She heard the crackle of the fire, felt her hands clasped tightly in her lap, saw wispy puffs of steam coming from the teakettle on the small range in the kitchenette.

Marina usually kept a low fire under the kettle during the day because she drank endless cups of hot tea while she worked. Now she stood and moved toward the kitchenette, making a point of avoiding Stephen's look as his eyes followed her.

In a voice that was oddly unlike her own, she asked, "Would you like something to drink? Tea or coffee?"

Behind her she heard him answer, "Whatever you're having will be fine."

Taking two gray stoneware cups and saucers from a cabinet, she set them down on the wooden counter. She focused all her attention on making the tea—putting just the right amount of a particularly spicy mint tea in a tiny bell-shaped strainer, then putting the strainer in a teapot.

What is it they always say? she asked herself. The pot should be taken to the kettle, not vice versa, for the very best tea. She set the teapot down near the kettle, then poured steaming hot water into it. Immediately, the clean, fresh aroma of mint began to fill the room.

From a bottom cupboard she took out a wooden tray and set the cups, saucers and teapot on it. Vaguely, she remembered that Stephen didn't take cream or sugar. She was glad of that for she didn't have cream or sugar bowls to match the gray stoneware teapot. Somehow, it would have been awkward to serve him with mismatched dishes, although it wouldn't have embarrassed her to do so with Rosie.

She carried the tray over to the raised stone hearth in front of the fire and set it down carefully. After checking to see that the tea had steeped enough, Marina poured a cup for each of them. When she handed Stephen's cup to him, his fingers closed over hers for just a moment. His hand was much bigger than hers, and stronger.

It was weeks since she'd felt a man's touch. She'd almost forgotten how different it was.

Slowly she pulled her hand away. Then she sat down in the rocking chair and cradled the cup in both her hands.

"Marina."

Something in his tone touched her in spite of her resolve to resist him. "Yes?" she whispered.

"Do you really think I'll take your sensitive, poignant story and turn it into a lot of jiggle and flash? Something that could only appeal to a few million randy teenagers?"

That was exactly what she thought. Mustering all her courage, she met his look and nodded silently.

He shook his head. "No way. If that was the kind of film I was after, I would've chosen another story. I chose yours precisely because it will be unlike what I've done up to now. Hell, it'll be in a whole different league."

"You've made a lot of money from making a certain kind of movie," she pointed out pragmatically.

"Yes."

"And somehow I think money matters to you."

"Of course it does. I'd be a hypocrite if I pretended otherwise. And while I may be a lot of things, I'm no hypocrite."

No, she thought, he wasn't that.

He went on, "Only people who are used to having money can pretend it doesn't matter."

"Maybe they're not pretending. Maybe it doesn't."

Surprisingly, he laughed, a low, throaty chuckle. "Maybe. I'm not used to it enough yet to say." He looked at her thoughtfully. "It doesn't matter to you, does it?"

"No. Not as long as I have enough so that I can write instead of working as a waitress."

"Is that what you've been doing? Working as a waitress?"

"Yes. Why do you seem so surprised?"

"I'm not sure. I guess I just assumed your life-style was a matter of choice and not necessity."

Marina's expression softened. "It's both, in a way." She could have said more, but she chose not to.

There was a silence between them as they both sipped their tea. It was actually a rather companionable silence. The light filtering in through the small, square windows began to grow dim as evening fell. A brisk wind came up, rustling through the eucalyptus trees near the cabin. But inside it was warm and cozy. Marina reached over to light a nearby Tiffany lamp, then got up to put another log on the fire.

"Let me," Stephen insisted.

He set down his empty cup, then picked up a log from a nearby wood box. He positioned the log to produce maximum heat, then closed the fireplace screen and sat down again.

Looking at Marina, he asked, "Well?"

She had been thinking, and she knew what she had to ask. "Why should I believe you when you say you'll respect the integrity of my story?"

She expected him to get angry. After all, it was a rather insulting question. Instead, he leveled a straightforward look at her and answered, "Because I say I will. And I always mean what I say."

She was tempted to ask sarcastically, *"Always?"* But somehow she didn't feel like being sarcastic with him any longer.

As if taking her silence for acquiescence, he went on matter-of-factly, "Here's the schedule. We want to shoot in the early spring so the movie can be ready for release by Christmas. That's the second-best time of year, box-office-wise, next to summer. And for a serious film it's actually the best time. For some reason people seem to prefer lighter films in the summer. So—"

She interrupted, using his first name without even realizing it, "Stephen, you're taking it for granted that I'll do the screenplay."

"Of course you will. I'm not about to let you refuse. And besides, you don't want to refuse."

Once more he was maddeningly arrogant—and right. She had no intention of refusing. But there was one thing seriously bothering her. "I think it may be very difficult for you and me to work together."

His smile reached his eyes. Suddenly the arrogance was gone and he simply looked immensely appealing. "I know it will be difficult. I'm not afraid of that. Are you?"

Her lips parted to respond, then she stopped before uttering a word. She had been about to say that of course she wasn't afraid. But the truth was just the opposite. In the beginning she'd been afraid he would ruin her story. Now her fear was much deeper—and far more intimate.

She couldn't answer his question. Instead, she said, "How long do we have to do the screenplay?"

"Till the end of January, at the latest. And that's pushing it."

She was stunned. It had taken her two years to write the novel. She didn't see how she could possibly write a screenplay in two and a half months.

Reading her mind, Stephen explained. "It has to be that fast if we're going to start shooting in February or March. Don't worry. We'll do it."

"Sure. No problem," Marina teased.

His laughter took the edge off her concern.

"But how are we going to do this?" she questioned. "Should I mail scenes to you?"

He shook his head firmly. "That won't work. Too time-consuming. And if there's one thing we don't have, it's time. Besides, if I'm going to teach you what you need to learn, we'll have to spend a lot of time together."

Something about the way his mouth curved slightly in an impudent smile made Marina suspect that his words held a double meaning. To her intense embarrassment, she felt herself blush, something she hadn't done in years.

To cover her embarrassment, she asked, "Then how are we going to arrange this?"

"There's a private apartment over the garage at the house I'm renting."

"You're renting that house?" Marina interrupted in surprise.

"Yes. Why?"

"Oh, no reason. I just thought . . . I assumed you owned it. I wondered why it was so empty."

She felt as if she was babbling and felt absolutely stupid. Why should it matter to her where he lived, if he owned or rented a house? she asked herself. His personal life was none of her business. And she wasn't interested in it, anyway.

Stephen explained, "The apartment has a separate entrance from the house, and a bathroom and kitchenette about the size of yours. I thought you could stay there while we're doing this."

"Stay there—at your house?" Marina asked.

"Yes. Of course, you'd have to come in to an office at the studio to work. There's an empty office near mine that you could use. It's small, but you won't need much room. That way, I can spend all my free time working with you."

Marina's head was whirling. It was all happening so fast. Two hours ago she'd been sitting there alone, working in the quiet, isolated atmosphere she was used to. *Casey* was something she had been going to put behind her.

Now, she was not only doing the adaptation, she was expected to move to Los Angeles for two and a half months to live in a strange house and work in a strange office. Her life was being turned upside down and she apparently had very little to say about it.

"What's wrong, Marina?" Stephen asked quietly.

"You're asking a lot of me."

"Yes. And in return, I'm giving you the chance to make *Casey* the movie faithful to *Casey* the book. Isn't that worth uprooting yourself for a couple of months?"

It was worth almost anything, she thought. Still, she hesitated.

He watched her intently. "Do you dislike L.A. so much? Or me?"

Her startled glance met his forthright one. "No, I don't even know L.A., really."

She hadn't answered the last part of his question, and he knew it. Suddenly his expression clouded as a new thought occurred to him. "Are you...involved with someone up here who you don't want to leave?"

"No." The answer came quickly—too quickly, Marina decided. That hurried, vehement denial revealed more than she cared to of her personal life.

She almost thought she heard him breathe a sigh of relief.

"Then what's the problem?"

"I'm used to working here," she insisted. "It's quiet and peaceful and—"

"And cut off from people," Stephen finished for her in a pointed tone.

She flared at his presumption. "And conducive to writing," she finished stubbornly.

"A writer should be able to write anywhere. I'm not asking you to work under difficult conditions." His eyes narrowed speculatively. "Why did you hide yourself way out here in the middle of nowhere?"

"I'm not hiding!" she snapped. "How dare you criticize my life-style. It's none of your business!"

"Maybe not. But I still say you're hiding from something."

"Damn it, Stephen, you're the rudest, most arrogant person I've ever met!"

"And you need to learn to face life, young lady, instead of running away from it."

"Oh! All right, if we're going to get personal here, would you like to explain why someone who could surely afford to buy a home would rent one, and an empty one at that?"

He was completely unruffled. "Because I don't want to put down roots until I get married. And when that happens, I intend to put them down permanently."

She was brought up short by the candor of his response. For a minute Marina simply sat there, staring at him. Then she said slowly, "There's no way we can work together without fighting."

"I'm not afraid of a good, clean fight. Are you?"

Actually, she was. But she was damned if she was going to admit as much to him. "No, not a bit."

"Good. How soon can you come down to L.A.?"

She hesitated, then answered, "The end of the week."

"Okay. I'll have the apartment and your office ready for you by Friday. Now then, how about dinner?"

"Dinner?"

"I understand there's a great restaurant around here called the West Wind."

"Yes, but—"

"Good. Do you want to change or is it casual enough for you to go as you are?"

Marina felt like a butterfly pursued by a steamroller. Stephen assumed so much—he assumed she would live at his house, work out of his office, go to dinner with him tonight. And somehow she didn't have the will to resist. The high spirit that many of the other men in her life had found too much to handle seemed to have deserted her.

"I'll change," she said, getting up from the rocking chair.

He stretched his legs out toward the fire and leaned back comfortably in the deep easy chair. "Okay. I'll wait." His entire demeanor suggested he had all the patience in the world.

Marina took some clothes from her closet, then disappeared into the bathroom.

Two hours later, after a delicious seafood dinner, they lingered over coffee. Watching Stephen over the rim of her cup, Marina thought about how at ease he seemed, while she was still rather nervous. She wondered if her nervousness was due to the simple fact that he was a man and she was still in the process of sorting out her new feelings about men.

She had intended to be perfectly cordial, but distinctly impersonal with Stephen. Instead, she found herself growing increasingly intrigued by him. He wasn't an easy man to pigeonhole. He was, by turns, easy and difficult, stern and humorous, self-centered and disturbingly perceptive.

All in all, she had to admit, her conversations with him hadn't been boring. Even the arguments had been stimulating. She'd begun by thinking he was a jerk who made mindless movies. Now she realized he was an extremely bright and ambitious man who didn't fit her preconceived notions of a Hollywood producer.

"A penny for your thoughts."

Startled out of her reverie, she glanced shyly at him. "I was just wondering what happened to your white Gucci loafers and gold chains."

He smiled dryly. "I left them at home."

She cocked her head to one side and eyed him thoughtfully. "And the jeep—that's not exactly run-of-the-mill Hollywood, is it?"

"I don't know. It suits me. That's all that matters."

Despite herself, she wanted to know more about him. Trying not to sound as if she were being personal, she asked, "How did you become a producer?"

"I left home at sixteen and headed west. L.A. was as far west as I could go. The only job I could get was as a messenger boy at a studio. The rest, as they say, is history."

Beneath the easy, self-effacing banter, Marina sensed that a red warning light had just flashed on. It said Don't Trespass Beyond This Point. He didn't want her to probe his psyche any more than she wanted him to probe hers.

Fair enough, she thought. Still, she was interested enough to hazard a couple of questions about his background— where he came from, what his family was like. He fielded the questions expertly, dismissing them with a brief, "I was born in New York, but we moved around a lot. I don't have any family left now."

It was clear he didn't want to discuss his early life. Which meant that he must have had a pretty rough time of it.

Obviously wanting to switch to the offensive, he asked about her background. She told him briefly that she was born and raised in San Francisco, went to U.C. Berkeley where she majored in English literature and had lived in Big Sur for two years.

"You weren't exactly poor, I'll bet." There was no edge to the observation. It was simply a statement of fact.

"No. We weren't exactly poor."

"And your family?" he persisted, when she didn't volunteer any information about them.

This was the tricky part. Marina wasn't about to explain her convoluted parentage. Instead, she answered, "My parents are divorced. My mother remarried recently and lives in Clovis."

"Clovis?"

"It's a small town in the San Joaquin Valley. Actually, it's a suburb of Fresno."

"Ah, yes. I know Fresno. We do sneak previews there sometimes. It's a good market for that. So, do you have any brothers or sisters?"

She shook her head. "Just . . . just my mother."

"It sounds like you don't care much for your new stepfather."

Stepfather. The word sounded strange, somehow. Possibly because it was inaccurate, she realized. Rafe Marin was her father, not her stepfather. But she wasn't about to go into that with Stephen.

Curtly, she said, "I don't know him very well." That, at least, was true. She didn't know him at all and wasn't at all sure she ever wanted to know him.

Before he could question her further, she went back to a question he hadn't really answered. "Why did you become a producer? For the power or the pleasures that go along with it?"

"You mean money, women, limousines at my beck and call?"

He was smiling wryly, but what he was saying was accurate. Marina knew enough about the film business to know that. She returned his smile. "Yes, all those things."

He shook his head. "No."

"Then is it an ego trip?"

"Of course it's an ego trip. I think the film business has cornered the world market in ego-tripping."

"And your ego is as healthy as any," Marina couldn't resist saying.

He laughed, that same low, throaty chuckle she'd heard once before. There was something rather seductive about it. As soon as she thought that, she pulled back and her defenses came up once more.

He seemed to sense that, for he watched her in absolute silence for quite a while. The piercing gaze from those deep blue eyes was unnerving. Marina felt like a specimen under a microscope.

She couldn't handle that kind of intense scrutiny from this particular man. She moved to steer the conversation onto safer ground.

"If you're going to start shooting *Casey* in the spring, are you already making preparations? Or do you have to wait until the screenplay's finished to proceed with the other things, like casting and so forth?"

"No, we're already in preproduction. Marty is my production manager on all my films. He does a good job of reining in my enthusiasm and keeping costs down. Of course, this is a relatively low-budget film, so that won't be a problem."

"How much will this movie cost to make?"

"About seven to ten million, depending on how high-priced the talent is."

Marina was amazed. "That's low-budget?"

He grinned ruefully. "I know. It sounds like black humor. I feel like that politician who was talking about the federal budget and said, 'A billion here, a billion there, pretty soon you forget you're talking about real money.'"

Marina laughed softly.

Stephen's expression sobered. The humor left his eyes and he said slowly, "You don't laugh enough. You should do it more often."

She felt acute self-consciousness and had no idea how to respond.

"By the way," he continued, "you look quite lovely tonight."

Marina's self-consciousness increased. She looked down at her nearly empty coffee cup as if it was the most fascinating object in the world. When she looked up again, she didn't quite meet his look.

"Tell me more about preproduction. What else goes on?"

"You'll see it all firsthand when you start working in the office. We'll hire a director. I have someone in mind, but I'm not sure he's available. Anyway, once the director's hired, then everyone else comes onboard—the art director, cinematographer, etc."

"What do they do exactly?"

"The art director is possibly the most crucial person besides the director. He's an artist craftsman who determines the 'look' of the film by designing the sets. He and the location manager decide where the movie's going to be shot."

"And the cinematographer?"

"His key responsibility is lighting. He brings the camera operator and focus man with him as a team. Then there's the wardrobe and makeup people, the editor and composer. Those are all what are called below-the-line costs. The big costs come when we start hiring actors. But I'm not looking for big names on this film."

"Why not?"

"Because I want the characters to be fresh and believable. The role of *Casey* is the kind that could make a new young actress. I'd like to find some great, undiscovered talent."

"You seem to have it all worked out," Marina observed.

"Everything but the script," he retorted.

For the first time it really hit her what was involved in writing a screenplay. All of the people Stephen had just been describing would be combining their talents to work toward one goal—putting her story on film. If it was a bad story, it would be a bad film. It was that simple. And that difficult.

Marina had been determined to adapt her novel for the screen. Now, she had her first flash of doubt as to whether or not she could do it. She'd never done it before. And as Stephen had said once, just because a writer could do a novel didn't mean she could do a screenplay.

What if she failed? Until this moment, that was an eventuality she'd never even considered. The thought was terrifying.

She was startled to feel Stephen's hand closing over hers where it lay on the table. There was just the slightest pressure from his fingers as he said in a husky whisper, "Don't worry, Marina. You're going to do just fine. I'll see to it."

As her eyes met his she saw a wealth of compassion in those dark blue depths. Her fear of failure began to recede. But it was replaced by a new, much more intimate fear as Stephen's touch sent a shiver racing up her spine.

Chapter Six

When they returned to Marina's cabin, she asked Stephen where he was staying.

"I don't know. I thought I'd find a motel somewhere."

"Obviously, you've never been to Big Sur before."

"No. Why?"

"There are very few motels in this area, and on a Saturday night they'll all be full. If you drive all the way up to Carmel or Monterey you might find something, but even there it will be difficult. Especially if there's a convention in town."

"How far is Carmel or Monterey?"

"An hour up the Pacific Coast Highway."

It was nearly eleven o'clock. He'd had a long, hard eight-hour drive up from L.A. and was exhausted. He obviously didn't relish the idea of getting back on a highway for another hour and facing the prospect of a possibly futile search for a motel room.

Marina had just made the same trip in reverse the week before when she'd gone to L.A. in one day. She knew exactly how Stephen was feeling. Taking pity on him, she said, "Look, why don't you stay here?"

Glancing around the single room, Stephen responded, "You're a little short on beds. There isn't even a couch."

Ignoring the impudent gleam in his eyes, Marina responded, "I'll stay with Rosie. I've done it before. She always has the welcome mat out."

"It's late. I'd hate for you to wake her up."

His tone was very suggestive. With a start, Marina realized he was teasing her in a not very subtle sexual way. An ironic voice deep inside her told her that this was called flirting. The man was flirting with her.

She rejected the thought immediately. No way. Stephen Kramer might be rather friendly with her now, but he hadn't done anything to indicate he particularly liked her. And aside from that one brief compliment during dinner, when he'd matter-of-factly said that she looked lovely, he hadn't betrayed any attraction to her. If he was at all interested in her sexually, it was in the most casual way. But to her, there was nothing casual about sex.

Why should he have any serious interest in her? Marina asked herself critically. She'd never bothered to look her best for him. In fact, she'd usually been at her worst. When she'd been in his office that one time she'd gotten a glimpse of what his life was like. He was surrounded by gorgeous actresses. He must be used to women who were not only beautiful but who made a point of flattering him because of his position in the film business.

No, she decided, he was just teasing her, period. There was nothing behind it.

"Rosie honestly won't mind putting me up for the night," she concluded. "And I won't be waking her up because she stays up to watch *The Tonight Show*. She has a thing about

Johnny Carson—says he's the over-fifty, thinking woman's sex symbol.''

As soon as the words were out of her mouth she regretted them. She hadn't intended to bring up the subject of sex, even in jest.

Stephen shot her a quick, curious look, then commented casually, ''Rosie's an interesting woman. Who do you find sexy, Marina?''

She felt absolutely tongue-tied. Finally, she said haltingly, ''Oh, the usual types, I guess—Mel Gibson, Al Pacino.''

''You don't find blond men sexy, I take it?''

Since Stephen had golden blond hair, that was a loaded question. Marina had no idea how to answer it. If she said yes, that could be construed as the wrong kind of encouragement. If she said no, it was insulting. So she simply changed the subject.

She took out some clean, neatly folded sheets from a wooden chest at the foot of the bed, set them on top of the chest, and began stripping the bed.

''I'll just change the sheets,'' she said, ignoring his look.

''Here, let me help,'' he offered, moving to the opposite side of the bed.

''Don't bother, I can handle it,'' she insisted.

''It's no bother. And it's the least I can do since I'm taking over your bed.''

Together they took the bedclothes off. Marina tossed the old sheets in a wicker hamper, then she and Stephen made up the double bed, working in unison. Not once did Marina look at him, but she was aware that his eyes were on her.

As they spread the patchwork quilt over the top, Stephen said, ''This is beautiful. Who made it?''

For the first time in several minutes she looked at him. ''I did.''

Surprise registered clearly on his face. ''You did?''

She smiled dryly. "Yes, I did."

He returned the smile. "Sorry. It's just that I associate quilting with little old ladies in sewing circles. You strike me as being much more modern than that."

"I am modern. I also enjoy making quilts. It's very satisfying somehow."

"How did you learn?"

"My mother taught me. She's quite talented when it comes to sewing and making things with her hands."

"I'm impressed," he responded, and seemed to mean it.

Embarrassed by the compliment, Marina tried to shrug it off. "A lot of people don't like quilts. They're too old-fashioned for their taste."

"Personally, I like old-fashioned things."

So do I, Marina thought but didn't say so. It struck her as odd that she and Stephen Kramer should have anything in common. Instead, she said, "I'll just check to make sure there are clean towels in the bathroom."

In the small bathroom, she quickly straightened up a few things, then turned to find Stephen leaning nonchalantly in the doorway, his shoulder resting against the jamb, his arms crossed.

Nodding toward the large, old-fashioned claw-footed tub, he commented, "That's the biggest bathtub I've ever seen. There must be room enough for two in there."

His tone was perfectly innocent, his expression blank. Yet Marina sensed the remark wasn't as careless as it seemed.

"I wouldn't know," she retorted, then brushed past him as she went back into the other room.

Taking her robe and gown from the closet, she flung back over her shoulder, "See you in the morning. Good night."

"Good night, Marina. Sweet dreams."

His voice sounded ironic. She fled from it, as if from danger.

As she walked quickly up the dirt road toward Rosie's, she glanced back at the cabin. In the light streaming through the window Stephen's dark frame was silhouetted, watching her go.

Somehow Rosie wasn't surprised to see Marina. "I thought you might be turning up tonight," she quipped as she turned off the television.

She went to the linen cupboard and took out a pillow, sheets and blankets, and started to make up a bed on the sofa. "So what happened?"

"I'm going to do the screenplay after all."

"I was hoping it was that. Had to be, of course. Why else would that young man come all the way up here? Unless maybe he's interested in you."

"I doubt that he's interested in me," Marina insisted. But even to her own ears, her voice lacked conviction.

"He's even handsomer in person than on TV," Rosie went on.

"I guess so. But he isn't my type."

Rosie raised one eyebrow quizzically. "Oh? Well, if a handsome, well-built, smart, successful, rich young man isn't your type I'd sure like to know who is."

"You don't know what he's like. He's incredibly egotistical. And rude. And argumentative. We can't talk for five minutes without fighting."

"Sounds like there's lots of sparks between you two."

"Well, they're the wrong kind of sparks. I have to work with him, but I don't particularly like him."

The makeshift bed was finished. Rosie sat down in a nearby chair and eyed Marina thoughtfully. "Then why'd you put on your best dress?"

Marina colored slightly. The gray suede dress *was* her best. She answered defensively, "It was the only clean dress in my closet. I know what you're suggesting, but I didn't dress up for Stephen. I don't care what he thinks of me."

"You don't much care about any man right now, do you?"

Marina sighed heavily. "Oh, Rosie, what does it matter? Men aren't the most important thing in life."

"No, but they have their uses. Sounds like you've talked yourself into a spot of celibacy."

"I've just decided to concentrate on my writing for a while and not bother with personal relationships. What's wrong with that?"

"What's wrong with it is that you're too young and pretty and full of life to turn into a miser with your affections. If you keep it up I'm gonna have to start calling you Scrooge."

In spite of herself, Marina laughed. "Look, I'll admit I don't have the highest opinion of men right now. Maybe I do have some sort of psychological hang-up about them. I don't know and I don't care. I only know that I'm just not open to a relationship at the moment. And even if I was, it wouldn't be with Stephen Kramer."

"Why not?"

"Because we rub each other the wrong way."

Rosie grinned slyly. "Then why not try rubbing each other the right way?"

"You are impossible. Look, Stephen and I are utterly different. He lives one kind of life, I live another. We're opposites."

"I've always heard that opposites attract."

Marina glared at Rosie in frustration. "You're not listening. I'm going to sleep."

"Okay. Sweet dreams."

Marina was startled to hear a repetition of Stephen's parting words to her. It almost sounded like a conspiracy to make her feel on edge. And it was working. She tossed and turned on the sofa for a long while before finally falling asleep.

The next morning she went back to her cabin. As she walked up to it, she heard the sound of wood being chopped. To her surprise, she found Stephen wielding her small ax with practiced ease.

"Good morning," he said brightly. "You were out of wood, so I took matters into my own hands."

Marina watched as he continued chopping. When he finished, he picked up two logs and carried them into the house.

"You're pretty good with that ax."

He smiled wryly. "You sound surprised."

"I am. Where did you learn to handle one?"

He dumped the logs in the wood box, then took an iron poker and stirred up the dying fire. "One of the many jobs I held in my misspent youth was cutting firewood. After several months of swinging an ax, I swore I'd never pick one up again. Which just goes to show you should never say never."

He took one of the logs he'd just cut and put it on the fire. In a moment the low fire began to blaze more brightly, cutting through the chill in the room.

Watching Stephen, Marina was strongly tempted to ask about his "misspent youth." But she knew he'd react as he had the previous night—by stonewalling.

She glanced over at her bed and saw that it was neatly made. There was no telltale evidence that he had slept there, between her sheets, his head resting on her pillow. It was an oddly disturbing thought. Had he slept well? she wondered. Or had he, like her, tossed and turned a great deal?

She decided this wasn't a productive line of thought, and quickly abandoned it.

"How about some breakfast?" she offered.

"Great. Can I help?"

"Certainly. You make the toast, I'll make the omelets."

"Sounds like a good deal."

"The bread's in that bread box. By the way, what do you like in an omelet?"

"Everything but the kitchen sink."

"Okay. Here goes."

A few minutes later they sat down to a simple but delicious breakfast of whole wheat toast, herb and cheese omelets and coffee. When they finished, Stephen offered to help do the dishes. By then Marina wasn't surprised by the offer. She'd learned that Stephen Kramer was a self-sufficient man who didn't expect to sit back and be waited on.

When the few dishes were washed, dried and put away, he said, "Well, I'd better be going. It's a long drive and I have an early meeting tomorrow."

"Okay. Well, I'll be down there by the end of the week."

"Good. I'll see you then. Come straight to the office and I'll get you settled in there. And I'll have a typewriter and desk set up in the apartment over the garage so you can work there as well."

"It sounds like I'll be working around the clock," she commented with a wry smile.

"We both will," he retorted, then went out to his car.

Marina followed.

As he opened the car door, he said, "Thanks for breakfast. And for the bed. It was quite comfortable."

"You're welcome."

His gaze became more serious. "I'm glad you're doing the screenplay, Marina." Before she could respond, he said, "See you later," and got into the car, closing the door.

She stood there watching as he drove off in a cloud of dust.

Marina arrived in L.A. late Friday afternoon. Her little Volkswagen was crammed to capacity with everything she felt she'd need for the next two months. She found her way to the studio without difficulty this time. When she reached the main gate, the guard informed her that she'd been assigned a parking place in the employee parking lot. As she pulled into her reserved space, she realized that she was now a member of the film community. For better or worse.

In the office, Stephen's young, red-haired secretary greeted Marina with a warm smile. "Hi, we've been expecting you. Stephen's in a meeting right now, but he asked me to show you where your office is. It's right over here."

She led Marina to a nearby room. It was small, but it was comfortably furnished and had the latest in high-tech typewriters. The typewriter made her old one at home look like a museum piece.

"I hope this is okay, Miss Turner," the secretary said.

"It's wonderful. You should see what I'm used to," Marina replied, laughing.

"Well, if you need anything at all, just let me know. By the way, my name's Brenda Simpson."

"And mine's Marina. Miss Turner sounds a little stuffy."

Brenda smiled warmly. "I'm glad you're going to be working with Kramer Productions."

"I imagine you were surprised, too, considering how things went the last time I was here."

Brenda laughed good-naturedly. "Well, yes. I have to admit it was something of a surprise. Stephen isn't known for changing his mind."

"Have you been with him long?"

"Just a few months. He's a wonderful boss."

At Marina's look of disbelief, Brenda laughed again. "Oh, he's difficult, all right. He knows exactly what he wants and he'd better get it or else. What a temper! I've known him to throw things when he's really mad."

"That doesn't sound wonderful."

"But you see, he never gets mad for no reason. And when he does, it's because he cares so much about what he's doing. He doesn't get mad and put people down just to exercise his power, like a lot of people in this business do. I've worked in the film business for two years, and believe me, Stephen's a prince."

Marina was beginning to suspect that Brenda's feelings for her boss went beyond business. But, as if reading her mind,

Brenda went on, "He introduced me to my fiancé, Richard. Richard's a stuntman who worked on *Rebels*. Stephen didn't approve of the guy I was dating before because he said he was an opportunist. Which he was, I guess. So he made a point of getting Rich and me together. Rich is just the sweetest guy in the world. When I compared him to my old boyfriend, I realized Stephen was right."

It was hard for Marina to picture Stephen playing Cupid. But Brenda was obviously happy about it.

"Well, I'd better get back to my desk instead of standing here telling you my life story. Let me know if you'd like to go to lunch sometime."

"I will. Thanks."

When Brenda left, Marina looked over her new digs. There was a rather droopy-looking plant in the corner, but nothing on the stark white walls. She decided her first order of business would have to be to water the plant, and as soon as possible, to find some pictures to brighten up the place. The important thing was that she had a window—small, but nevertheless a window. She couldn't have stood being in a closed-in room with no view of the outdoors. Even though the outdoors here consisted of a blank wall a few feet from her window.

Stepping outside her office, she asked Brenda where she might find a paper cup and water. Brenda responded that there was a small coffee room at the end of the suite of offices. As Marina walked toward it, she saw Marty come out of his office. His arm was around a petite, dark-haired woman, who was rather plain yet quite appealing.

"Don't be late," she was saying to him.

"I won't be. What's for dinner?"

"Fish."

He grimaced and she went on, "I know, I know. But it's healthier than red meat. And to make up for it, there's a very special dessert."

"Oh, what?" he asked with interest.

Standing up on tiptoe, she whispered in his ear. He chuckled, then squeezed her arm affectionately. "That's healthy, too," he said.

As the woman walked off, his eyes followed her until she'd left the office. His expression betrayed such love that Marina felt like a Peeping Tom.

Suddenly Marty noticed her. "Hey, Marina, good to see you. Where you headed?"

"To the coffee room for some water. The plant in my office looks like it's on its last legs."

"I'll go with you. Around this time of day I need one last cup of coffee to keep me going."

He led her into a tiny cubicle that held an automatic coffee maker, a tiny refrigerator, a purified-water cooler and a few odds and ends like napkins and plastic utensils. On a cake stand were the crumbly remains of a chocolate cake someone had brought.

As Marina filled a plastic cup with water, Marty poured himself a cup of coffee, adding a little cream and sugar. When he was finished, he walked back to her office with her and remained standing in the doorway, sipping his coffee while she watered the parched plant.

"It's good to see you again, kid."

"Thanks. You know, Marty, I don't think I'd be here if it wasn't for you. I owe you a lot."

He tried to shrug off the compliment, but she insisted, "No, I mean it. I'm not sure why Stephen changed his mind about giving me the chance to adapt *Casey*. But I know it had something to do with the conversation we had when I went out to his house. I wouldn't have been able to find him, if you hadn't told me where he lives."

Marty put a finger to his lips. "Ssh. That's our little secret, remember?"

Marina grinned. "Don't worry. I'll carry that secret to the grave."

"Good. Even though it worked out, I'm not sure Stephen's ready to thank me for what I did. Anyway, I'm glad you're here. You're the perfect person to adapt your book."

Marina's smile slowly faded and was replaced with concern. "I hope so."

"Hey, don't worry, kid. Stephen told me he's going to work with you. He'll teach you the craft you need to learn, and you'll do just fine."

"I'm glad you're so confident. Somehow, I'm not."

"It's a piece of cake. By the way, I'd like to invite you to have dinner at my place once you get settled. My wife, Amy, is dying to meet you."

"That would be nice, thanks."

Just then they were interrupted by Brenda, who said that Stephen was ready to meet with Marina.

As Marina walked toward his office she felt an odd fluttering deep in her stomach. She chalked it up to exhaustion and hunger. Nevertheless, it was irritating.

The door to Stephen's office was open and she walked right in. It was a large room, furnished simply but tastefully with a beige sofa and chairs and a round conference table. Stephen sat behind a huge desk piled high with scripts, books and papers, all in casual disarray.

As Marina walked in, he got up and came toward her.

He looked strangely different than she remembered; even more attractive and less intimidating.

"Hi, good to see you. How was the trip down?"

"Long," she answered with a shy smile. "I'm glad I won't be doing it again for quite a while."

"Did Brenda get you settled in?"

She nodded. "And I found the coffee room. I'm all set."

"Is the office okay?" he asked with real concern.

"It's just fine. I appreciate the window."

He smiled. "The view isn't quite what you're used to. But the National Studios' lot isn't Big Sur."

"I'll be okay. As long as I have some real, honest-to-God sunlight instead of that fluorescent stuff, I'm fine."

"Well, you'll find the view at my place much nicer. The apartment has a big window looking out at the ocean."

The reminder that she'd be staying at his house—even though in an apartment over the garage—made her feel awkward somehow. Marina looked away for a moment, gathering her wits, then said, "Well, I'd better get started, I guess."

"It's five o'clock on a Friday afternoon. This is no time to start anything. I arranged it so I could leave early today to take you out to the house. We'll work out there over the weekend. By the time you come in here Monday morning you'll have a better idea what to do."

"Okay. Shall I follow you out there?"

"I didn't bring my car in today. I got a ride with someone. I'll ride out there with you."

"Oh . . . okay. Well, I'll just get my purse, then, and be right back."

Later, in the intimate confines of her small car, Marina felt that same fluttering deep in her stomach. Stephen's broad shoulder lightly brushed hers, and his muscular body seemed to fill the little seat. She was so intensely aware of him—of his sheer physical presence—it was all she could do to concentrate on maneuvering along the narrow, twisting Pacific Coast Highway.

On this rapidly darkening mid-November evening, the highway was packed with people either going home or leaving the city for the weekend.

Stephen watched her in silence for some minutes, his expression, as usual, unreadable. Once or twice she opened her mouth to speak, then realized she wasn't sure what to say.

As it turned out, he was the first to speak. "Do you know L.A. well?"

"Hardly at all. I've only been here twice."

His smile was as dry as vermouth. "I suppose you have the typical San Francisco superiority complex where L.A.'s concerned."

She met his smile with her own. "Of course. It's inbred. San Franciscans are taught that we have the best restaurants, the best scenery, the best weather. While L.A. is flashy, trashy and, as the English say, not quite *quite*."

Stephen laughed. It was an appealing sound, husky and genuine. "Well, all that's true, I guess. But there's nothing in San Francisco to beat a Trancas sunset. We're too late to see it now, but tomorrow night..."

He let the sentence trail off suggestively.

Yes, Marina thought, tomorrow night... There would be a lot of sunsets, a lot of nights spent in close proximity to this man.

He interrupted her thoughts. "What part of San Francisco were you raised in?"

"Hillsborough."

She knew there was a wealth of meaning in that one word. With a quick glance at Stephen, she saw that the meaning wasn't lost on him.

"Hillsborough," he repeated thoughtfully. "Big houses, big money." He looked at her. "And now you work as a waitress and live in a cabin."

She tried to make light of it. "Thanks to you I'm no longer working as a waitress. I can afford to be a full-time writer now."

"Why couldn't you be one before? If your family is wealthy..."

"They're not anymore. My... my father lost everything shortly after I graduated from college."

"I think it must be harder to have it and lose it, than to never have it at all."

Marina was caught off guard by the genuine note of caring in his voice. It prompted her to be more revealing than she would have been otherwise. "I don't know. Strangely enough, it wasn't all that hard—going broke, that is. What was tough was losing my illusions about my family."

"You mean because of the divorce?"

"Yes. It made me realize what matters and what doesn't. Money—at least big money—isn't what matters. I've been happy with my life-style the past couple of years."

"You don't miss having things?" he probed.

"Oh, no. I miss—" She stopped. She'd been about to say that she missed that absolute certainty of who she was and whom she belonged to.

When she didn't continue, Stephen asked, "Are you close to your parents?"

It was a personal question, and for a moment Marina hesitated about answering. Finally, she said as matter-of-factly as possible, "I was never very close to my father, though I liked him well enough. He was a classic workaholic and didn't have a lot of time for family things."

"And your mother?"

"I was very close to her when I was growing up. But lately we've sort of grown apart."

"Because of her remarriage?"

That was the second time in their short acquaintance that he'd questioned her about her feelings regarding her mother's recent marriage. It irritated Marina and she let her irritation show.

"I'd rather not talk about that."

"Did I hit a nerve?"

"Look, Stephen..."

"You'd better keep your eyes on the road," he interrupted calmly. "There are a couple of sharp turns here."

Marina gritted her teeth and stared ahead. Well, she thought angrily, what's sauce for the goose, etc....

"Where were you raised?" she asked pointedly.

"I think I told you we moved around a lot."

But she wasn't about to let him finesse his way around the question. "Where, for instance?"

He hesitated, and for a moment she thought he wouldn't answer. Finally, he said with studied nonchalance, "Oh, all over the Southwest: Phoenix, Tucson, Houston."

"Why did you travel so much?"

It was a logical question, and not necessarily all that personal—though in Stephen's case, Marina sensed it was quite personal.

His voice was tight. "My father kept looking for something better. He never found it."

Marina knew she should let it drop there, but somehow she couldn't. It wasn't just a desire to get back at him for his relentless probing into her own sensitive areas. She felt an urgency to know more about Stephen, to understand him. Somewhere there was a key to his difficult, intriguing personality, and she wanted to find it.

"Did you have any brothers or sisters?"

"I had...a younger sister."

The admission was almost torn from him, as if it were a closely held secret. And with that admission the tension that had been slowly building between them reached a danger point. Marina felt Stephen holding himself rigidly under control. He didn't want to talk about himself and bitterly resented Marina's probing.

Common sense, as well as sheer politeness, required that she drop the subject. But with a recklessness that she hadn't had the courage to feel for quite a while, she threw caution to the wind.

As she turned onto Gull Drive, she asked, "What happened to your family?"

There was a moment of absolute silence within the small car. Then as she pulled up in front of Stephen's garage and turned off the car, he faced her. His face was white and strained, and for once the expression in his normally unreadable dark eyes was all too clear. Marina saw a poignant anguish that caught at her heart.

"They died." His voice was hard and cold. "My father was an alcoholic. He passed out one night with a burning cigarette in his hand. My mother and little sister died immediately. My father lived just long enough to realize what he'd done. I wasn't home that night. I spent as much time out of the house as I could. If I hadn't been gone, if I'd been there...maybe..."

Marina felt torn by profoundly conflicting emotions. She wished she hadn't pressed so hard. She wished she could offer him some comfort. And more than anything else, she wished he didn't feel the terrible pain and guilt that he obviously felt.

"No one but Marty knows about it," he went on coldly. "In this business, most people aren't concerned with where you come from. They're only concerned with whether you're going up or down. But being a writer I suppose you have a professional curiosity about the dark side of people's lives."

The coolly worded insult was like a slap in the face. Marina felt awful—mean and small. She would have given anything to take back that last question. And yet, part of her was glad she knew. It explained so many things: why he didn't drink, why he was curious about her gilded childhood.

Reaching in his pocket, Stephen took out a house key, which he tossed on the dashboard. "That's the key to the apartment. You can let yourself in. We'll start work in the morning."

He got out, slamming the car door behind him, and went into his house.

For several minutes Marina just sat there, her hands still gripping the steering wheel, her lower lip trembling with barely suppressed emotion. Finally, she got out and began carrying her things up to the apartment.

It was a lovely, spacious apartment, with a living room, bedroom, bath and kitchenette. But she didn't notice anything about it. She couldn't get over the way he'd looked. And the way he'd sounded when he'd accused her of probing his psyche out of a cold professional curiosity.

Mechanically, she unpacked, but she was hardly aware of what she was doing. When the last suitcase was empty, she pushed it aside. She was so preoccupied that if she'd been asked where she'd put her things, she wouldn't have been able to answer.

Absently, she walked over to a large curved window at one end of the living room and looked out onto the dark beach. A full moon shone intermittently through patchy clouds. During one moment when it was unobscured, Marina saw a man standing out on the beach, staring out to sea.

She knew immediately who it was. That blond hair glistening white-gold in the moonlight, those broad shoulders, that commanding stance, were all unmistakable. His hands were shoved in his pockets and he didn't move. He just stood there, alone, and there was something very forlorn about him.

Marina knew what she had to do. Slipping on a red windbreaker, she left the apartment, walking slowly down the stairs and onto the beach. Her tennis shoes sank into the soft sand, making no sound as she made her way toward Stephen. A brisk ocean breeze brought a flush of color to her otherwise pale cheeks, and her hands were clenched tightly in front of her in the pockets of the windbreaker.

He didn't sense her presence until she was nearly abreast of him. Even then, he didn't look at her but continued watching the ocean.

Tears stung the corners of her eyes. She told herself it was that cold wind, but she knew it wasn't.

Gathering all her courage, she said in a tremulous voice, "Stephen, I'm sorry. I hurt you and I think I meant to do that. I'm not sure why except that you were getting too close to things that are very painful for me and I wanted to defend myself by attacking you. I'm not proud of that. But it

wasn't professional curiosity. It wasn't..." Her voice broke
and she couldn't go on.

Unable to face him any longer, she turned away and began slogging through the sand back toward the house.

"Marina!"

The sound of her name brought her up short. She heard
him coming toward her, but she didn't turn around. She
waited, at once hopeful and terrified. And every nerve ending in her body seemed electrified.

When he reached her, he spun her around to face him.
For an instant she looked into those blue, blue eyes. And
before she knew what was happening, he pulled her roughly
against him, pressing her so tightly against his hard chest
that she thought she would be crushed, and bent his face
toward hers.

She felt panic start to rise and her first instinct was to
struggle. But that was replaced by an even stronger instinct, a more primeval one, as she felt his strength and
caught his male scent. As he held her against him tightly she
felt the arousal she produced in him. And instead of fighting him, she wrapped her hands around his neck and raised
her lips to his.

Chapter Seven

Stephen's rough skin brushed against Marina's softer skin as their lips met. He drew her even tighter against his body so that her breasts, under a cotton blouse and thin windbreaker, were rubbed hard against the warmth of his chest.

There was nothing gentle or tentative about the kiss. His lips were harsh and seeking. Want and need obliterated more tender emotions. All that leashed power that she'd sensed in him the first time they'd met was unleashed in a torrent of desire.

For a moment Marina felt overwhelmed by his strength and the force with which he claimed her. Frightened, she tried to pull back. But he wouldn't let her. His lips forced hers open, demanding more of her.

Suddenly she felt a piercing pleasure unlike anything she'a ever known. It shot through her body like a burst of flame, igniting nerve ending after nerve ending. She gave way under it, her resistance dissolving as she surrendered herself to his need and her response to that need.

She stopped trying to pull back from him and instead let her body go limp in his fierce embrace. Her tight muscles slackened and—as if it were coming from someone else—she heard a sigh of contentment deep in her throat.

"Marina." His lips moved against hers, less urgent now, his voice husky with desire.

Slowly his hold on her grew more gentle and she pulled back just enough to breathe more easily. But at the same time he began to stroke her body, molding it against his own. His hands moved under the windbreaker to cup her small firm breasts through the thin cotton of her blouse.

She shuddered at his touch. Instinctively, not conscious of what she was doing, she pressed against him, her thighs against his, her breasts against his chest, her lips seeking his. Their bodies fit so perfectly together, as if they'd been made for each other.

He whispered hoarsely, "My God, I want you. Can't you feel how much I want you?"

She could feel it and it both frightened and excited her. With a low moan she arched her slender body against his stronger one. She was aware of nothing but the surge of pleasure that raced through her, a pleasure aroused by him that she had no wish to control.

When he spoke again, he sounded like a man possessed, a man who has lost all reason and control, who is obsessed with one thing and one thing only.

"I'd like to take you right here, on the sand. I'd like to see the moonlight shining on your bare skin and feel the cool sand beneath us. And there would be nothing but the ocean lapping softly behind us and the breeze caressing us as I took you again and again."

A thrill of excitement raced up her spine as she listened to his blatant words. She wanted to give herself to him there and then, to feel everything he described, to let him take her as tenderly or as roughly as he chose.

But at the back of her mind where some semblance of reason remained she realized that they weren't alone. There were other houses on this beach, with lights shining through the windows. The beach wasn't their private domain where they could abandon themselves to pleasure.

Sensing her thoughts, he took her arm and led her toward his house. It took less than a minute to reach the redwood deck, then enter through a sliding glass door. But during that minute Marina's mind began to function clearly again, to regain control of her wayward body.

Embarrassment and chagrin began to replace the passion she'd felt only a moment earlier. What had she done? she asked herself furiously. She couldn't want this man. She didn't even particularly like him. And even if some part of her did want him, it was madness to think about giving in to that.

Stephen seemed to have regained some control as well. In the living room he let go of her and made no move to kiss her again. But he watched her, his eyes piercing in their intensity.

"I...I have to go," she whispered, and turned toward the door.

"Don't go." It was a request, not a command, and it stopped her as a command wouldn't have done.

She faced him across a space of only a few feet. Yet those few feet seemed to have an impenetrable barrier.

He stood there, hands clasped tightly at his sides, his blond hair windblown. Looking at him, Marina felt irresistibly drawn to him, and it was all she could do not to reach out and touch him, to brush a wayward lock of hair from his eyes. As it was, everything within her strained toward him.

"I didn't plan what happened out there," he said in a quiet, compelling voice. "I didn't bring you here to seduce you."

She had begun to wonder about that, to think that possibly his only thought was to get her into his bed instead of concentrating on the movie. But even as she'd thought it, she knew it was ridiculous. This man didn't have to go to such lengths to find a bed partner.

He went on with a hint of a smile, "Until a moment ago, I didn't even realize that I was attracted to you. But I know it now. The knowledge was brought home to me quite forcefully. And I know that you feel the same about me."

The raw statement of fact embarrassed her terribly. Marina felt herself blush, and would have given anything not to do so.

Pulling herself together, she responded firmly, "No, I don't feel that way. What happened out there was . . . a mistake."

He raised one eyebrow curiously. "A mistake? How can feelings be a mistake?"

She didn't have an answer to that. She stood there, completely at a loss.

"We wanted each other, pure and simple," he pressed.

Her cheeks flamed with color. Was that all it meant to him? she wondered. Sheer chemistry and nothing more?

"It doesn't matter," Marina insisted, her voice tight and low and on the verge of breaking. "It can't happen again."

"Why not?" He asked the question matter-of-factly, as if they were having an academic discussion instead of a dialogue about intimacy.

"Because I don't want it to happen," she insisted desperately.

Now Stephen was smiling openly. "Oh, I doubt that."

Marina thought he was being flip, and it both hurt and angered her. Apparently, she deduced, he thought it would be perfectly all right to explore each other's bodies without first exploring each other's hearts and minds. But she couldn't be that impersonal about it.

"I mean it, Stephen. I'm here to work, not for anything else."

"Marina, I—"

She interrupted. "I know in your world you're used to taking sex casually, but I don't feel that way. I can't."

His hand reached for her, but she stepped back and it fell.

Forcing her eyes to meet his, she continued, "I want to do this screenplay. It means a great deal to me. But I don't want to get involved in the . . . the Hollywood life-style. So we'll just work together and . . . and that will be all. What happened tonight must never happen again."

Deliberately, fighting not to let him see the turmoil raging within her, she turned and walked toward the door.

"Marina . . ."

Without stopping or looking back, she went out the door, closing it with finality.

In the apartment she went into the bathroom and splashed cold water on her face. Her reflection stared back at her in the mirror above the basin. There was very little physical evidence that she'd just been through an emotionally and physically wrenching experience. She was paler than usual and her lips were slightly swollen from Stephen's impassioned kisses—that was all.

She told herself over and over that nothing important had happened. Nothing at all.

She almost believed it.

In the kitchen, Stephen went through the motions of making dinner. He defrosted a steak in the microwave, then put it under the broiler in the oven. He threw together ingredients for a green salad and mixed oil and vinegar for the dressing. But when he sat down to eat a few minutes later, he had absolutely no appetite. He picked at the salad, munched desultorily on a few bites of steak, then pushed all of it aside.

For a few minutes he sat alone at the table, thinking, remembering. Then, growing angry, he shoved back his chair and went into his bedroom. As he began to strip off his clothes, the phone rang. He picked it up and answered curtly, "Hello."

"Stephen, darling, it's Laura."

He had no desire to talk to her, but knew that he should. His response was perfunctory. "Yes?"

There was a silence over the phone, then she said awkwardly, "I got the roses—and the note. I don't understand."

"I thought it was fairly clear."

"But why? Why are you 'setting me free' as you so quaintly put it?"

"I assumed you wanted your freedom."

"But what on earth would make you think that, darling?"

He cut through the innocent protest. "Where were you last weekend, Laura?"

She didn't answer immediately. Then, in a voice that was determinedly cheerful, she said, "Oh, for heaven's sakes, you know where I was. Working my little fingers to the bone."

Stephen wasn't in a mood to play games. "I don't believe you."

"Stephen, don't be ridiculous." Her tone betrayed nervousness rather than innocence.

"I wish you all the best, Laura. I mean that. Goodbye."

"Stephen! Look, this is silly. All right, I admit I wasn't working, but I didn't want to hurt your feelings. It's stupid to break up over a little episode. It didn't mean anything."

"You think that makes it better? After spending two years with me, you don't seem to know me very well, Laura. Goodbye."

This time she didn't protest. He hung up and breathed a long sigh of relief.

Despite their differences, he had truly cared about Laura. If this had happened two weeks earlier, he'd have been very angry and very, very hurt. Now all he felt was disappointment that their relationship had ended in such a tacky way.

As he finished taking off his clothes, it wasn't Laura he was thinking about. It was Marina.

He stepped into the sauna off the bathroom. After grabbing a towel from a rack, he knotted it low on his hips, then sat down on a small wooden bench. As steam filled the small, wood-paneled room, he leaned back against the wall.

It was early, not yet nine o'clock, and yet he was physically and emotionally exhausted. A feeling of intense dissatisfaction washed over him along with the hot, damp steam.

What *is* it? Stephen asked himself, angrily slamming one tightly balled fist against the bench.

But he knew perfectly well what was wrong. He wanted Marina. Wanted her with a hunger he hadn't felt in years. In a sense it was like the hunger for success that had propelled him from the very bottom to the very top in just a little more than ten years of struggle. At sixteen he'd been broke, on his own, a high school dropout. At twenty-six he had had his first hit movie and had worn a silk shirt for the first time.

He'd wanted success so much he could taste it.

And now he wanted Marina in the same way. He remembered how well her body fit with his. Even though she was fully clothed, he could still feel the curves, the hollows, the fullness in just the right places. She was his physical and emotional opposite—as soft as he was hard, as yielding as he was demanding.

There was passion there, whether she wanted to admit it or not. A passion so fierce, it fired his own in a way no other woman had ever done. She might not be his type, as he'd tried to tell himself before, but there was sure as hell *some-*

thing there that he responded to. It had taken all his self-control not to take her there on the deserted beach.

Why did this stubborn, difficult young woman fire his blood in a way no other woman had done? Stephen shook his head in perplexity. There was no easy answer to that. Physically, she didn't begin to compare to Laura, or any number of other women he could have if he chose. She was far from voluptuous, and while she was pretty, she wasn't beautiful.

And her personality certainly wasn't the answer. She'd been hard to get along with from the beginning. And when she'd stood there earlier and all but accused him of being the worst kind of shallow Hollywood philanderer, he could have cheerfully throttled her.

How dare she make a snap judgment like that? As if he spent all his time lolling in hot tubs, lecherously pursuing every young woman who crossed his path.

Stephen felt himself growing furious all over again just thinking about it.

So if it wasn't her looks and it certainly wasn't her personality, why did he want her?

A word stole into his thoughts—*character*. Marina Turner had character. And that was one commodity sorely lacking in his business. Her values were solid and honest, her thinking straight. She was the kind of woman a man could depend on to be there for him, through thick and thin, and not just during the good times. It wouldn't matter to her if his movies grossed a hundred million or disappeared from theaters in three days.

Stephen couldn't picture her ever doing what Laura had done—coolly lying to him in order to be with someone else, then insisting he shouldn't be angry because it didn't mean anything. He could have forgiven Laura much more easily if she'd been swept away by real feeling for another man.

When Marina made a commitment to a man, he'd bet it was for a lifetime, not just while it was convenient. And she'd certainly made it clear that she didn't take sex lightly. Hit-and-run sex wasn't her style.

Along with the character was passion—a deep womanly passion that she probably didn't realize she possessed. But he'd realized it as soon as he took her in his arms and their lips touched. Every fiber of her being reached out to him; after a brief, initial resistance, nothing was held back.

He wondered what it would be like to make love to her instead of stopping at just a kiss. The thought brought a sharp ache deep in his abdomen. The knowledge that she was so close, only a few yards away in the apartment above the garage, made it worse.

Steam filled the room. Stephen's body glistened darkly now. His smooth, hard chest was dotted with beads of perspiration. Drops of water trickled down the flat plane of his stomach. Closing his eyes he reveled in the sensuous sensation of warmth and dampness.

Marina... what on earth was he going to do about her?

The next morning Marina went into the kitchenette and discovered that it was fully stocked. She made tea and toast for breakfast, but had no appetite for it. She was just looking at the cold toast, telling herself she should eat it, when she heard a knock at her door. She knew who it must be, of course, and as she answered the door she felt an attack of nervousness.

Stephen stood there, looking cool and collected.

"Good morning, Marina. Ready to get to work?"

Clearing her throat, she responded, "Yes. Are we working here?"

"No, I have an office downstairs. While we're out here I thought we'd work there. The rest of the time you'll be working at the office, of course."

"All right."

Grabbing her copy of the galleys of *Casey*, along with her unfortunate treatment, she followed Stephen downstairs to his office.

Apparently he wasn't going to make any reference to what had happened between them last night. Good, Marina thought with relief. That would certainly make things easier. Yet the relief she felt at this was mingled with a gnawing disappointment.

His office was a large room facing the ocean. A double set of French doors opened onto the beach. The four doors let in plenty of sunlight and the room was bright and cheerful. It would be a pleasant place to work, Marina realized.

There was a good-sized desk, a massive, impressive-looking typewriter and a home computer with a printer.

"I assume you'd rather work on the typewriter than the computer," Stephen said.

She nodded. "I don't know the first thing about computers and I have no desire to learn. I'm going to have to be dragged kicking and screaming into the computer age."

"I'm not surprised after seeing your typewriter. You should have that thing bronzed."

"It works. And it doesn't intimidate me. It's truly user-friendly."

"Okay, you take the chair at the desk, by the typewriter, and I'll sit over here."

As Marina sat down, Stephen plopped into a big over-stuffed armchair on the other side of the desk. Having the desk between them made her feel secure somehow. She was glad they would be working this way, instead of poring over pages together, side by side.

"Okay," Stephen began, "before you put one word on paper I'm going to give you a lecture on screenwriting. So just sit and listen. Feel free to take notes or ask questions. But don't even try to argue. I know what I'm talking about, and you're just learning."

Marina couldn't resist impudently saying, "Yes, professor."

Shooting her a dark look, Stephen continued. "All right, what is a good screenplay? When you read a good one, you know it immediately, from page one."

"Is it a question of style?"

"That and the way the story is set up, the grasp of dramatic situation, the introduction of the main character and the basic premise of the story. All these things have to be set up in the first few pages."

"Which I didn't do in my treatment," Marina admitted.

"Exactly. Unlike a novel, a screenplay has to take off fast. You only have about two hours to tell a story in movie form. You can't waste half of it getting started. By the end of the first ten or fifteen minutes we should know who the main characters are and what the story is all about."

"Well, in *Casey* she's the protagonist and the story is about her affair with a married man."

"Yes. The question is, where do we open up? Your treatment opened with her graduating from high school in San Francisco, went on to describe what she did during the summer, then finally got her down to Big Sur where she meets the married artist and the affair takes place. We don't have time for all that."

"But I only spent a few pages describing all that."

"One page equals about one minute of screen time. You spent ten pages, ten minutes of screen time, setting up unnecessary scenes."

"What if there's a lot of action, or a lot of dialogue?"

"Doesn't matter. The point is, you have to get your story rolling faster than that."

"Are you saying it should open when she arrives in Big Sur?"

"You bet."

"Then how do we know about her background?"

"That's called exposition and it's a clumsy thing to handle in a movie. You have to be careful or it sounds like what it is—filling the audience in on what they need to know about the back story."

"So how do we do that?"

Stephen gave Marina a pointed look. "*You*, as the writer, do it as cleverly as possible. Whatever you do, show, don't tell. Action is character. Don't have Casey telling someone her life story. Reveal her character through what she does. The director will help. He'll focus on physical things that help tell the story visually—like a graduation announcement, for instance, or a bumper sticker on her car that reads 'Class of '86.'"

Marina had been thinking furiously as Stephen talked. Now she said excitedly, "How about if I open up when she walks into the restaurant and is hired as a waitress? I could use the scene from the book where the manager has her set a table and she wants to do it in the elaborate, formal way she's used to, with two forks, two knives, soupspoon, dessert spoon, etc."

"Good. That will show right up front what kind of life she came from and what a step down it is for her to be working as a waitress."

"Then what happens after the opening?"

"Maybe I'd better explain the whole structure of a screenplay to you. A feature film, like this one, as opposed to a TV movie, is divided into three acts. Act 1 is the beginning. It's the setup and you have about thirty pages to set up your story."

"I see. By the end of that first thirty pages, and thirty minutes, we have to know who the main characters are and what the main thrust of the story is going to be."

"Yes. So in our movie we should know who Casey, Mark and Sheila are. We should know that Mark is a talented but struggling artist who asks Casey to pose for him, and that

Sheila is his wife who works to support him while he paints. All by the end of the first thirty minutes.''

"I took a hundred pages to do it in my novel."

"As I've said before, and will probably say again, a novel isn't a screenplay. Now, at the end of the first act, there is a plot point."

At Marina's blank look, he explained, "That's an incident or event that hooks into the story and turns it in a new direction. And it usually happens around page twenty-five in the script."

"I guess the plot point in this story would be when Casey and Mark become lovers."

"Right. Now the story goes in a new direction. And this is where act 2 begins. It's the biggest chunk of the screenplay, from about page thirty to page ninety. This is the middle action part, where most of the confrontation takes place."

"You mean when Casey confronts Mark over her love for him, and he has to confront his own mixed feelings—being in love with her but also feeling loyalty to Sheila," Marina commented.

"Yeah, that defines the need of your protagonist—Casey needs Mark, she wants him to leave Sheila and marry her. That's her goal. But since this is drama, there have to be obstacles to that goal. The obstacles are Mark's loyalty to Sheila and his determination to put his art above his personal life. Being with Casey is good for him creatively because she inspires him to be better than he's ever been. But being with Sheila is good financially because her support allows him to paint."

"And all those obstacles generate conflict, which is at the heart of drama," Marina finished for him. "I do know something, you see."

He smiled and Marina returned the smile. For the first time all morning she began to feel at ease with Stephen. And she was learning so much. Already she had a much better grasp of screenwriting than she'd had going in. And they were just starting.

Stephen went on, "There's a plot point at the end of act 2, also, that moves the story in a new direction."

"Sheila's pregnancy," Marina answered quickly.

"Right. That complicates Mark's decision. It was hard enough to leave a wife, but now he has to consider leaving a child as well."

"And since he was abandoned by his father," Marina said eagerly, "he has strong feelings about not abandoning his own child."

"Right." Stephen looked at her appraisingly. "You know, one of the things I liked so much about your novel was the really thorough way you developed your characters psychologically. It made each one very compelling. They stayed with me for a long time after I finished reading the book, and that doesn't happen very often."

The simple, sincere praise shook Marina. She couldn't meet Stephen's look. Instead, she looked down at the page where she'd been taking notes and asked, "What about act 3?"

"That's the resolution of the story. It takes place between pages ninety and one hundred and twenty—unless we're making a major epic, which we're not."

Ignoring the gibe, Marina said, "All right, now we come to the ending. I assume you'll want to keep the ending I have in the novel."

"No."

She sat up straight in her chair. "What?"

"It's too ambiguous. The days of ambiguous endings in movies are over."

"There are plenty of good movies that have ambiguous endings that worked beautifully."

"Yeah, and you know how old they are? Nowadays audiences want a resolution, whether it's happy or sad. They don't want to go out of the theater shaking their heads and wondering what it was all about and what was going to happen next."

"Stephen, the ending is the most powerful part of my story."

"Wrong. It's the weakest part. I'm surprised the editor let you get away with it. Casey decides to do the honorable thing and leave because she can't hurt Sheila and the child. That's good, but then you have Mark undecided about whether or not he should go after her. And you end with him still being undecided. I guess it's okay in a novel, but it won't work in a movie."

The ending was dear to Marina's heart and she wasn't about to change it to a pat conclusion. Glaring at Stephen, she said, "You mean it won't work in a commercial movie. Damn it, Stephen, this isn't *Rebels*, where life is simplistic and everyone lives happily ever after."

He had been sprawled comfortably in the chair. Now Stephen sat up abruptly and met Marina's angry look stubbornly. "It's about time we had this out. I understand how you might have felt that way before, but there's no excuse for it now. This movie means every bit as much to me as it does to you. I intend to make a fine, serious film. The only thing it will have in common with my other three films, including *Rebels*, is that I will do it as well as I possibly can."

"Then why do you want to ruin the ending?"

"I'm not ruining the ending, I'm improving it. Believe it or not, Marina, you don't know it all. You're a good writer and you'll probably get even better with experience. But you're not perfect, not all of your words are golden."

She was livid. "You want to make it pat and predictable...."

"That's not what I want to do and if you were capable of being objective about it you'd realize that."

"Objective! Look, I wrote this story, I know it better than you ever will. And I know that ending works."

"A strong ending resolves the story in order to make it understandable and complete. There's nothing particularly clever about leaving the audience hanging because you weren't sure which way to have your character go."

"That wasn't it at all! In real life people often have a hard time making a decision about love versus duty. In real life—"

Stephen interrupted impatiently, "This isn't real life, Marina, it's a novel. It isn't enough to say that something would happen a certain way in real life. You have to make it believable and satisfying dramatically."

"I think my ending's believable," she insisted, refusing to back down.

"It's esoteric. That's okay in a novel, it's not okay in a film."

"There have been esoteric films," Marina shot back.

"Yes, there have. Almost without exception they played in art houses in L.A. and New York to very limited audiences."

"We're back to numbers again. I don't know why you're so concerned with how many people will see this movie."

"I don't know why you're so unconcerned with it. Do you really want a film that has such little appeal that only your mother and best friend go to see it?"

No, she didn't. For the first time in the argument, she had a twinge of self-doubt.

Seeing this, Stephen went on in a calmer tone, "Look, Marina, when you begin a screenplay you should know exactly where it's going, how it's going to end, and everything in the script should lead to it. It's your goal, and once you lose sight of it the power of your script becomes diffused. This is a powerful story, but if it builds to a climax where the hero is left wallowing in confusion, the power evaporates."

Marina didn't speak for a moment. There was something to what Stephen was saying. Her editor at the publishing house had said much the same thing, but hadn't pressed Marina to change it.

Stephen took a deep breath. "Casey's the protagonist. The movie should end with her, not Mark. And it should end decisively. There should be a resolution to the problem, not anticlimactic B.S."

Marina looked out the windows. Outside, waves crashed on the beach and sea gulls screeched. But inside the office there was a tense silence.

Stephen leaned forward in his chair, his hands clasped between his knees, his expression urgent. "I want this film to be absolutely fine. I want it to be so fine that critics have to grudgingly admit that maybe I'm more than a schlock merchant after all. I'm not trying to make it commercial. I want it to have an audience, but I know damn well it'll never be half as commercial as any of the other movies I've made. But if you don't believe that, then we're both wasting our time here."

His eyes locked with hers. He wouldn't look away.

Inside her, Marina felt some hard core of resistance slowly begin to melt. After what seemed like an interminable silence, she said in a low voice, "Okay."

Stephen looked startled, then wary. "Okay... what?"

A hint of a smile lifted the corners of Marina's mouth. "Okay, you're right and I'm wrong."

For a moment he looked as if he didn't believe her. The knowledge that she could surprise him pleased her somehow.

"Just like that?" he asked.

"When you're right, you're right. What can I say? You're right—this time."

Slowly his expression softened into a warm smile. "Are you, by any chance, laughing at me?"

Her voice was little more than a whisper. "Only a little."

"Arguing with you is very stimulating. I think I enjoy it."

She smiled. "Of course—you won."

He shook his head. "No, we both won."

Then, before she could reply, he went on, "I don't know about you, but I didn't eat much breakfast. Suddenly I'm starving. Want to go out to a little deli near here that has the best strawberry blintzes this side of the Bronx?"

"I'd like that."

As they both stood up, Stephen said, "Working with you is going to be interesting."

Indeed, Marina thought.

Chapter Eight

When they returned from breakfast they continued working through the afternoon, pausing only long enough to eat a light lunch of fruit and cheese. The entire day was spent outlining the first ten pages of the script. When Marina complained that they were getting bogged down in it, Stephen gave another lecture.

"The first ten pages of a script are absolutely crucial," he insisted adamantly.

"I understand. I just think you're being arbitrary in insisting that it take no more than ten pages to set up the main characters and the conflict."

"You're in an unusual position here, Marina. I'm working with you on the script. Normally, if you did a screenplay it would go to a 'reader.'"

"What's that?"

"Someone who reads scripts so a producer doesn't have to bother. It can be someone hired to do the job. Or it can be any number of people—a wife, a girlfriend, a secretary.

The point is, the reader has to be hooked in the first few pages or he won't continue reading. And he certainly won't recommend it to the producer. If the producer does read it, he'll scan the first few pages—about ten, to be exact—and make a decision about whether he should toss it or keep reading."

"That's very discouraging."

"That's reality. Audiences do the same thing when they watch a movie. After the first ten minutes they either like the movie or they don't. And if they don't, it's hard to overcome that resistance, no matter how good the movie gets later."

"I'm not sure I agree with that. I'm willing to give a movie more than ten minutes to prove itself."

Stephen smiled dryly. "Oh, I doubt that. Remember the opening of *Star Wars*?"

"Sure, it was wonderful. That great shot of a small spaceship being pursued by a larger one that seemed to come right out of the edge of the screen, lasers blasting...it was wonderful."

"Right. George Lucas captured the audience's attention immediately. You knew in the first two minutes you were going to enjoy the movie, and you sat back in the seat and did just that. After that terrific opening, you knew you were going to like that movie."

"Are you saying all movies should start that fast?"

"No, of course not. Serious films, like ours, can take longer to capture an audience. But they shouldn't take more than ten minutes."

At Marina's look of stubborn disagreement, he went on, "Tell you what. We'll go see a movie tonight. There are a couple of interesting ones playing at the Malibu Cinema. You see how long it takes you to make a decision about whether the movie is worth the price of admission. I'll bet it'll take you no more than ten minutes."

"Okay. But only if I can have popcorn."

He smiled at her. "You can even have extra butter."

She returned the smile. But inside she felt a twinge of something she recognized as fear. She and Stephen were getting along now, in spite of the intermittent disagreements. They were even joking with each other occasionally. She knew that she should feel more relaxed with him than she did.

But she couldn't get the previous night out of her mind. As they worked throughout the afternoon, she would go for long stretches of time without thinking about it. Then something would happen—he would lean over her to see what she'd typed, and their shoulders would touch...or she would look up and catch him watching her intently....

And then the atmosphere between them would change, ever so subtly, so that it wasn't just work, but was something more. Something very personal.

Since Marina had no idea what the format of a screenplay was like, Stephen showed her the script of *Rebels*.

"This is the shooting script," he began.

"You mean the final draft that the movie was shot from?"

"Right. So all the scenes are numbered. But that isn't done until we're down to the final draft. Now then, basically a film is composed of several thousand feet of frames that are spliced, edited and run on reels to make the movie. A frame is like a photograph—it's the square the camera reveals. There are definite boundaries. For instance, you might write, 'half a treasure chest showing in frame.'"

"Or half a souped-up '58 Corvette," Marina interrupted, referring to a famous scene in *Rebels*.

Stephen looked at her in surprise. "You saw the movie?"

"Yes."

"I thought your less-flattering references to it were based on reviews, not personal viewing."

She met his look. "Actually, I enjoyed it. I just didn't want *Casey* to be that kind of light, escapist film."

He gave her a direct look. "It won't be."

Something in his voice made Marina look at him intently. For the first time, she began to trust that he really would make *Casey* with all the integrity she'd hoped.

After a moment, he went on, "Frames are called shots. You have to visualize your story scene by scene and identify the subject of each shot."

"Like Casey, Mark or Sheila?"

"Yes. Or a beach or a sunset or a car moving along a highway. It's identified in capitals and followed by dialogue or narrative describing the action taking place. And when the camera moves to a new shot, you have to identify it as a new shot."

"Then what comes after the subject?"

"The setting—is it inside or outside? It's written INT.—DAY or EXT.—NIGHT. If all the shots are taking place in the same place and time, you don't have to repeat the setting."

"But understand," Stephen continued, "that the director has the final say about how it will be shot. You may as well understand now that screenwriters don't have the same control over their work as novelists."

Her tone was dry. "I'm beginning to get that impression."

"Writers get upset over it and complain about their work being ruined. But film is a collaborative medium. It's craft, not art, because it isn't one person's vision."

"What if the same person writes and directs a film?"

Stephen grinned slyly. "Getting delusions of grandeur already? I'm creating a Frankenstein's monster here."

"It just occurred to me that it would be nice to be able to protect what I've written."

"A lot of screenwriters feel that way. But even those who are able to do that, like Woody Allen or Mel Brooks, are still at the mercy of other people—the cinematographer, the actors and so on."

"Maybe I won't try to become an *auteur*, after all," Marina said with a sigh.

"I never have believed in that theory. The idea that one person is responsible for a film, like an author is responsible for a book, is inherently ridiculous. But enough of that. Let's talk about the opening."

"You've already made it clear you don't want to use the same opening that's in the novel."

"No, and I've explained why. We're adapting your book, and that means changing it into a screenplay, not faithfully copying everything in the book. It's not a filmed novel. They're two different forms. We're writing a screenplay based on other material, but basically we're still writing an original screenplay."

"Now, hold on," Marina interrupted angrily. "You're playing fast and loose with my story."

"Your story dealt with the internal life of characters, especially Casey—their thoughts, feelings, emotions. But a screenplay can't do that. It has to deal with externals. A screenplay is a story told with pictures. You have to learn to see it that way."

Marina was thoughtful. She knew Stephen was right. Much as she resisted the idea, she knew now that she was going to have to look at her story in a whole new way. Even when she and Stephen were outlining the first few pages, she still had hoped to include some of the earlier scenes somewhere. Now she realized that the story would have to make a clean beginning in Big Sur.

But there were several scenes in those first hundred pages that were dear to her heart. One scene in particular, where Casey breaks completely with her emotionally cold, snobbish parents, Marina felt was the best scene she'd ever written. And now it would have to go.

It occurred to her, though, that she might do something interesting with the scene where Casey described that breakup to Mark. Instead of sliding over it quickly, as she had in the book, she might be able to make it very dramatic.

The more she thought about it, the more excited she became at the prospect.

Looking at Stephen, she said, "Okay. Let's talk about the new opening."

They discussed the opening in great detail and drew up another outline. By midafternoon they had a scene they both agreed on. While Marina typed up the script, Stephen went into the kitchen to make coffee. When he returned a few minutes later with steaming mugs of coffee for both of them, she handed him the first page of the screenplay.

A minute later he looked up to find Marina watching him anxiously.

"Well?"

"It's fine," he said quietly.

"That's all? Fine?"

"Very fine."

For an instant she felt intense disappointment. Then she caught something in his look and somehow she sensed that he was even more pleased than he could admit.

"All right, boss, what do we do next?"

They worked until six o'clock, at which time Stephen said, "Enough. Let's have dinner."

Marina was glad to break for the day. Her mind was exhausted. She'd taken in so much new information, and knew that there was still a great deal to learn. Stephen was a good teacher; much more patient than she would have expected, and not nearly so difficult to please.

If only it could go on like this—professional, impersonal—everything would be all right, she thought. She would finish the screenplay, then return to Big Sur.

And forget that kiss.

In the apartment, she changed from jeans and a sweater to a cowl-necked chambray dress that was cinched tight at the waist with a tan leather belt. The full skirt came down past the tops of her tan boots. Because it was a cool November evening, she threw a blue-and-tan shawl across her shoulders.

Stephen met her downstairs by the garage. A raised eyebrow and a smile of approval were silent compliments at her transformation.

He'd changed into a dark blue V-neck cashmere pullover that revealed his tanned, muscular chest. The matching slacks fit his flat stomach and hard thighs smoothly. As always, he looked wonderful. His features were so strong, even and appealing, his build so muscular, Marina knew that he must photograph well.

A sudden thought occurred to her, and without thinking, she asked as they drove off, "Why did you become a producer instead of an actor?"

Stephen was startled by the question. "What makes you think I was ever interested in acting?"

Because you're handsome enough to be an actor, she wanted to reply. But she couldn't say that. Instead, she replied awkwardly, "Oh, I don't know. I guess I just assumed that most people who want to be in the film business want to be actors."

"Many, perhaps, but not most. I was certainly never interested in being in front of the camera."

"Why not?"

"It's too hard; the insecurity, the rejection. You're either too young or too old, too ugly or too handsome. You're constantly told you're not the right type. There are more than twenty thousand members of the Screen Actors' Guild, and only a handful earn a living at their craft. It's a tough life."

"I never realized how tough it must be until I was waiting in your office that first day and saw actress after actress come in, all hoping to be cast in a role that was merely a walk-on."

Stephen cast a quick glance at Marina, straining to see her in the darkened car. "I mistook you for an actress that day."

Marina smiled at the memory. She could see the humor in it now, though at the time she'd been furious.

"You could be an actress," Stephen went on.

"Me? You're kidding."

"Nope. There's a freshness about you—an innocence. You would shine on film."

Marina smiled ruefully. "I can't see myself as an actress."

"Don't get me wrong, I'm not suggesting a career change. Like I said, acting's too tough a profession for me to recommend it to anyone. Besides, you're a talented writer. It would be a shame if you stopped writing."

"I'll never do that," Marina said with feeling. "Writing's the most important thing in my life."

Stephen glanced at her again as they reached a straight stretch on the Pacific Coast Highway. "Is it the only thing in your life?"

The pointed question caught her off guard. Irritated, she retorted, "Is producing the only thing in yours?"

Instead of being angry, Stephen answered evenly, "Yes, at the moment it is. But I don't intend to let that always be the case."

"I take it you want marriage and children?"

"Definitely. Don't you?"

Marina's answer came fast and sure. "No."

His eyes flicked to hers, then back to the road again. "You sound pretty definite about it."

"I am."

"Don't you think you're kind of young to make that kind of decision? You're only what—twenty-two, twenty-three?"

"Twenty-four."

"Oh, pardon me," he teased. "So at the ripe old age of twenty-four, you've definitely decided you don't want marriage or children."

"Not every woman is cut out to be a wife and mother," she snapped.

"No, that's true. But I would have said you are."

In spite of herself she couldn't resist asking, "Why?"

Without looking at her, keeping his eyes on the highway, he said matter-of-factly, "Because you have so much love to give."

At that moment they reached the restaurant in Malibu where Stephen had made reservations earlier. While Marina was still digesting his last, rather startling remark, he went on calmly, "Here we are. I think you'll like this place. They have fabulous lobster."

They sat at a small table for two in a quiet corner near a window overlooking the beach. Floodlights lit the beach, and birds could be seen playing tag with the low, frothy waves that broke gently on the sand.

On the periphery of her vision Marina saw the candlelight flickering in hurricane lamps, the diners at the adjoining tables, the waiters carrying trays of food.

She looked back at Stephen. A slow smile spread across his face. Marina felt her heart race and a flush suffuse her cheeks. His smile was absolutely dazzling when it reached his deep blue eyes, as it did now, crinkling them at the corners.

Fortunately, at that moment the waiter arrived to take their order. Marina felt slightly disoriented, and ordered the first thing that came to mind—the lobster that Stephen had recommended. He ordered the same thing, and as the waiter left, he said, "I think you'll like it."

"I'm sure I will," she murmured noncommittally.

A moment later the waiter returned with steaming bowls of clam chowder, and Marina concentrated on her soup. But when that was finished there was a long wait before the main course was ready, and she had no excuse to ignore Stephen any longer.

Crossing his arms on the table, he leaned toward her. "There's something I'd like to know. Something personal. You don't have to answer if you'd rather not."

He'd never been so polite about probing into her personal life before, and Marina's curiosity was piqued by this sudden burst of good manners.

"What is it?"

"I get the feeling there's a lot of you in *Casey*. You told me it isn't autobiographical, except on a superficial level. How autobiographical is it exactly?"

It wasn't an easy question to answer, but at least it wasn't as personal as she expected. She answered slowly, "I never had an affair with a married man. But I had a terrible crush on one during my freshman year in college."

"A professor, of course."

She smiled. "Of course. He taught a creative writing class. It was such a cliché; he was older, more mature, more sophisticated. I worshiped him."

"I take it he was attracted to you."

"Yes. I was so flattered. He made my high school boyfriends seem like such children. And he told me I had real talent as a writer."

"Well, he was right about that."

"Thank you."

"What happened?"

"Well . . . he wanted to have an affair. And I seriously considered it. He said his marriage was sterile, that it was a marriage in name only—all the usual lines."

"But you believed them?"

"I wanted to believe them. Then I found out that this was his second wife. He'd been married before. He had had an affair with a graduate student who was his teaching assistant, and ended up marrying her. I met her once. She was young and pretty, but she didn't look very happy."

"I'll bet she wasn't."

"Anyway, when I realized what was happening between us wasn't grand passion but just another affair, I ended it. I felt like an absolute fool."

"But you didn't behave like one," Stephen reassured her.

"Well, I did up to a point."

"We all have behaved like fools up to a point. Especially at eighteen."

Looking at him, she dared to ask, "Have you ever made a fool of yourself over someone?"

"Several times. But I like to think I haven't committed the ultimate foolish act."

"What's that?"

"Hurting someone in the name of love."

"Oh." Marina's voice was small and helpless. She had no idea what to say in the face of such honesty, such integrity. When she remembered how she'd despised Stephen at first, had accused him of lacking integrity, she felt sick.

"I think I owe you an apology," she said slowly, forcing herself to look at him instead of turning away.

He raised one eyebrow quizzically. "Oh. Why?"

"For giving you a great deal less credit than you deserve."

"I see. As a producer, you mean."

He didn't really mean that, she knew. He was simply pressing her to spell out exactly what she felt about him. The next words were the hardest she'd ever had to say in her entire life.

"That, too. But mainly...as a man."

He didn't smile. Didn't speak. But there was something in his eyes Marina had never seen before. It shook her profoundly, turning her inside out, and leaving her feeling limp.

His gaze held hers until she couldn't bear it any longer and had to lower her lashes demurely, in a way that was very unlike her.

"Tell me about your life," he asked.

It was a plea rather than a command, and she found she couldn't resist it.

She smiled softly. "Everything?"

He returned the smile. "Everything. Start with your earliest memory and go on from there."

"Ah…my earliest memory. Well, I think that must be my mother reading bedtime stories to me. We'd sit in my bed together, both of us under my covers, and she'd hold the book so I could see the pictures. She read with such feeling—she really threw herself into the stories, changing her voice and expression. Her wicked witch in *Snow White* was truly scary."

"Sounds like she was a wonderful mother."

"Yes, she was. The kind of mother who was waiting at home with cookies and milk after school. You know."

He shook his head slowly. "Actually, I don't know. My life was very different from yours."

There wasn't a trace of self-pity in the words. It was a plain, unemotional statement of fact. Yet there was something poignant about those words that caught at Marina's heart.

She would have stopped talking about her mother, but Stephen continued, "Go on. Tell me more about your mother. What's her name?"

"Caroline."

"A pretty name."

"Yes. I like it. If I—"

Marina stopped. She'd been about to say that if she ever had a daughter she wanted to name her Caroline. But since she'd just told Stephen in no uncertain terms that she didn't intend to marry or have children, that was stupid.

Changing the subject, she said, "She sewed my Halloween costumes. I can still remember the year I was a witch. My hat was so tall, it kept falling off. I didn't know whether to grab my hat or hold on tight to my trick-or-treat bag."

Stephen laughed, then he noticed that Marina's expression had grown sober. "What is it? What's wrong between you and your mother now?"

Marina didn't answer for a long moment. Finally, she said, "Nothing, really."

But she could tell that he didn't believe her. Still, she was relieved when he didn't press the issue.

Instead he asked, "What was your life like growing up? Was your family part of the social set in San Francisco?"

Her smile was rueful. "Sort of. All of that mattered to my father. He came from a family that had been wealthy but had lost everything. He wanted desperately to regain what he'd lost. All he could think about was making more and more money, being one of the social elite in the city."

"It must have devastated him when he lost everything."

"It did. Mom and I didn't care, really. But he did. I guess I can understand why he..."

She stopped, reluctant to continue. But Stephen urged her to finish. "Why he what?"

"He...he fell in love with another woman. She was much younger, not a great deal older than I am, in fact. And she was quite wealthy."

"Oh. I see."

She sensed that Stephen really did see.

"How did your mother take it?"

"My mother has a lot of... well, class, for want of a better word. When he asked for a divorce, she gave it to him. I know she must have been deeply hurt, but she didn't let it show. And she wasn't bitter or vindictive."

"She sounds remarkable. I'm glad she found someone else to be happy with."

Marina didn't echo the sentiment. She knew it was churlish of her not to, but she just couldn't.

Watching her, Stephen asked bluntly, "Why do you dislike your stepfather so much?"

"I don't know him well enough to dislike him. He doesn't matter to me."

"I don't believe you."

Her temper flared. "Well, I don't care what you believe. It's the truth."

"No, it isn't. And since it isn't like you to lie, it makes me very curious about him. When you first mentioned your parents' divorce and your mother's remarriage, I assumed you resented your stepfather out of a feeling of loyalty to your father. But now I don't think that's the case."

At that moment the waiter brought the lobster.

Breathing an inward sigh of relief at the interruption, Marina pointedly ignored Stephen and concentrated on her food.

When they finished they had a scant five minutes to make it to the movie theater, so there was no time for further discussion of her family. Marina was intensely relieved. She didn't want to go into the intimate details of her parentage with Stephen.

When the movie was over Marina had to admit to Stephen that he was right: she'd been hooked in the first ten minutes of the film.

As they drove back up the highway toward Trancas, just north of Malibu, Stephen said, "I won't say I told you so. But keep it in mind while you work on the next nine pages of the script."

"I will."

After that they lapsed into a companionable silence.

It had been a very nice evening, actually, Marina thought happily. There had been difficult moments, especially when Stephen asked about her mother's remarriage. But the rest of the time they'd gotten along amazingly well. She felt more comfortable with him than she would have thought possible.

But just as she was telling herself that, they arrived at his house. And suddenly she felt a vague apprehension begin to grow within her. It was confusing at first, until she realized what it was. They'd had a date. No matter how she tried to tell herself otherwise, that was really what it had been. She had dressed up and Stephen had taken her out to dinner and a movie—typical date protocol.

Though he'd originally said that the point of it was to see a movie and help her understand the importance of the first ten minutes of a film, that had played only a small part in the evening. Pleasure, not business, was the order of the evening. They had talked about personal subjects, not work—still more typical date protocol.

And now he was walking her to her door. As she climbed the steps just ahead of Stephen, Marina felt a growing panic. What would he expect at her door? A good-night kiss, or even more?

She took out her key with shaking fingers and opened the door. Then she said over her shoulder, "Thank you for taking me to the movie. You were right, it was quite educational."

"Marina."

His voice was low and compelling.

When she answered, her own held a tiny quaver. "Yes?"

"Look at me."

It was a command. She would have liked to turn her back on him completely and hurry inside the apartment, but she knew that would be rude and ridiculous.

Forcing herself to assume a composure she didn't feel, she turned to face him. As Marina looked into his eyes, even darker than usual on this moonless night, she saw what she had known she would see—desire.

Her mouth felt suddenly dry and her hand shook as he took it in his larger, stronger one. Very gently, with exquisite slowness, he raised it to his lips, turned it over and kissed her tender palm.

"Marina..." He leaned toward her, his voice husky.

He was very close to her now. She could feel his warm, sweet breath against her skin, his powerful body close beside her own trembling one. She felt helpless to resist, as if the moment was inevitable and right and she shouldn't fight it.

Without realizing what she was doing, she leaned toward him.

With a low groan deep in his throat, he gathered her to him, his mouth seeking hers. The kiss was gentle this time. The passion was there, just beneath the surface, but it was held in check, as if he didn't want to frighten her away.

Marina was shaken to the very roots of her being, and her breath caught in her throat. And all she could think, over and over again, was, "I want this . . . I want it so. . . ."

Gently he cradled her in his tender embrace, running his fingers through her tousled hair, kissing her mouth, her forehead, the lids of her closed eyes. Then he stopped kissing her and simply held her against his chest so that the thudding of her heart was in concert with his.

Then he took her hand, the hand he still held, and kissed it again.

Marina said nothing; she wasn't capable of speech. She felt filled with an extraordinary joy, more intense than any happiness she'd ever known. She knew it must be apparent in her eyes, in the smile she gave to him. She simply couldn't hold it in, couldn't deny it.

As his eyes looked into hers, she thought she saw something very nearly like that same joy in those dark blue depths.

He smiled as he slowly, gently released her. Then, pressing one last kiss against her palm, he whispered, "I think I'd better leave you now. Good night, Marina."

Don't go, she wanted to say. But she held her tongue.

As his hands let go of her and his body moved away from hers, she felt an acute sense of abandonment. He turned and walked down the stairs. When he was out of sight, Marina finally went inside the apartment.

Chapter Nine

Marina awoke in the middle of the night to the sound of a heavy rain beating down on the roof and slashing at the windows. A fierce wind howled around the corners of the house.

Ever since she was a child she had been terrified of storms. It had begun one night when she was very small and got tangled in her bedclothes. It had been a stormy night and she'd wanted to go to her mother's room, but she couldn't untangle herself. The more desperately she struggled, the more trapped she became. It had seemed to take an eternity for her mother to hear her cries and come to her.

After that she'd never been able to sleep calmly through a storm if she was alone. She could only bear it if someone was with her.

Now she got up, turned on the lights and curled up in a chair with a wool throw pulled tightly around her. Outside, the storm was rapidly growing worse. Massive waves crashed on the beach, sounding like the roar of battle. The waves sounded so close to her, as if at any minute they would come smashing through the house.

Marina went through the familiar litany of reassurance that she always used on herself: there was nothing to be frightened of, storms were exciting, not terrifying, she was all right, she was all right.

But it did no good at all. To make matters even worse than usual, she was in a strange place without anything familiar and reassuring around her. She had begun to tremble the moment the storm woke her. Now she shivered uncontrollably. Despite the fact that she wore a long fleecy nightgown and had a heavy blanket wrapped around her, she was cold—so cold her fingers were numb and her teeth chattered.

As she sat in the chair, curled up in a tight ball like a child, she wondered how she would get through this terrible night....

In his bedroom, Stephen awoke to the sound of the wind and rain. Ignoring it, he turned over to go back to sleep when he suddenly realized his window was slightly open. He always left it open a bit because he couldn't stand to sleep in a stuffy room. Now he saw that rain was coming in. Already a small area of the carpet near the window was soaked.

Swearing under his breath, he got up and strode to the window. A narrow gust of bitter-cold wind, along with a spray of rain, hit his naked body just before he firmly closed the window.

Just as he was turning away, something caught his attention out of the corner of his eye. Looking through the window he saw that a light was on in the apartment over the garage. He stood there for a couple of minutes, waiting for it to go out, but it remained on.

He didn't understand it. It was three o'clock in the morning. Surely, he thought, Marina wasn't making tea or reading at this hour, even if the storm had awakened her. And then it occurred to him that she might be ill.

He put on slippers and a knee-length burgundy velour robe, then ran out of the house and up the stairs as quickly as possible. He knocked lightly on the door. Then, realizing that he couldn't be heard above the storm, he pounded on the door.

She answered it with a blanket pulled tightly around her shoulders. Her face was nearly as white as the gown she wore, and her gray eyes were huge and round and terrified.

She didn't say a word. She simply seemed intensely relieved to see him.

He came in and closed the door. Taking her in his arms, he asked tenderly, "Are you frightened?"

Stephen felt her smooth cheek move up and down against his chest. She was trembling so hard she could hardly stand. Only once before in his life had he seen anyone so physically terrified, and then it was a stuntman who had narrowly avoided death after a dangerous stunt went wrong.

He picked her up bodily and carried her to the bed. Gently he laid her down, then lay down beside her, keeping his arms around her. He stroked her hair tenderly and murmured vague words of reassurance.

"It's all right, Marina, you're safe, you're not in danger. It's all right, I'm here with you, you're not alone. I won't leave you. I'll never leave you."

It was only after he said it that he realized how sincerely he meant it—he never wanted to leave her again.

Glancing down at her, he saw that her face was still buried against his chest. She didn't seem to mind the dampness of his robe. Her hands clutched at it in tight little fists, like a child's.

He reached out with one free hand and turned off the bedside lamp, casting the room into darkness. Gradually the terrible shivering abated and her breathing grew steady.

Marina fell asleep, relaxing against him with a soft, whimpering sigh.

A slow, warm glow spread all through Stephen as he held her. She felt so good in his arms, so right. His body stirred with desire, as urgently as it had done earlier when he'd kissed her. But now, as then, he controlled it.

What he felt for her was too important to be treated carelessly. He could take her physically, but he wanted much more than that. From the moment when she'd come out to him on the beach and apologized for hurting him, he'd known she wasn't just another woman. And he didn't want to have just another affair with her.

His hunger for her was powerful, and when they made love for the first time he wanted her hunger for him to be just as powerful. When they made love it would be more than a quick slaking of desire. He needed to be emotionally intimate with her as well as physically intimate, and he knew she wasn't prepared to give herself in that way yet.

But he could be patient when he was certain that something was inevitable. And he was absolutely positive that it was inevitable that he and this woman would be together.

It was just a matter of time.

As he fell asleep next to her, it occurred to him that for the first time in years he didn't feel alone.

When Marina awoke the sun was shining with the almost blinding intensity that happens only after a storm. Walking into the living room, she saw sunlight pouring in through the tall, curved windows, brightening the room that had seemed so dark and dreary during the night.

The storm had passed, leaving no evidence beyond an unusual amount of seaweed and driftwood on the beach.

After putting on some water to boil, Marina sat down and tried to recall the events of the night. Had Stephen really been there, or was it all a dream? Remembering his arms around her, his voice murmuring reassurance, it seemed much too vivid for any dream.

Yet he wasn't there now. And there was nothing to indicate he had been there.

The whistling of the teakettle brought her out of her reverie. After making a cup of tea, she curled up in the chair once more and tried to think.

Something had to be done. Maybe Stephen hadn't been there during the night, maybe it had been a dream. But Marina knew she had not dreamed that kiss at the door. That was all too real. Even now, hours later, she could remember how she'd given way to him, melting in his arms as easily as a tallow candle melts.

It had been wonderful, more wonderful than she'd ever imagined a kiss could be, even in her wildest romantic fantasies. When he'd let her go, she'd felt a sharp pang of loss; she hadn't wanted it to end there. And yet the fact that he didn't press her had made the experience all the more special.

But none of that changed the fact that it mustn't happen again, she told herself. And the sooner she made him understand that, the better.

Marina dressed quickly in white linen slacks and a light beige sweater, then went down to the house. Apparently Stephen had been waiting for her, because he opened the door almost immediately. He made a move toward her, but something in her expression stopped him.

As he stepped aside to let her enter, he asked, "Would you like some breakfast?"

"No, thank you," she replied in a scrupulously polite voice.

They walked into the living room. Without sitting down, Marina began in a tone that was determinedly matter-of-fact, "We have to talk."

"Yes."

Somehow she wasn't prepared for his easy acquiescence. Her voice was a little less controlled as she went on awkwardly, "Yes, well, the thing is—"

He interrupted, "Can we sit down while we talk?"

Since Marina couldn't think of a good reason why they shouldn't, she said yes. He sat down at one end of the sofa, clearly expecting her to join him. Instead, she sat in the chair.

She wanted to remain objective and impersonal, but as she looked at the powerful man opposite her she was struck by his strength. It occurred to her that he would be as demanding in bed as he was in his work. She remembered the expert touch of his large, strong hands, the thrust of his body against hers the first time they'd kissed with such abandon, and the warm, insistent pressure of his mouth on hers. The memory shot through her body like a flame, making a mockery of her defenses.

"Are you all right this morning, Marina?" he asked.

Instantly she knew that he *had* been with her the night before. She hadn't dreamed it. She colored as embarrassment washed over her. He'd been with her, he'd lain beside her in her bed. But he hadn't touched her, except to hold her. That, at least, was reassuring.

Still, things had gone too far. The knowledge strengthened her resolve to stop what was building between them before it went further.

"I'm perfectly fine," she insisted.

Then, taking a deep breath, she repeated, "The thing is, our relationship seems to be getting too personal and I'm not happy about that."

Stephen crossed his legs and watched her every movement as she fidgeted in the chair. "You're not happy?"

He didn't seem to believe her.

"No," she insisted. "I'm not happy about it. I came down here to work with you on the screenplay, not to indulge in a little—" she paused, searching desperately for the right words "—extracurricular affair."

"Is that what you think?" His voice was cold with anger.

She tilted her chin defiantly. "Yes."

He leaned forward, fury glinting in his deep blue eyes, which were as cold and hard as a sapphire.

"You've got me neatly pegged, haven't you? Typical lecherous Hollywood producer, a starlet on each arm and a hot tub ready for action."

"Stephen—"

"No, you're going to listen to me, young lady. I've had about enough of this. I dismissed it as just plain naive at first, but now it's insulting. Especially under the circumstances."

She wasn't sure what he meant by that. Before she had a chance to question him, he went on. "I'm thirty-two years old. Since I was sixteen, I've worked eighteen hours a day, 365 days a year to get where I am. I've made three movies and every one has made a big profit. That kind of success didn't happen on the side, while I was busy seducing every woman between fifteen and fifty. And when I'm not working, I'm usually at home by myself."

Stung by his tone, Marina retorted, "I suppose you'll try to tell me you're lonely."

"No, not lonely exactly. But alone more than I would care to be."

"There must be any number of women who'd be happy to provide some companionship," she said with angry antagonism in her voice.

"Possibly. But I don't want them. I want you."

She froze. So, she thought with a sinking feeling, she'd been right. All he wanted was to seduce her. He probably didn't even care about the screenplay, that was just an excuse to get her where he would have easy access to her.

But even while she was telling herself all this, her body stirred. She felt an irresistible pulse of attraction begin to grow....

He reached out one hand toward her. "Marina..."

She pulled back as if she'd been hit and forced her eyes to meet his. When she spoke, her voice was low and urgent. "Stephen, I don't want you."

"I don't believe you. I know better."

"I don't even particularly like you," she insisted.

"*Like?* I'm not talking about liking someone, Marina. I've liked women in the past, and I'm sure you've liked men. I'm talking about wanting someone so badly you can taste it. Wanting them so much you can hardly stand it. But forcing yourself to stand it because rushing things might ruin it. That's how I feel about you. And you know exactly what I'm talking about because that's how you feel about me."

"That's not true!" Marina answered hotly, on her feet now. "I came down here to work."

Stephen stood up and faced her. "And I brought you down here to work. At least that's what I believed. But something else has happened, something that most men and women want desperately to happen and never experience."

"I don't want to hear any more. I won't listen to any more!"

"If you won't listen, then I'll show you."

Suddenly he was next to her, and before she could move he pulled her roughly into his arms. He held her as tightly as he had done that first night, so tightly that her arms were pinned at her sides. With a cold determination he wrenched her face around so that she was looking directly at him, and then he kissed her.

She shuddered once, then relaxed. Stephen pressed his body against her so that through the thin linen of her slacks and her sweater she could feel its pulsing hardness, the strength of those powerful muscles. His skin was rough against her face, and his lips forced her reluctant ones to part.

Suddenly frightened, she began to struggle, but he held her until he had finished the kiss, until he could feel her body's arousal. Then, and only then, did he pull back, just a little, still holding her tightly. His face was only a few inches from hers, their eyes level. His eyes blazed at her.

"Now, Marina, tell me again that you don't want me."

Her whole body was shaking. Her pulse raced and her breath came fast and hard. She was torn between shame and anger.

"So I was right! All you wanted was to get me into your bed. Why not admit it instead of talking all that rot about being alone? You're usually more direct than that!"

"Very well, I'll be direct."

She realized her fatal mistake and tried to push him away, but he held her too tightly.

His mouth came down on hers again, catching her just before she turned away. This time the kiss wasn't rough and demanding, but smooth and assured and incredibly seductive. Again she felt a throb of deep pleasure through her entire body.

Still he held her arms at her side, with an ease that was almost contemptuous. She couldn't move, couldn't get away. With one free hand he began to caress her, bending her back slightly so that his hand could trace the curve of her hip, her narrow stomach, up to the gentle swell of her breasts.

She trembled with desire and her breath caught in her throat. She felt the blood pounding in her head, and a low moan of pleasure escaped her lips.

Stephen groaned in response. Easily, urgently, his hand slid under the light sweater and found the wispy satin and lace bra that was scant protection for her quivering breasts.

In spite of herself, she swayed against him. With a flick of his thumb and forefinger he undid the front clasp of the bra, and his fingers caressed her naked flesh. Slowly, with exquisite gentleness, he stroked her breasts until her nipples were hard.

He lifted his head, and as she looked at him she saw through a haze of increasing desire the same fierce desire in his eyes.

"I want you, Marina. I never knew I could want a woman like this, so much that it's all I can do not to take you here and now."

Within her, a voice whispered urgently, *Take me, Stephen, here ... now. ...*

"And you want me, Marina. Just as bad."

Summoning all her will, she tried to pull out of his embrace, but he wouldn't let her go.

He caught her hand. "Feel how much I want you, Marina."

He forced her to touch him, so that there was no doubt about what he felt for her.

His voice was ragged with emotion. "That's what you do to me. That's what I've tried to control for two long nights and two long days."

Her lips parted with fear and desire. There was something in his expression—something poignant and desperate—that made her long to touch him, kiss him, reassure him. But she forced herself not to respond, to hold herself back from him as much as possible.

"I don't want you, Stephen. ..."

"You're a fool or a liar. It doesn't matter which."

There was humor in his voice now, not anger.

When she opened her mouth to respond angrily, he stopped her words with his lips, his kiss softer this time, almost as gentle as the good-night kiss he'd given her the night before. He released her hand and took his other hand from her breasts.

Marina could have pushed him away now, but she no longer had any wish to do so. She was going under in a swell of physical pleasure such as she had never known. It went beyond anything she'd ever experienced or dreamed.

Sensing her surrender, Stephen relaxed and the aggression left his body. Now, he was cradling her in his arms, as tenderly as he would a baby. He molded her body to his, and this time it didn't resist.

With a tenuous bravery she let herself respond to him. Her lips opened more fully to his, her hands began to slide over his chest and around his broad shoulders. Slowly, enjoying every moment of it, she let her hands explore the hard, corded muscles of his arms and shoulders.

Gathering all her courage, she took his hand and guided it back under her sweater to press it against her rapidly beating heart. Her breath came fast, too fast, so that she felt a little breathless. But it felt so good, so sweet. She wanted him. She had never wanted anyone or anything the way she wanted this man.

Slowly, as if it were the most difficult thing he'd ever done, he pulled away from her. Marina drew in a long shuddering breath as some semblance of reason began to permeate her mind again. Tears started in her eyes. Gently he bent to kiss them away.

When he spoke, his voice was different than she'd ever heard it before. It was both triumphant and chastened.

"Marina, I want to make love to you. Now. Do you want to make love to me?"

She was no longer embarrassed or ashamed, but something odd seemed to have happened to her voice. She couldn't speak, she could only nod helplessly.

"Oh, sweetheart." His voice broke as he gathered her to him again. Then, his lips brushing her hair, he whispered, "I want it to be right for you. More than right—perfect. If you're really not ready, I'll wait."

She smiled up at him. "I'm not sure I'm ready. But I don't want to wait."

The smile that met hers was warm and tender. "I'm glad, because despite my noble words I'm not sure I could let you walk away from me this time. I'm not exactly famous for my self-restraint, Marina, and you've sorely tested what little I have. Last night . . ."

"Yes. Last night."

"Last night, if you hadn't looked so much like a babe in arms, I would have . . ." His voice trailed off.

As she leaned against him, she whispered, "I don't think I would have stopped you."

He chuckled, a low, throaty sound that was very seductive.

Without saying a word, he picked her up as easily as if she were a rag doll and carried her into his bedroom. Her arms went around his neck, and her gray eyes were wide with anticipation tinged with just the slightest apprehension. She wasn't a prude, but she had never made love to a man for the first time in the middle of a bright, sunny morning. There was no darkness to cloak her embarrassment. Suddenly she felt as nervous as a bride.

"Stephen?"

"Yes, sweetheart?"

"I just wanted to hear your voice."

He smiled tenderly as he laid her down on the bed. "Don't be afraid, Marina. I won't go any faster than you want me to."

She thought she would feel awkward and ill at ease undressing in front of him. Sensing that, he did the job for her. Slowly, he slipped her sweater off her, along with her bra. Her shoes, slacks and underwear came off next in quick, deft movements.

When she lay naked before him, his eyes slowly traveled the length of her slender body.

"You are beautiful," he whispered hoarsely.

Lying there, she exulted in the way he made her feel, as if she were the most beautiful, most desirable woman in the world.

She wasn't uninhibited enough yet to undress him. But she watched in frank appreciation as he shed his clothes. Then he laid down next to her, and she felt his bare skin along the length of her body. His fingers entwined in her tousled hair as he kissed her over and over again. He brushed his lips against her forehead, her cheeks, her eyelids.

At the same time, her hands went to the back of his neck to draw him even closer.

He slid one leg between hers and held himself poised just above her, as if afraid that he might easily crush her. His hands slid down her back, past her narrow waist, to the tiny indentation at the base of her spine.

"You feel so right," he whispered. "That was all I could think the first time I held you, that you feel so unexpectedly right."

Her lips curved in a slow, seductive smile that was all the sexier because it was completely unaffected.

"Do you know what I thought the first time you held me?"

His smile was impudent. "You probably thought that I had a lot of nerve kissing you when I'd only seen you a few times before in my life. And we argued every single one of those times."

She shook her head slowly, amusement evident in her expression. "No. I thought that if you tried to take me there and then I wouldn't have the will to resist."

"*Marina.* Some day I'll find a nice deserted beach where I can test that statement. Until then you'll have to make do with a prosaic bed. But at least you'll notice the bedspread isn't tawdry velvet, it's a nice, practical wool. And there are no mirrors on the ceiling or pink champagne cooling in a silver ice bucket."

She colored with embarrassment. "Stephen, I'm sorry for those awful things I said—"

He interrupted easily, "It's interesting to see you blush when you're naked. Do you realize your whole body is slightly pink?"

Which made her blush even more furiously.

She gave up even attempting to appear sophisticated and experienced. Instead, she said with touching humility, "You reduce me to my bare essence. I can't pretend with you."

"I don't want you to pretend. I want you just as you are, sweet, infuriating, honest and passionate."

"You're more than a little infuriating yourself, Stephen Kramer. And not at all sweet. But you are very passionate."

He didn't answer because his lips were busy nuzzling the tender curve of her throat. As his lips moved lower and he buried his face in her breasts, she felt a shock wave of desire ripple through her.

Cradling his head against her, she murmured vague, unintelligible words of comfort and affection. Through it all, only a word now and then was clear.

Then his mouth found one taut nipple, and as he teased it gently between his teeth, she arched her neck and breasts, offering herself to him fully. She was on fire now, her entire body smoldering with a desire that demanded fulfillment. She couldn't have held anything back from him now if she wanted.

As his lips moved lower down her abdomen, he whispered huskily, "I hear your heart beating, Marina. It's beating almost as fast as mine."

Her hands moved down to his shoulders, her fingers kneading the hard, corded muscles in his shoulder blades, her nails digging into his hard flesh.

A heavy ache deep within her intensified sharply as he drank in the soft fullness of her body. Suddenly her need for him was almost unbearable.

"Stephen, I need you so. I need to be part of you."

He looked up at her. "I know, sweetheart, I know. I need you, too. I need you more than breath itself. But I'm not going to take you quickly. This means too much to let it be anything less than absolutely perfect."

"Oh, Stephen, it is perfect."

"Then I'm going to give you even more than perfection."

She smiled seductively. "More?"

"More." The word was a promise of ecstasy, and somehow Marina knew that promise would be fulfilled.

His lips moved to the pulse beating madly at the base of her throat. "There's still so much of you to explore. I'm going to know every square inch of your skin before..."

He let the words trail off, but she knew what he meant.

Her voice was a breathless whisper. "Stephen..."

He stopped her speech with his lips, then murmured, "The journey's just begun, sweetheart. And the trip is every bit as important as the destination."

If she had any doubts, they were quickly subdued. She'd never imagined there could be anything like the sweet agony that filled her entire being as he discovered the planes and hollows of her body, the secret places that responded to his touch with profound arousal. His hands and lips roamed her body slowly, sensuously, pausing just long enough to bring each place to a fever pitch of feeling.

There was no resistance on her part; she opened up completely to him, secure in the knowledge that whatever happened he wouldn't hurt her. He used his strength to dominate only in the most tender way. His touch was exquisitely gentle.

As long as he possibly could, Stephen controlled his own desire in order to bring Marina to a height of feeling that was almost unbearably intense.

Then he began to move more quickly and his gentleness turned to urgency. The deep ache within her was at burst-

ing point now, and she begged him to take her, to give her
the ultimate fulfillment.

Completely uninhibited now, she moved wantonly against
him. He could no longer hold back. Reason and control
were beginning to slip away, as pure physical need took over.

Now his body told him, *now*.

She opened herself to him, welcoming him. In her soft
velvety depths he found more than satisfaction. He found
peace.

And as he shuddered against her, she found a pleasure
and a joy that were so intense, they were bittersweet.

A moment later he positioned his body beside hers, leaving one arm lying possessively across her breasts. Looking
at her, he was concerned to see tears at the corners of her
eyes.

"Marina, what is it?"

She smiled through her tears. "It's all right, Stephen. It's
just ... I never knew it could be like that. I never knew...."

His finger gently brushed her tears away. When he spoke
there was an awkward tone in his voice that she'd never
heard before. It took her a moment to realize it was sheer
embarrassment. He was quite simply so touched by what
she'd just said, that he was embarrassed.

"Marina, if you'd spent years thinking of the one absolutely right thing to say, you couldn't have said anything
more wonderful."

Ever so lightly he brushed his lips across hers. "You are
mine. Absolutely. Understand that. You belong to me now.
We belong to each other."

"Yes, Stephen. Yes..."

They continued to lie together for several minutes, neither speaking. The important things had been said. There
was no point in saying anything else.

Marina felt no regrets. Once she faced how much she
wanted him, the outcome was inevitable.

She didn't know what would happen now. She couldn't think beyond the immediate moment. They were together. That was all that mattered. Everything else paled in importance compared to that one simple fact.

Strangely, she felt no concern or insecurity. She didn't need promises from him. Promises were too easy to break. The crucial thing was integrity. He had that. Now she knew him for what he really was—an honorable man, a man who was nothing like her initial view of him.

Whatever happened between them, she knew this was no more a passing affair for him than it was for her. How long they would remain together was a question that only time would answer.

After several minutes Stephen said slowly, "Why were you so terrified last night?"

"I have this thing about storms," she admitted reluctantly. "I always have...since I was little. It's only bad if I'm alone. If someone's with me, I'm all right."

"I know...when I held you it only took a few minutes for you to fall asleep. You slept like an exhausted child."

She smiled shyly. "I always do, afterward. Fear is very tiring."

He kissed the tip of her nose. "You won't be frightened again, because you won't have to be alone."

She didn't know what to say to that, so she said nothing. Inside though, she felt an incredible lightness, as if some terrible weight had been lifted from her.

She leaned her cheek against his chest. Without looking up at him, she asked softly, "What are you afraid of, Stephen?"

For a moment she thought he wouldn't answer. Then he said in an almost inaudible voice, "The past."

There was something haunting about those two simple words. Wrapping her arms around him, she held him as tightly as she could.

For a while neither spoke.

Then Stephen said in a determinedly cheerful voice, "I have an idea."

"Do you now?" she teased.

"I do. There's a sauna in the bathroom—"

She interrupted slyly. "Ah, I knew you were all tinsel and glitter after all."

Ignoring the thrust, he went on, "We could sit in it for a while...."

"That is a good idea."

"And then take a shower. Together...."

"A *very* good idea."

"And then get to work on the script."

She adopted a rueful expression. "Slave driver."

"You writers are all alike—you hate to write."

"Of course. It's the second hardest thing in the world."

Reaching down with one finger, he tilted her chin up so that their eyes met. "What's the hardest thing?"

She hesitated. Then, her eyes still locked with his, she answered, "Being honest about our feelings."

A slow, bittersweet smile spread across his even features. "You are so right."

She laid her head against his chest again and sighed with contentment.

After a moment, he sat up and patted her derriere. "Come on, tiger."

Marina groaned as he pulled her up. "Oh, Stephen, why can't we stay in bed all day?"

"Give me a week and I'll think of an answer to that."

He led her into the sauna and handed her a large bath sheet, which she wrapped around herself. After tying a smaller towel around his waist, he turned up the sauna, and they sat down facing each other.

Marina leaned her head against the wood-paneled wall and closed her eyes.

Watching her, Stephen was filled with a sense of wonder. He never would have expected this morning to turn out the way it had. And he certainly hadn't planned it. He had assumed they would go out again, he would kiss her again, and gradually—not for a while, perhaps, but eventually—her resistance to him would crumble. As far as he was concerned, their joining was natural and right, and it was only a matter of persuading her of that.

Instead, they had both been caught up in a passion so profound that they were powerless to resist it. She'd come to him an hour earlier, determined to put him in his place. Instead, she'd found a place by his side. It was ironic—and wonderful.

He'd never realized a woman could give so much. So much tenderness. So much passion. So much heart.

What they had just shared made every other relationship he'd ever had with a woman seem shallow and meaningless. He couldn't understand now how he'd ever wanted to spend the rest of his life with Laura. Compared to Marina's generosity of spirit and openness, Laura was a phony. Period.

And yet he couldn't shake a gnawing feeling that Marina was holding something back. He didn't know why he felt that way. It was nothing she'd said or done. It was simply a feeling he had, almost like an instinct.

He looked at her, sitting there, her eyes closed, her body glistening with tiny beads of perspiration. Remembering how she had just given of herself, he told himself he was being stupid. She wasn't holding anything back.

But the feeling continued to gnaw at him.

Chapter Ten

O kay," Stephen said, "we've got the first ten pages now."

They were in his office, it was the end of the afternoon and Marina was very tired. But she felt exhilarated. The screenplay had gone well, much faster than the day before. She was beginning to understand the form and have a feel for it.

As Stephen glanced through the pages once more, he continued, "This is good. Very good. It's a unit, a sequence that builds nicely to Casey's first meeting with Mark. That gets us to the place where we should be at this point in the script. The setup is over."

Marina stretched tiredly in the chair behind the desk. Looking at her, Stephen smiled warmly. "I've worked you pretty hard today, haven't I?"

She returned his smile. "Yes. But I've enjoyed it. I feel like I'm finally beginning to understand what a screenplay is all about. It's so different from a novel."

"Can I say I told you so?" Stephen quipped.

Picking up a pencil, Marina threw it at him playfully. "No, you cannot."

"Then how about dinner?"

"Mmm, sounds great. I'm starved. I'll even cook."

"I'll let you. I hate to cook. Tossing a steak on a broiler is as far as I'll go."

"Let's go see what you've got in your refrigerator."

Stephen's refrigerator turned out to be woefully empty. Looking at it, Marina said dryly, "This is definitely the refrigerator of a man who hates to cook. Since it isn't really possible to survive on diet sodas and moldy cheese, I take it you eat out a lot."

"Of course. That's why God created restaurants."

Ignoring that, Marina continued to rummage in the refrigerator and the cupboards. Eventually she found enough ingredients to make a quiche. While she was putting it together, Stephen drove to a nearby market and bought a loaf of crusty French bread.

Later that evening they sat on the floor in front of the fireplace in the living room, finishing the last of their dinner.

Leaning over, he kissed the tip of her nose. "Thank you. That was a marvelous dinner."

"It was pretty simple. You're easy to please."

He shook his head slowly. "No, I'm very hard to please. Ask anyone who works for me. But you are a terrific cook."

"Hopefully, I'm becoming a terrific screenwriter as well."

"You are. I suspect that by the time this is finished, you'll be good enough to have a full-time career as a screenwriter, if you want."

Marina's expression grew serious. "No, I don't think so. Even if I get to be pretty good at it, it's not what I want to do, at least not full-time. I like writing novels. There's a satisfaction there that I don't get from screenplays, even though they're challenging and interesting to do."

"I can understand that."

"You see, I have more control with a novel than I do with a screenplay."

He looked at her appraisingly. "Is control important to you?"

She didn't answer for a moment. It was a serious question and her feelings about the subject ran deep. Choosing her words carefully, she finally said, "It isn't just important, it's crucial. Not because I want to control others. I honestly don't. But I don't want to be controlled by any—" She stopped. She'd been about to say, "By any man." Instead, she finished, "By anyone."

"I see."

Something in his tone told her that he did see.

The atmosphere between them had changed subtly. Instead of light teasing, it was a bit more serious. And there was just a hint of tension in the air.

"Marina, what are you afraid of?"

He'd asked her that question before, and she'd evaded it. Now, she knew, she had to answer. The time for evasions was past.

"I watched my mother devote herself to my father, because he wanted it that way. She's very creative, an artist, actually. But she didn't pursue that because he wanted her to concentrate on taking care of him and seeing to his comfort. She cooked and cleaned and decorated and entertained. She was defined solely as his wife. When he took that identification away from her and bestowed it on someone else, she was crushed. Eventually she recovered, and went on to pursue her artistic ambitions. But it was damn hard."

"I understand."

"No," Marina replied fiercely, "you can't possibly understand. Because that will never happen to you. That's the difference between men and women."

He was silent for a long moment. Then he said slowly, "You're determined that it will never happen to you."

"Yes."

"I don't think you have to worry about it, you know."

"Why not?"

"Your mother came of age in a different time. She did what she was expected to do. There were other options, but they were hard to achieve."

"You think it's different now?" Marina asked in a harsh tone that clearly revealed her feelings on the subject.

"Yes, I do. I don't want a woman who will be fulfilled only through me. I want a partner, in every sense of the word. Someone who's doing more interesting things than washing my socks."

Marina's voice was dry. "It almost sounds as if you mean it."

To her surprise, Stephen leaned toward her and cupped her face in his hands, forcing her to look directly into his eyes. "Understand this about me. I always mean what I say."

Marina pulled back. "Let's change the subject."

"Why? I'm not afraid of a good, healthy argument if it clears the air and helps us understand each other better."

"I don't want to be understood, Stephen!"

She had spoken more sharply than she intended. She saw a hurt look cross his face, and guilt washed over her.

"I'm sorry," Marina whispered. "You're being too good to be true and in return I'm being awful. I don't have an excuse. I don't even have an explanation."

He pulled her onto his lap and wrapped his arms around her. "If this is what you consider being awful, then all I have to say is that you don't know the first thing about it. Mildly difficult is how I would describe it."

She smiled shyly. "You're indulging my bad temper. You shouldn't do that. It will only encourage me."

His lips brushed the top of her head. "Obviously, you're incorrigible. That's okay—I am, too."

For a while they were both silent. She felt comfortable and secure wrapped in his gentle embrace. His cashmere sweater felt soft to her touch and she snuggled against him happily. A soft sigh of contentment escaped her lips.

In the fireplace the wood snapped and crackled. A brightly burning twig dissolved in a shower of sparks.

Reaching up to the lamp, Stephen turned it off, and they sat there in the dark, their faces lit by the glow of the firelight.

His thoughts were a great deal more serious than he had let Marina see. He wasn't angry with her, but he was concerned. He knew now that his instinct that something was wrong, that she was holding back from him, was accurate.

The simple, obvious explanation was exactly what she had told him—she had seen her mother be deeply hurt and she was naturally concerned about not letting the same thing happen to her. The fact that she obviously felt her father had abandoned her as well as her mother made matters even worse.

And yet somehow Stephen didn't feel that was the whole explanation.

Marina had so much to give. He'd learned that much about her already. If she was holding back, not giving everything, there was a damn good reason. Of course, he speculated, they'd known each other a ridiculously short time. That was a good reason for holding back.

But that didn't seem to explain it completely either.

He told himself he was being unrealistic. Things had moved so fast between them, faster than either was prepared for. He hadn't expected it and, obviously, neither had she. If he was more ready for it than she was, that was only because he was older and experienced enough to know what he wanted.

It would just take time, he thought, for Marina to feel less overwhelmed by it all. Fortunately, time was something they had in abundance. She would be living with him for another two months while she wrote the script. And after that, he had no intention of letting her return to Big Sur.

Bending down, he whispered something in her ear. She smiled seductively up at him. "Here?"

He nodded.

"Now?"

He nodded again.

Without saying another word, she slowly began to unbutton her blouse....

Marina was in the coffee room at the office the next morning when Marty came in, whistling cheerfully.

"Good morning, Marina. Gorgeous day, isn't it?"

"It is. I drove in with Stephen and the ocean was magnificent. On a clear, sunny day like this it's just about the most beautiful sight imaginable."

As he poured a cup of coffee, he replied, "I'll bet it's really magnificent up at Big Sur."

"Oh, yes. It's lovely down here, but up there are the most stunning cliffs and plateaus and promontories. The scenery is breathtaking."

He smiled. "Well, Malibu and Trancas ain't too shabby."

"No, definitely not."

"So how are you settling in down here?"

She hesitated. "Oh . . . fine. Just fine."

"I know Stephen can be hard to work with. But his bark is definitely worse than his bite. I've seen him reduce a secretary to tears when he was angry about a mistake. Then when he realized how upset she was, he sent her roses every day for a month. It made her boyfriend so jealous, he proposed, which she'd been waiting three years for him to do. So I guess it worked out in the end."

Marina chuckled softly. "Oh . . . I'm not afraid of Stephen. We started working on the script and it's going very well."

"Good, glad to hear it."

Cocking her head to one side, Marina observed, "You're awfully chipper this morning."

"Yes, I am. And you know why? I'm going to be a father."

"Marty! Congratulations. Is this your first?"

He nodded happily.

"When's it due?"

"I don't know."

Taken aback, Marina said, "You don't know?"

"Amy isn't pregnant yet. We just decided last night to start trying. But as a production manager I know how to get things done," he quipped. "By next Thanksgiving there'll be a new deduction at our house."

Marina laughed. "I'm sure there will be. Well, I'd better get back to work. Stephen's in meetings all morning, but he said that when he breaks for lunch he expects me to have something for him to read."

"Okay. If you need any help, just let me know. I mean that."

"Thanks. I appreciate it."

Back in her office, Marina worked hard without a break. She lost track of time and was startled to find Stephen watching her from the doorway.

"Lunchtime already?" she asked, looking up from the typewriter.

"It's past lunchtime, actually. Nearly two o'clock. I have another meeting at two-thirty. Want to grab a quick lunch at the commissary?"

"Sure." Picking up three neatly typed pages, she asked, "Will you have time to glance at these?"

"Yeah, I'd like to."

Noticing her wastebasket half full of discarded pages, he commented, "Having a hard time?"

"In a word, yes," she said with a sigh. "I wrote ten pages, then culled it down to these three. And you'll probably say they're too long and need to move faster."

In a few minutes they were sitting in the commissary and had ordered hamburgers. Stephen read Marina's three pages carefully. Then, he took a red pen from his shirt pocket and began to cross out lines of narrative and dialogue.

"It's too long, Marina. You knew it, you just needed me to confirm it."

"Yes, but I'm not sure I understand why it's too long. What's wrong with it?"

"The purpose of a scene is to move the story forward. If it doesn't do that, then it's useless and slows down the pace of the movie. Of the two scenes you've done here, one is completely unnecessary, and the other is too wordy."

Glancing over the pages he handed back to her, she said, "But why is the scene where she explains her lack of money unnecessary?"

"It's not completely unnecessary, but it can be done very quickly and without dialogue."

"Without dialogue? How?"

"For instance, by showing her driving to a nearby motel and pausing to look at the sign that says what the rates are. She doesn't go in, but drives to a second motel. It's seedier and the rates are a lot lower. She goes into that one and we know that she's going to take a room, although we don't have to bother going through the whole process of showing her talking to the manager and being shown to the room."

"That's brilliant."

He grinned. "Of course."

"Seriously, Stephen, that cuts right through all the wordy business I had and gets right to the point."

"That's what I was just saying. In a screenplay every word, every shot has to count. Or it isn't necessary and you throw it out."

"When I think about those ten pages I had—"

"Don't worry about that. Quite often you have to overwrite, then cut it down to get to the essentials."

"Well, that makes me feel better anyway. I was beginning to think I'd wasted a lot of time this morning."

Their hamburgers arrived and they started to eat. Between bites, Stephen said, "There's another thing that's helpful to know. It can be very effective to dramatize the scene against the grain, instead of taking the obvious approach."

"I don't understand."

"You know how some actors will play an angry scene smiling softly, hiding their anger but letting the audience know it's there."

"Jack Nicholson does that beautifully."

"Yes. Well, you can do that as a writer, too. For instance, in this scene where Mark and Casey really talk for the first time, you've taken a pretty conventional approach. He says to her, 'I want to get to know you better. Let's talk.' And as they talk, he realizes she's more interesting than the airhead teenager he originally thought she was."

"What's wrong with that?" Marina asked defensively.

"Nothing. It's perfectly all right. But it would be stronger and more original if you took a less head-on approach."

"For instance?"

"You're the writer. Think about it. Be creative."

As Marina finished the last of her hamburger she was thinking furiously. She was still thinking as they walked back toward the office.

Interrupting her thoughts, Stephen said, "Look, they're shooting a scene over there."

On the street to the right of them, a flashing red warning light stopped traffic.

"That's a second A.D.—assistant director," Stephen explained, pointing to a young man talking into a portable phone. "His job is to take care of all the mundane stuff—making sure the actors and equipment are in the right places—so the director isn't bothered. The guy riding with a Panaflex camera on a crane is the director."

"It's absolute chaos," Marina commented as people milled around, looking as if they didn't know what to do next.

"Organized chaos," Stephen corrected her. "This street on a back lot in L.A. will turn into a New York alley on the screen. And the audience will believe it." He looked at Marina. "*Casey* will be the same. The characters and story that were in your imagination, then on paper, will become real on the screen. And an audience will believe them and suffer with them and finally triumph with them."

Meeting Stephen's look, she said, "I'm beginning to understand why you love making movies."

He nodded. "Yes, it's unlike anything else. I don't know why so many people in this business seem to need drugs and alcohol. Making a movie, no matter what part you play in it, is a natural high."

Suddenly Marina had an idea. "Stephen, listen to this. What if Lucy suggests to Mark that he paint Casey, and he says no, she's pretty but not interesting enough. Then, as he's turning away, he sees her doing something totally unexpected, that doesn't fit in with his view of her. And he looks at Lucy and says, 'Maybe I was wrong.'"

"What is she doing?"

Marina stopped. "I don't know yet."

"Well, figure it out, because that's exactly what that scene should be."

His tone was flat, almost unemotional. Yet Marina sensed he'd just given her high praise, indeed. She basked in the warm glow of it.

Back in the office, she worked hard all afternoon. By seven o'clock, when Stephen was finally ready to leave, she was exhausted and ready to quit.

They stopped at a Mexican restaurant in Santa Monica for a dinner of spicy chili con carne, then continued the long drive to Trancas. They were nearly there when Stephen said, "Do you realize Thanksgiving is Thursday?"

Marina had been feeling tired and full and pleased with what she'd accomplished that day. Now a pang of guilt shot through her. *Thanksgiving.* Her mother wanted her to come to Clovis for the holiday.

"Yes," she said finally, "I realize it."

"Do you have plans with your family? Because if you don't, Marty and Amy have invited us to eat with them."

Marina hesitated. Although she had made tentative plans with Rosie, she was still unsure about what she was going to do. She was torn between not wanting to hurt her mother and not wanting to be with Rafe, the man she was determined never to call father.

Misinterpreting her hesitation, Stephen went on, "Don't worry about hurting my feelings. I understand if your parents are expecting you to be with them, then—"

"No," she interrupted abruptly, "they're not expecting me."

She didn't look at him as she spoke. She knew if she did he would see that she was lying.

"Are you sure, Marina?"

"It's a long drive up to Clovis, too long for a one-day trip. And I'm so deeply into the screenplay now, I don't want to take off more time." Marina made a mental note to call Rosie about the change of plans.

Stephen was so glad she would be staying with him, that he didn't question her rather lame explanation.

"Okay. In that case, would you like to come over to Marty and Amy's? She's really looking forward to meeting you."

"Yes, that would be nice, Stephen."

Her voice was small and subdued in the darkness of the car.

Not noticing, Stephen continued. "You'll like Amy. She's very nice. Very genuine. There's no tinsel and glitter about her."

She smiled at what had become an "in" joke between them.

"I'm sure I will. I like Marty a lot."

"Marty's the best. Just the best. We've known each other since high school. He's the one person in this whole business who I trust completely."

"He thinks a lot of you. In the beginning, when you and I were at odds, he tried to make me understand you, and not be so mad at you."

Stephen put an arm around Marina's shoulder and squeezed it gently.

"Well, then, that's just one more thing I owe him for."

"I haven't actually met Amy, but I saw her in the office. She and Marty seem very happy."

Stephen hesitated, then said thoughtfully, "I think they are now. You know, we've gotten into a real 'disposable' mentality nowadays—disposable cans, disposable diapers, disposable marriages. I think Marty and Amy have managed to get past that."

He smiled and finished wryly, "They have all their ducks in a row."

Marina shot him a curious glance. "Is that Hollywoodese? Liz told me I was going to have to learn a whole new language if I wanted to get by in the film business."

"Yeah, it's definitely Hollywoodese. Like 'points.' They're not the ends of sharp sticks, you know."

"Oh, what are they?"

"Percentage of profit. And everyone who is anyone gets them."

"I'll keep that in mind when Liz negotiates my next screenplay contract," Marina teased.

"Then there's 'take a meeting.' You don't *have* a meeting or go to a meeting. You 'take' it."

"Why?"

"Who knows? That's just the way we all talk. It was hard for me to get used to at first. I wanted to pronounce Rodeo, as in Rodeo Drive, the way they do in western movies, with the accent on the first syllable. It took years for me to learn to automatically pronounce it with the accent on the second, so that it sounds vaguely French."

Marina chuckled softly. "Ah, but you learned."

"I learned. But sometimes when I'm at some social function that I haven't been able to avoid, and I look around at all the sleek, privileged people, I still feel like an outsider."

"Does it bother you?"

"Not really. In a way it's reassuring. It means I haven't started to believe all the B.S."

"Is that why you drive a jeep instead of a Porsche? As a way to hang on to who you were before all this?"

"Sort of. But, you know, I'm not proud of who I was. After all, I was a high school dropout, never went to college."

Until he put it that way, Marina had never fully understood how different their backgrounds were. She told him as much.

"I know," he responded pensively. "We come from totally different places, you and I. I imagine you were pretty excited when you graduated from high school."

"Oh, yes. I thought I was totally grown-up and knew it all."

"And you enjoyed college."

"Yeah, once I got over the initial shell shock from realizing I didn't know anything."

Stephen laughed easily. There was no envy in his tone or expression. But when he said in a low voice, "My children will have all that and more," Marina knew he realized just how much he'd missed.

Suddenly she wished she could give it to him, erase all those hard, lonely years and make everything all right. It was a childish wish, she knew, the wish to magically make it all better, to make all the hurt go away instantly. And it was quite impossible.

Tenderly she whispered, "I'm sorry, Stephen."

He kept his eyes on the road as he replied. "It's all right, Marina. It wasn't your fault. Hell, it wasn't really anyone's fault."

She didn't say anything, but she reached up to clasp his hand in hers.

Marty and Amy lived in an old Spanish-style house on a tree-shaded street in Santa Monica. When Stephen and Marina arrived there around noon, Marty was watching a football game and Amy was putting the finishing touches on the turkey. Stephen joined Marty in front of the TV set and Marina went out to the kitchen with Amy.

"We're not very liberated, when all is said and done," Amy said dryly.

"No. Maybe it'll be different for our daughters."

"Or our granddaughters."

"Is there anything I can do to help?" Marina offered.

"Not really," Amy replied, taking a casserole out of the oven and setting it on top of the stove. "I'm not much of a cook, so I planned a very simple meal. Just turkey, dressing, green salad and broccoli casserole. And, of course, pumpkin pie for dessert. It came from a bakery so you don't have to be afraid to try it."

"Sounds marvelous."

"Thanks. But it's all quite easy. And everything's ready except for the turkey. Fortunately, when it's done, Marty will have to assume some responsibility and carve it."

"It was awfully nice of you to invite me to join you today."

"Not at all. I've been dying to meet you. When Marty told me that you really gave Stephen a taste of his own medicine, I was intrigued, to put it mildly."

"Well, I've since discovered that he's not such an ogre."

Amy eyed Marina shrewdly. "Have you? Good. Stephen's actually sweet."

Sweet wasn't exactly the adjective Marina would have chosen to describe Stephen Kramer. Powerful, definitely. Sexy, undoubtedly. Even, at times, surprisingly tender. But *sweet*?

She repressed a smile.

Amy went on, "Marty brought home a copy of the galleys of your book. I loved it. I cried at the end."

As always, Marina was embarrassed by praise about her writing. She never knew quite what to say. Now she murmured an awkward, "Thank you."

"When will it be published?" Amy asked.

"In the spring."

"It should be a best-seller."

Marina smiled. "That would be nice, but it's not very likely. My agent has made it clear to me that I can't expect too much from a first novel."

"Seems to me you've done all right, so far. You made a movie sale to one of the hottest producers in the business."

"Yes. But I don't think that was due to my wonderful writing. I get the feeling Stephen was looking for a certain type of project and my book fit his requirements."

"It's true he wanted to do something serious, something on a small scale. A relationship story, rather than a big, commercial vehicle. He wants to prove to everyone that he can do good work as well as popular work."

"I think he'll do it."

"I think he will, too," Amy agreed wholeheartedly.

"How long have you known Stephen?"

"As long as Marty has. We all went to high school together in Houston. Stephen had to drop out, but he kept in touch with Marty. And when he came to L.A. he persuaded Marty and me to join him. We were married by then. I wasn't too sure about moving here, but I figured, 'Where he goeth, I goeth,' or however it's phrased.''

"It must have been hard at first."

"Oh, yes. But somehow I had faith in Stephen. I knew he wouldn't let Marty down. He's very responsible, you know. If he cares about someone, then he takes care of them. He's quite paternal, actually. He'll make a marvelous father someday."

"Perhaps. But the film industry isn't conducive to happy families," Marina observed soberly.

"You're right, it isn't. But you know, I've met a lot of people in the business who have their heads on straight, who have strong marriages and well-adjusted kids. You don't have to get sucked into all that unhappiness. You have a choice—you go with what you know, deep down, is right, or you let yourself get carried away. I know what matters to me, now. And I won't let anything destroy what Marty and I have."

Just then Stephen and Marty came into the kitchen.

"Can we help?" Marty asked.

"Don't tell me, it's halftime," Amy quipped.

"How'd you guess?"

She and Marina laughed.

"All right," Amy went on, "this darn turkey must be ready by now."

She took it out of the oven and Marty carved it, putting several thick slices onto a platter. Then they went into the dining room and enjoyed a delicious meal. Afterward, they watched football and played Trivial Pursuit. And when Amy and Marina insisted that the men help do the dishes, the men gave in good-naturedly. Even the washing up was fun, as the four of them had a bad joke contest to see who could tell the dumbest joke.

It was a thoroughly nice day, Marina thought when she and Stephen finally left that evening. But her happiness quickly faded as she sat quietly in the car on the way home. She knew that this must have been a less than happy day for her mother. And she felt incredibly guilty about it.

She had sent her mother a brief letter, telling her what she was doing in L.A. and explaining that because of work she wouldn't be able to come home for Thanksgiving. She knew that her mother wouldn't buy that excuse. Her mother was all too aware of the truth—that Marina wanted nothing to do with Rafe.

"You're very quiet," Stephen observed, as he negotiated the sharp curve where the Santa Monica Freeway merged into the Pacific Coast Highway.

"Am I?" Marina said, stalling. "I guess I just ate too much and now I'm feeling full and tired."

He risked a quick glance at her, then returned his eyes to the road. "I hope you enjoyed spending the day with Marty and Amy."

"Oh, I did. They're wonderful."

"I guess you missed your mother, though."

"Yes." That was true. She just didn't miss Rafe.

"I'm glad you like Marty and Amy. They like you. Amy told me you're a regular person. That's quite a compliment coming from her."

Marina smiled. "I think she's a regular person, too. Marty's a lucky man."

"They're both lucky."

"He told me they want to have a baby."

"I know. It's about time. After all, they've been married ten years. There's no reason to wait."

Marina gave him a dry look. "They may have felt there was a reason to wait. You don't necessarily know what's best for the rest of the world."

"Of course I do," Stephen responded with a perfectly straight face.

For an instant Marina wasn't sure if he was joking or serious. Then his mouth curved in the barest hint of a smile, and she chuckled softly.

Unable to restrain her curiosity, she asked, "Why did they wait?"

"Until recently, Amy worked full-time. She didn't want to have a child and farm it out to a nanny. But she didn't want to quit working. Then she grew disenchanted with her career and quit."

"So now she'll be a full-time mother?"

"For a while. Eventually, when the child is older, she'll probably go back to work. She isn't the type to sit home doing her nails and having lunch with the girls."

"I can understand that. I would never want to quit writing."

Stephen gave her a sharp look. "You wouldn't have to. It's the perfect career to have at the same time you're having kids."

Marina smiled ruefully. "Obviously, you haven't given too much thought to midnight feedings, childhood illnesses and the terrible twos."

"I wouldn't expect my wife to handle all that alone. I'd like to be part of it. All of it."

Watching him, seeing the sober expression on his face, Marina knew he meant what he said. He wouldn't be the kind of father who only sees his children when he pats them on the head as they're on their way to bed at night.

Marina had never given much thought to children, beyond assuming that someday she would have some. At the moment her feelings about motherhood were decidedly mixed. But she knew that if she did have children, she would only do so if she were married to a man like Stephen. A man who would actually share in raising them.

But thinking about marriage and children, even in a vague, at-some-point-way-down-the-line way, bothered her.

It made her feel intensely uncomfortable and she immediately shifted her thoughts to another area.

"Stephen, have you hired a director yet?"

He shook his head. "No. The guy I wanted isn't available, after all."

"Why not go with a woman?"

"Now, Marina, don't jump on your feminist bandwagon."

"Damn it, Stephen, don't be a jerk. At least consider the possibility. Amy was telling me about a picture she saw at a screening for studio employees. It's called *Heartaches* and it's by a new director, a young woman. She said it was fabulous."

"I've heard of it. It's a National Studios release. In fact, there's going to be an official screening of it tomorrow night on the lot, with a party beforehand."

"Could you go?"

"Of course. But . . ."

"Stephen, if it was a man would you go?"

He was silent for a long moment. Finally, he said, "All right. We'll go."

"We?"

"We. You're coming, too. If I'm going to subject myself to one of these studio affairs, I want you there, too."

"But I hate big, impersonal cocktail parties. I won't know anyone—"

He interrupted with a smile, "Misery loves company. Either you come or I don't go."

She sighed. "Okay. But that's blackmail."

"Yes. Successful blackmail."

"You're impossible."

He smiled. "You've told me that before."

"And I suspect I'll tell you again."

"I suspect you will—while you stand by my side tomorrow night, helping me make small talk with people I don't know and don't want to know, while people who are only

nterested in what I can do for them try to catch my atten-
ion."

"You make it sound like such fun." Marina's tone was
utterly dry.

"It's even worse than it sounds. Just remember, it was
your idea."

"If she turns out to be a wonderful director and you hire
her, I'll expect an apology."

"You'll get it. At the main gate of the studio, at high
noon."

Marina grinned slyly. "I'll hold you to that, you know."

"I'll bet you will."

They had arrived at his house. As he pulled into the garage and shut off the engine, he added in a husky voice, "In
the meantime, I can think of a much better thing for us to
do than argue."

Marina raised her eyebrows in studied innocence. "Oh?
And what might that be, pray tell?"

"Rather than tell you, I think I'll show you."

And with that he put his arms around her and kissed her
slowly, expertly.

When she finally drew away from him, she said in a voice
that wasn't entirely under control, "Show, don't tell, *is* one
of the first maxims of screenwriting, after all."

"You're right. Why don't I show you some more?"

"Why don't you do that?"

Before she'd finished speaking, his lips were on hers
again, and she was no longer capable of witty banter.

When they drew apart, Stephen said thickly, "I'd better
get you inside. Necking in cars is for sixteen-year-olds.
Grown-ups have other options."

"Indeed," Marina whispered, as he helped her out of the
car.

Chapter Eleven

The next morning Marina dressed with special care. Since there wouldn't be time to go all the way out to Trancas again before going to the party and screening of *Heartaches*, she would have to wear the same clothes from the office to the party. Stephen reassured her that most of the other people there were in the same position—they'd be coming straight from work, too, and would be casually dressed.

"It isn't a star-studded premiere, with furs and jewels and the whole bit," he explained. "It's strictly business, for studio employees and the people who worked on the picture."

Still, Marina felt nervous about how she would look. Because it was a cold, dreary day, she chose charcoal-gray wool slacks and a matching silk broadcloth blouse, with a gray and blue tweed jacket. It was casual and comfortable enough for work, but nice enough for the party.

At the office, Marina got down to work quickly. Now that she had a rough draft of the first ten pages of the screenplay, and was faced with the remaining one hundred or so pages, she felt overwhelmed. Stephen was too busy to work with her as closely as he had done the previous weekend. As she flicked through the galleys of her novel, trying to decide which scenes to use and which to leave out, she grew more and more confused.

Between meetings, Stephen came in and found her looking harried. He suggested that she begin working with three-by-five index cards. It was a good way to organize scenes and sequences. She wrote the idea for a scene or a sequence of scenes on a card. Then she could arrange the cards any way she wanted. It was easy to rearrange them, add some or delete some.

As soon as she began to use this system, she felt less overwhelmed. Suddenly the screenplay was manageable again. By seven o'clock that evening, when it was time to knock off work and go over to the commissary for the party, she had most of the major scenes from the screenplay outlined on cards.

"Ready for your first Hollywood bash?" Stephen asked as they walked across the lot together.

"Sure. Will there be swinging from the chandeliers and general carrying-on?" she teased, trying to appear nonchalant.

He grinned. "I doubt it. Will you be disappointed if it's quiet and dull?"

"Actually, I'll be relieved."

He squeezed her arm. And as they entered the brightly lit commissary, he whispered in her ear, "Don't worry, Marina. Ten of these people aren't worth one of you."

She didn't have time to do more than smile at him as they were surrounded by people.

The commissary was full of people talking in small groups, milling around with vaguely purposeless expressions or looking self-important. One thing that relieved Marina was the casual dress. She fit right in with the jeans and pantsuits. Stephen had been right when he said this was work, not play. Everyone seemed to have come straight from an office, mostly on the lot, and the talk was almost exclusively of work.

At one point Stephen was taken aside by the president of the studio, a large, florid man whom he didn't seem particularly happy to talk with. Reluctantly, he left Marina to fend for herself. Since she didn't know anyone else there, she simply grabbed a glass of Perrier from a passing waiter, ensconced herself in a corner and watched the ebb and flow of people around her.

It was easy to pick out the actors from the studio executives. They were the ones with great charm and a great sense of their own importance. The executives were the ones whose eyes kept flicking to the studio president.

Then a young woman invaded Marina's corner. She looked as though she was a few years older than Marina. Her shoulder-length blond hair was straight and not particularly stylish, and her attire was the most casual imaginable—faded jeans that had obviously been mended more than once, and under a black cotton blazer a black-and-white T-shirt emblazoned with the logo, The Best Man for the Job Is a Woman.

She smiled warmly at Marina. Then, gesturing at the crowd, she said in a surprisingly confident, authoritative voice, "Quite a turnout. Somehow I didn't expect this many people."

"I didn't know what to expect," Marina admitted. "This is my first time at one of these affairs."

"I'm not exactly a seasoned veteran myself. I've only gone to a few of these, and then it was because I knew the director. Now I know how they must have felt—like Daniel walking into the lions' den."

Suddenly Marina realized whom she was talking to. "You're the director of *Heartaches*?"

The woman smiled. "Yeah. Carla Brooke."

"I'm Marina Turner."

"Pleased to meet you, Marina. Are you new at the studio?"

"I'm not really with the studio. At least not permanently. Stephen Kramer bought a novel I wrote and I'm adapting it."

"How wonderful for you! Everything he touches seems to turn to gold. I hope the spell holds and you have a mega-hit."

"Thanks, but I'll settle for a good film."

Carla eyed her curiously. "Now that's something I don't hear every day. It's how I feel, too. You know you're probably the only person in this room who's a soul mate."

"Thanks. Tell me about your movie. I'm afraid I don't know much about it except that I've heard it's wonderful."

"I'm happy with the way it turned out, especially considering how little money we had to work with."

"Didn't the studio finance it?"

"No, they're just releasing it. A group of Canadian investors looking for a tax write-off put up the money."

"What's the story?" Marina asked with real interest.

"It's about a group of single women who are friends. They're all looking for Mr. Wonderful."

"Judging by the title, I assume they don't find him?"

"Well, one does, sort of. She finds Mr. All Right. The others end up kissing a lot of frogs, as the saying goes."

Marina smiled ruefully. "Sounds like something most single women can relate to."

"I think so. I certainly related to it. Then I married the art director halfway through the film, and my direction became a little less sharp-edged after that."

"Congratulations. Is he here tonight?"

"Yes, somewhere in the crowd. He's very social and loves to mingle. I'm just the opposite. He keeps telling me I'm going to have to learn to mingle more if I want to make it in this business. Contacts, connections, are so important."

"How did you get into directing?"

Carla took a sip of the Coke she was holding and answered, "I went to A.F.I.—American Film Institute. Then I worked for an advertising agency doing commercials. Three years ago I got the chance to direct a very low-budget film. It was so low-budget we couldn't even afford to use a union cast and crew. At least *Heartaches* was union."

"Is it tough being a woman in such a male-dominated area of the business?"

"Very. There are only three or four women members of the Directors' Guild, you know. And I'm not one of them yet. But it's going to change, it has to. Women have special talents to bring to filmmaking. We have our own special sensitivity about personal relationships. And we see female characters more accurately, in less stereotyped ways, than male directors do."

"I agree," Marina responded wholeheartedly. The more she talked to Carla, the more convinced she was that Carla would be a good choice to direct *Casey*.

She asked with studied casualness, "By the way, have you met Stephen?"

"Nope, haven't had the pleasure. We don't exactly travel in the same circles. I do low-budget films that play in art houses, and he gets mentioned on the front page of *Variety* every other day."

There was wry humor in her tone, but no real envy.

"Would you like to meet him? I'll introduce you," Marina offered.

"Sure, why not?"

Scanning the room, Marina finally glimpsed Stephen making his way toward her through the crowd. People anxious to talk to him kept stopping him, but he refused to linger. When he reached Marina, he said, "Sorry about deserting you. Chuck needed to talk to me."

"Stephen, this is Carla Brooke. She directed *Heartaches*."

"Of course. Nice to meet you."

"Nice to meet you, Mr. Kramer."

"Please call me Stephen. And I'll call you Carla, if I may."

"Sure."

Carla seemed a little surprised at Stephen's down-to-earth friendliness.

He went on, "Chuck was telling me that he's really high on your movie. He thinks it could grab some Oscar nominations for the studio."

"I hope he's right. That wouldn't hurt the box office."

"No, it wouldn't." Stephen glanced at his watch. "Well, we'd better be getting over to the screening room. It's nearly eight o'clock."

"Right, I'd better not be late for my own movie."

"Would you like to come with us?" Marina offered.

"Thanks, but I'd better find my husband. Hopefully, I'll see you two over there."

"Yes, I hope so, too."

Stephen took Marina's arm and led her through the crowd that was beginning to leave the commissary and walk en masse to a nearby screening room.

The room was like a small movie theater. Stephen found seats for the two of them as close to the door as possible, "For a fast getaway afterward," he explained.

When everyone was seated, the lights went out and the movie began. It was beautifully shot, well written and well acted. A minor masterpiece, Marina thought. And Carla's directing was faultless. There was a sensitivity toward the four female characters that made them appealing rather than pathetic.

By the end of the movie, when The End flashed on the screen and the lights came back on, Marina knew Carla was definitely the right director for *Casey*. All she had to do was make Stephen realize that.

To her surprise, he turned to her and said, "You can say 'I told you so.' What an eye that woman has! She directed the hell out of that story."

"I agree. What do you think about her directing *Casey*?"

For a moment he was absolutely silent. *He's marshaling his argument,* Marina thought. She felt anger begin to well up within her. If he refused to consider Carla, it would be only because she was a woman. And if he did that, Marina was going to let him have it.

He said thoughtfully, "She can certainly handle relationship stories. And I like the subtle way she handled the sex scenes. That's how I want them handled in our film. I want a PG-13 rating with *Casey*, not an R."

"So?" Marina pressed.

They had risen to their feet and were about to join the crowd moving through the exit when Carla and her husband passed by. Stopping her, Stephen congratulated her on the movie.

She seemed thrilled with the compliment. "Thanks. It's nice of you to say so. By the way, this is my husband. John, this is Marina Turner and Stephen Kramer."

The two men shook hands. Then Stephen turned back to Carla. "Marina and I have a project you might find interesting. Could you and your husband come out to my place in Trancas tomorrow to discuss it?"

Carla was stunned. She obviously hadn't expected anything like this. Watching her, Marina felt thrilled. She was excited for Carla and very proud of Stephen.

"Why...yeah, sure," Carla replied, with a quick look at her husband.

"Good." Taking a card from his pocket, Stephen went on, "That's my address. It's easy to find. Why don't you come around noon and we'll have lunch?"

"Okay," Carla agreed readily.

She shot Marina a pleased, grateful look that suggested she knew very well Marina was at least partly responsible for this.

A few minutes later, when Marina and Stephen reached his car, Marina threw her arms around him and gave him a long, lingering kiss. When they finally drew apart, he asked softly, "Was that my reward for having the sense to recognize talent when I see it, despite the gender, and not being a male chauvinist pig?"

A slow smile spread across her face as she looked deep into his eyes. "No. That's just because I enjoy kissing you."

"Do you now?" he teased.

"I do."

"Then let's get home so you can have plenty of opportunity to do more of the same."

During the long ride out to Trancas, Marina felt her passion growing. The longer she knew this man, the more she wanted him. The better she came to know him, the more she liked and respected him. Their relationship was proceeding at a pace that was giddy and exciting. It was different now than it had been a week earlier. And worlds removed from what it had been two weeks earlier.

She had no idea where it would be in the future. She didn't even want to think about that. She just wanted to enjoy every moment of it.

Looking at Stephen's profile as he looked straight ahead at the road, she thought, *I want you. I want you so much it almost hurts.*

She had no inhibitions where he was concerned, and certainly no shame. There was a very special chemistry between them. She knew he felt it as strongly as she did.

Now, she placed her hand lightly on his thigh. Through the fabric of his gabardine slacks, she felt his muscles tense at her touch, then slowly relax. The knowledge that her mere touch could affect him sent a frisson of excitement racing through her.

When they reached his house, he didn't even bother to turn on the lights. He led her through the darkened house to his bedroom and there made love to her with a hunger and abandon that left her absolutely exhausted—and absolutely satisfied.

As Marina fell asleep in his arms, she knew she would never stop wanting him.

With the unpredictability of Los Angeles weather, especially beach weather, Saturday dawned warm and clear. Marina and Stephen dressed in shorts and went for a walk on the beach. Marina could see the entire curve of Santa Monica Bay in the distance. Azure waves broke in a white froth against the pristine white beaches. There wasn't a cloud in the clear blue sky.

Marina felt exhilarated. It was a perfect day for walking on the beach, barbecuing hamburgers for lunch and making plans for a really fine film.

When they had walked quite a way, they sat down together on the sand to rest for a minute before heading back. Stephen put his arm around her and she leaned her head on his shoulder.

"What a gorgeous day!" she exclaimed happily.

"As gorgeous as the days in Big Sur?"

"Nothing is as gorgeous as a really perfect day in Big Sur."

Gesturing around them, Stephen insisted, "But the bay, the beach, the sun..."

"Big Sur has bays, and beaches and a dazzling sun. And the most magnificent scenery that makes this look only mildly pretty in comparison. But there's one thing Trancas has that Big Sur doesn't."

"Ah, what might that be?"

She looked at him. "You."

Her tone was low and even. But something in her look caught at his heart and left him speechless for a moment.

When he finally found his voice, he said, "I don't want you to leave, Marina. When the screenplay's finished, don't go back to Big Sur. Stay with me."

She wasn't surprised at the request—but she was pleased. It was proof, if she needed any, that he felt about her as she felt about him. Still, she was torn.

"My home is there," she said slowly.

"You could make your home down here," he insisted. "You can write anywhere."

That was true. And she wanted to be with him. She hadn't thought about leaving him, but now that she did so, she felt a sharp jolt of loneliness and loss.

"I didn't expect this," she said honestly. "I didn't want it."

He kissed her forehead. "I know, sweetheart."

"I'm not sure I'm ready for it."

He offered her a slow, lazy smile. "I'm not sure anyone ever is ready for something this strong. All you can do is give in to it. There's no way to fight it."

"I know. I tried to fight it, and I went under so fast I didn't know what hit me."

"Will you stay?" he pressed.

She didn't answer immediately. She felt his body tense and knew that he was worried about her answer. And at the same time she knew that there was only one answer she could give.

"Yes," she whispered. "I'll stay."

He didn't say a word. But his body relaxed, and he expelled a long, pent-up breath.

They sat there in silence. A cool breeze lifted Marina's hair from the nape of her neck and caressed her bare skin. Overhead, sea gulls screeched and circled and dipped. Sandpipers minced along the shore, tripping in and out with the waves.

The beach was surprisingly quiet and empty for a weekend. Marina felt that she and Stephen were in their own little world, a paradise of sun and sea and sand.

Stephen was looking out to sea. Without looking at Marina, he said slowly, "There's something I want to tell you about."

Something in his tone alerted her to the importance of what was to come.

"Yes?" she said in a quiet voice.

"I told you that my family—my mother, father and sister—died in a fire. I didn't care about my father then, although over the years I've learned to feel pity for him. But I did care about my mother. And, especially, my little sister."

"What was her name?" Marina asked gently.

"Beth. That's a pretty name, isn't it?"

"Yes. Very pretty."

She waited for him to continue.

After a moment he went on haltingly, "She was ten years younger than I was, so I was very much a big brother. She was a cute little thing, blond hair and big blue eyes. I think she would have been very pretty when she grew up."

His voice cracked and he paused for a moment. When he went on, he had himself in hand. But there was tremendous emotion behind his carefully controlled voice.

"I took care of her a lot. My mother was busy dealing with my father and didn't have a lot of time or patience for Beth. Because she was so little, everything that was going on, all the problems, were harder on her than they were on me."

Marina thought what a great deal of responsibility Stephen had taken on his young shoulders. She could imagine him trying to be a parent to his little sister, wishing he could make life better for her, feeling guilty because there was no way he could, of course.

"I didn't mind taking care of her," he went on, as if in response to some unspoken criticism. "She was so sweet and she needed me and loved me...."

His voice trailed off into another, longer silence.

Marina knew that he didn't want her to say anything. He just needed her to listen. Somehow she sensed that he'd never talked of this to anyone. She wasn't sure why he was doing so now. Except that it meant he was opening up to her in a way that touched her deeply.

She sat there, with his arm around her, holding one of his hands in her smaller ones.

"I guess I'll always miss her," he finished simply.

They continued to sit there in silence for a long while. Stephen didn't say anything further, and neither did Marina.

When they returned from their walk, the doorbell rang. Glancing at her watch, Marina saw that it was twelve o'clock exactly. They had taken longer on their walk than she realized. Stephen answered the door and admitted Carla and John.

"Glad you could make it. Why don't you two go out to the deck with Marina, and I'll get some drinks. Is Coke or Perrier okay?"

"Fine," Carla and John agreed.

As Marina led them through the living room out to the deck, she caught the surprised looks on their faces. They had expected something different from Stephen Kramer's house, too, she realized humorously.

A moment later Stephen joined them on the deck and poured drinks for everyone. Then he asked Marina to explain the story of *Casey* to them. She did so with great detail and enthusiasm. When she was done, Carla said, "It sounds marvelous. I love the fact that it's a female-coming-of-age film. That hasn't really been done."

Stephen replied, "I know. It's usually male-coming-of-age. But I think people have had enough of that for a while. I think this story will appeal to a lot of people. Not that it will be another *Star Wars*. But I think the marketing people at the studio, who are always down on anything that doesn't have blockbuster written all over it, will be surprised by this."

"Are you interested in the story, then?" Marina asked Carla.

"Definitely."

"I'll give you a copy of the galleys of the novel to take home with you," Stephen said. "Marina's doing the screenplay and it isn't ready yet. But we want to start shooting in February."

Carla's husband, John, looked startled. "February? That doesn't give you much time for preproduction."

"No," Stephen admitted. "But I want this to be a Christmas release, and Chuck has agreed to it. Can you work that fast?"

Carla thought for a moment, then, with a quiet confidence said, "Yes, I can."

"Good. Have your agent call me first thing Monday morning and we'll get a deal memo together."

Now it was Carla's turn to look startled. "You mean that's it?"

Stephen nodded. "Yes. Assuming you want to do it."

"Oh, I want to do it!" She exchanged an excited look with John. "Boy, do I!"

"Good. I'm glad you feel that way because I was very impressed with your movie last night. I think you're the perfect director for our project."

"Thank you. I don't know what else to say."

Stephen smiled. "Say you'll bring it in on time and under budget."

Carla returned his smile. "That's a promise!"

"When Marina gets a rough draft of the screenplay finished, you can see it. We'll have another meeting to make sure we're in agreement on that. In the meantime, as John pointed out, we don't have much time for preproduction so we'd better get started now. Marty Stein is production manager on all my films. But the other slots are open. Do you have any ideas on who you'd like to fill the below-the-line slots?"

Before she could answer, he added quickly, "I'm assuming John will be your art director again?" Turning to John, he said simply, "I loved your work on *Heartaches*."

"Thanks," John replied. He and Carla exchanged a relieved look. Marina realized they'd been concerned about Stephen not wanting them as a package deal.

Carla named some of the crew from *Heartaches* as people she'd like to work with on this project. Stephen agreed, then offered his own ideas for the other positions.

Since Marina knew nothing about this part of the process, she excused herself and went into the kitchen to get lunch ready. It was an easy chore since they had stopped at a nearby deli at the tail end of their walk and bought a selection of cold cuts and cheeses for sandwiches. After arranging everything on a tray, she carried it outside to a round redwood table on the deck.

She rejoined the three of them just in time for a discussion about casting. Though she didn't know any more about casting than she did about the below-the-line positions, she was vitally interested in it. She had very definite ideas about what type of people should play Casey, Mark and Sheila.

There was a very spirited four-way discussion, as each of them suggested possible actors and actresses.

Finally, late in the afternoon, Carla and John left.

"I'm going to read these galleys tonight," Carla promised Marina. "Can I call you in the morning and let you know what I think?"

"Please do. And I'll tell you what I've done with the screenplay so far."

"Okay. Talk to you tomorrow, then."

When they were gone, Marina and Stephen went into the kitchen to get something to drink.

"I like them both," Stephen said, sipping a Coke from a can.

"So do I. Oh, Stephen, I think Carla's absolutely the best possible person to direct our movie."

"I think you're right."

Marina clasped her hands around his neck. "And you know what else I think?"

His eyes were warm with amusement and affection as they met hers. "No, what else do you think?"

"I think you're the best possible person to produce it."

He put down his Coke, slid his arms around her waist and pulled her against him. "I was wondering when you were going to get around to admitting that."

"Are you suggesting I've been too proud to admit I was wrong?"

"I'm not suggesting it. I'm coming right out and saying it."

She laughed softly. "Well, you were right. I was proud. But now I'm beginning to feel that where you're concerned I have no pride at all."

"Good. Because where you're concerned, I don't, either."

He kissed her tenderly. As she felt herself melt in his arms, she thought that she'd never been so happy in her life. And she thought that so much happiness was a little bit terrifying.

Chapter Twelve

Now that a director had been hired, preproduction on *Casey* moved into high gear. Actors were auditioned, screen tests were made, a location manager went up to Big Sur to scout locations. In Stephen's suite of offices, the cubicles that had been empty were filled now with the crew hired to make *Casey*. Carla and John were given adjoining offices.

Whenever she had a free minute, Carla would pop into Marina's office to check on the script. Marina enjoyed discussing it with her. They saw the story very much the same way. But as a slightly older, more experienced woman, Carla had insights that Marina lacked.

She made several suggestions that improved the story. Marina only wished that she could go back and rewrite parts of her novel. But it was too late for that. All she could do now was make the screenplay even better, in its own way, than the book.

She was well into it now, up to the plot point that came at the end of the second act. In that scene Sheila told her husband, Mark, that she was pregnant, just when he was on the verge of asking her for a divorce. It was the second most pivotal scene in the movie and had to be handled very carefully.

Despite the fact that Marina was well into it and had both Carla and Stephen to help, writing the screenplay didn't get any easier. It was an amazing, almost mysterious phenomenon. One day she was excited, confident, convinced she'd finally mastered the craft. The next day she was down in the dumps, confused, unable to produce anything that satisfied her.

It was exactly as it had been when she was writing the novel—one day it worked, and the next day it didn't. She didn't know how or why. It was the creative process and it defied logic.

One day she was having a particularly hard time. She was scowling at her typewriter when Stephen came into her office.

"If anything made me as mad as that typewriter's obviously made you, I'd shoot it," he said with a grin.

She turned her scowl on him. "Very funny. I just want you to know one thing. While you and Carla and John and Marty and everyone else here are complaining about how hard your jobs are, there's only one person facing a blank piece of paper. And that's me."

He stopped smiling. "I know. Nothing involved in making a movie is as hard as writing it. I do know that. And I respect the special talent you have that enables you to do it."

Her scowl dissolved. "You're buttering me up."

"Yes. Is it working?"

She smiled. "Yes."

"Anything I can do to help?"

"You can fix my wretched dialogue."

Marina handed him the pages she'd been working on. He sat down in a chair facing her desk and read through them slowly. When he finally put them down, Stephen said, "You're right. This is stilted, unnatural. It doesn't flow."

"I know all of that. I just don't know how to fix it."

"All right, I'll give you my patented lecture on writing dialogue."

Marina picked up a pencil and pad of paper. "I'm ready."

"Okay. Here it is—remember that the purpose of dialogue is to move the story forward, to give information, establish relationships, reveal conflicts, character or emotions. Dialogue that doesn't serve one of those purposes is unnecessary and boring. So every time you write some dialogue, ask yourself if it accomplishes anything. If not, cut it out."

"Okay. That means cutting out everything I've written today, because none of it serves any purpose at all."

She sounded tired and frazzled, which was exactly how she was feeling.

"Listen, take the afternoon off. Go shopping, go to a movie. You need to relax a little."

"You're giving me permission to play hooky?" she asked with a grin.

"Yup. I'd do it with you, but I've got to look at a couple of screen tests."

Seeing her reluctance, he continued, "Go on. You deserve a break. You've been working seven days a week on this thing."

"Okay, I think I will." She slid the cover over her typewriter, then stood up. "I'll check out Rodeo Drive and spend some of the money you're paying me."

Stephen took his car keys out of his pocket and tossed them to her. "Well, take your time. I won't be ready to leave until seven o'clock, at least."

After making sure no one was looking through the open door to her office, Marina kissed Stephen. He gave her an odd look, which she ignored as she left. She knew what that look meant. He didn't understand why she was reluctant to let people know they were personally involved. She wasn't entirely sure she understood the reason herself, only that she wasn't ready yet to deal with the inevitable results of public acknowledgment of their relationship.

A half hour later she made her way through the crowds on Rodeo Drive. The sidewalks were filled with shoppers carrying extravagantly wrapped packages. There was no snow on the ground, but the shops had managed somehow to create a festive, Christmassy atmosphere. Windows were gaily decorated, and beautiful blue decorations and lights hung across the streets.

Marina did a lot of window shopping. She was amazed at the fabulous goods for sale—and the fabulous prices. Then her eye was caught by something in a jewelry shop window. Among many more expensive pieces was a small, old-fashioned cameo. As soon as she saw it, she knew her mother would love it.

She looked closer to read the price tag—two hundred dollars. That was a bargain compared to the pearls, diamonds, emeralds and rubies that filled the rest of the display. Quickly making up her mind, she went inside the store and emerged five minutes later with a tiny but exquisitely wrapped present.

She breathed a sigh of relief. That was one name she could scratch off her shopping list. All that was left now was Rosie and Stephen.

In an art gallery she found the perfect gift for Rosie, a lovely sketch of a Hopi Indian girl, executed by a Hopi artist. Rosie loved Indian arts and crafts, and the small picture would go perfectly with the other things in her home.

Stephen was more of a problem. What could she possibly get a man who had so much more money than she did? Marina wondered. And it wasn't just a question of money. He lived so simply, it was clear he wasn't interested in expensive possessions.

Marina looked in store after store. Nothing was right. She wanted a personal gift, something special, something with meaning. She looked at and rejected an eelskin wallet, a silk tie, a platinum comb-and-brush set and a cashmere sweater. She nearly bought the sweater because it was exactly the color of his eyes—a deep, cobalt-blue. But she finally decided against it—to the annoyance of the impatient clerk—because it simply wasn't personal.

Anyone could give Stephen a sweater like that. He could easily buy one, or a dozen, for himself. She wanted to give him something that no one else could give him, something... Marina stopped as an idea struck her. Suddenly she knew exactly what to give him.

She hurried to a pay phone and called Rosie.

"Marina! It's so good to hear your voice. How are you?"

"Just fine."

"Are you turning Hollywood on its ear?"

Marina laughed. "I don't think so. This is a tougher business than I realized."

"You can handle it, kid."

"Sure. Tell me what's going on at the ranch."

"The usual—I had to buy a load of hay for the horses. At those prices, I might as well feed them gold."

"How's Homer? Is he behaving?"

Rosie chuckled good-naturedly. "Course not. But every time I catch him doin' something wrong, he just gives me that pity-me-I'm-a-poor-orphan look, and I don't have the heart to discipline him."

"That dog has your number."

Rosie sighed. "Yeah. What can I say? By the way, we've got a new boarder here."

"Boarder" was how Rosie referred to the various stray animals she adopted.

"Who's this one?"

"Ugliest little kitten you ever saw. Typical mangy gray tomcat. Someone must've brought him out to the country and dumped him, 'cause there's no way he could have made it out here on his own."

"What are you calling him?" Marina asked with curiosity. Rosie's choice of names was always interesting.

"Well, I waited 'till I'd observed his character for a couple of days. Then I decided to name him Aristotle."

Marina suppressed a giggle. "Now, why would you name a mangy gray tomcat Aristotle?"

"He's a deep thinker. Sits staring into space for a long time."

"How's Homer getting along with Aristotle?"

"He tries to ignore him, but it's hard when Aristotle jumps on him and pulls his ears."

"Oh, Rosie, it's so good to talk to you," Marina said with a laugh.

"It's good to talk to you, too. But I'll bet you didn't call all the way from Los Angeles just to hear about Homer and Aristotle. What's up?"

She asked Rosie to do her a favor. When she explained what it was, Rosie seemed confused. "You want me to send *what* to you?"

Marina explained that it was going to be a Christmas present.

Through the telephone, she sensed dawning awareness in Rosie's tone. "Oh . . . I see. I take it you and Stephen Kramer are getting along better now?"

Marina didn't want to get into an intimate discussion of her relationship with Stephen over a public telephone with shoppers bustling past, so she simply said, "Yes, everything's working out fine."

"Sounds like it," Rosie responded.

Marina couldn't suppress an embarrassed smile. Rosie was nobody's fool.

"Well, I've got to go. I'll call you again when I have more time."

"Okay. There's just one more thing, Marina. Your mother called. She doesn't have an address or phone number for you down there, and she wanted to get in touch with you. Why don't you give her a call?"

Marina hesitated. She knew she should have given that information to her mother, but she'd been reluctant to talk to her or communicate with her in any way beyond the short note she'd sent. But this couldn't go on. Rosie was right, she should call her.

"All right," she said heavily. "I'll do that."

"Good. You'll both feel better if you talk. Well, if I don't talk to you before then, have a very merry Christmas."

"You, too, Rosie. Bye."

She stood at the pay phone for several minutes. It wasn't until a woman standing nearby gave her an irate look that she realized other people might want to use the phone. If she was going to call her mother, she'd better get it over with. Hopefully, Rafe wouldn't answer.

She dialed the familiar number and was relieved when she heard her mother's voice.

"Mom, it's me."

"Marina! I'm so glad you called. How are you? *Where* are you?"

"I'm still in L.A. I'll be down here for another month or so working on the screenplay. And I'm fine."

"Good. I'm so glad everything's going well for you."

"How are you?"

"I'm fine, too."

There was a pause, and Marina knew that her mother was waiting for Marina to ask about Rafe. But Marina had no intention of doing so.

When that became apparent, her mother said slowly, "Your father and I were both very touched that you came to our wedding. I don't think you realized what it meant to us, especially to him."

"I know what it meant to you," Marina said pointedly. "That's why I came."

"Oh, Marina, when are you going to give your father a chance? This is tearing him up inside. It's like losing you all over again."

"Mother, I don't want to talk about it."

"I know you don't. I know how hurt you are, and that's why I haven't tried to force the issue. But, darling, it's been months now."

"I know exactly how long it's been. I remember the day when you told me that my father wasn't my father after all, that a stranger was. A stranger who abandoned both of us before I was even born."

"Marina, he didn't abandon us. I've tried to explain that to you, but you refuse to hear it."

"Well, I'm not interested in hearing it now."

Marina's tone was sharper than she intended and she immediately regretted it. She adored her mother and didn't want to hurt her.

"Look, I'm sorry," she continued. "I didn't call to argue with you. I love you."

Her mother's voice was poignant. "I know. I love you, too. You've always been the most important thing in my life."

"Even...now?"

"Marina, your father hasn't taken your place in my heart. You each have your own place there. My love for him is something entirely different from my love for you."

When Marina didn't respond, her mother went on. "Oh, darling, he could give you so much love, too. He wants to. Just as he's given me so much. If you'd just give him a chance."

"Mother, I have to go," Marina said quickly. "I'm at a pay phone and I can't talk any longer."

Profound disappointment was evident in her mother's tone. "All right, darling. I understand. There's just one last thing. I'm asking you, for my sake, to come home for Christmas."

Marina was torn between wanting to go home, wanting to please her mother—but not wanting to be with her father.

There was a long, tense silence. Finally, she said slowly, "I'll think about it."

"Thank you. I hope I see you then. Take care, darling."

"Bye, Mom."

She hung up and left the phone to the heavily laden shopper who'd been waiting impatiently for ten minutes.

As Marina was hurrying back to Stephen's car, she tried to put her conversation with her mother out of her mind. Instead, she thought about the gifts she'd bought, and the special one she'd thought of for Stephen. She was sure he'd be surprised and pleased.

She congratulated herself on getting all her Christmas shopping out of the way so quickly. Then she realized that there was one person she had conveniently forgotten—her father.

Her happy expression faded. She didn't want to buy him a gift. After all, what would she write on the card: *To Dad, with love from your daughter, whom you didn't see for twenty-four years*?

But if she bought her mother a gift and didn't buy one for her father, she knew how deeply hurt her mother would be. It would ruin her mother's enjoyment of the cameo.

She sighed heavily as she drove back to the studio. Problems, always problems. They had started when the man she'd thought was her father walked out on her mother and her. And they'd gotten worse when her real father had entered the scene.

Her joy at Christmas shopping and talking to Rosie dissolved.

In his office, Stephen leaned back in his tall leather chair and grimaced. Facing him across the wide desk, Marty said, "I know...we've looked at every actress between seventeen and twenty-seven, and none is quite right."

"I wish Carol Needham had been available. She was so right for the role of Casey."

"Yeah, she's hot. That's probably why someone else signed her to a picture."

"It always boils down to who's available. It's rare to be able to get exactly who you want."

"At least the role of Sheila won't be so hard to fill. There are any number of good, thirtyish actresses desperately looking for a meaty role."

"Yes. Which says something about sexism in our industry," Stephen commented bluntly.

Marty gave him a startled look. "I sense Marina's had an effect on you. You didn't used to be so sensitive."

"Thanks."

"Seriously, how's it going with her? Is she doing okay on the screenplay?"

"The first draft's coming along fine. It should be done by Christmas. Then we'll tinker with it for a while, and by the end of January we should have a shooting script."

"Great. Boy, this project's really rolling along like gangbusters. Unlike some I could mention."

He and Stephen shared a knowing smile. "Yeah," Stephen responded. "Remember how long it took to get a studio to finance our first movie?"

"Three long, hard years. I swear I will never eat peanut butter or tuna again."

"Amen to that. By the way, how's Amy?"

Marty grinned. "She felt a little faint yesterday—which has never happened to her in her life. We're gonna wait another couple of weeks, then she's going to the doctor."

"I'll keep my fingers crossed."

"Thanks. You know, of course, we expect you to be the godfather."

"Of course. If you'd asked someone else, I'd have never spoken to you again. But what does a godfather do exactly?"

"Buy expensive presents, mostly."

Stephen smiled. "I can handle that."

Marty's expression grew more serious. "And if something should happen to Amy and me, well, you'd be the child's guardian and raise him."

"Nothing's going to happen to you. But if it does—I'd be happy to raise him."

"Thanks, buddy."

Stephen went on, "Well, enough of this morbid talk, though. I need your advice about something."

"Shoot."

From his desk drawer, Stephen took out a small velvet-covered box. "This is Marina's Christmas present. Do you think she'll feel it's too gaudy?"

Marty took the box and opened it. He whistled appreciatively, then gave Stephen a sober look. "Does this mean what I think it means?"

"Well, I've never given a woman a diamond solitaire before. To me, it means I'm asking her to marry me."

"When did all this happen? A few weeks ago, you two hated each other. Then you decided to be friendly. And now..."

"Now I want her to be my wife and have my children. To tell you the truth, I think I knew it the minute I laid eyes on her. I just couldn't believe it could happen that fast."

"I think it can happen that fast."

Stephen's expression was bemused. "You think it's pretty corny, huh?"

"Yeah, I think it's pretty corny. And pretty wonderful. Congratulations."

"You approve?"

"I do. And so does Amy. You know what she said when you guys left after Thanksgiving?"

"I can imagine. She always seems to know both of us better than we know ourselves."

"She said that you'd finally met a woman who could stand up to you and at the same time give you what you need."

"I think she's right. You know, even when Marina and I fight, I don't worry. Because I know that when it's over we'll be as close as ever."

"In that case, marry the girl, the sooner the better."

"I intend to. I don't believe in long engagements. But about the ring—do you think it's too much?"

"You mean because it's as big as my fist?" Marty teased.

Stephen looked genuinely worried. "I wanted to give her something special. But she's so down-to-earth. Do you think she won't like it?"

"Hey, I've never heard a woman say she preferred a small diamond. Marina may not be into conspicuous consumption, but I'll bet she'll love this."

"I hope so."

"Have you asked her to marry you?"

Stephen shook his head. "I haven't even told her I love her."

"Well, I hate to sound negative, but has it occurred to you that this may come as a surprise to her?"

"Doesn't matter. She doesn't have any choice."

Marty grinned. "That's the Stephen Kramer I know and admire. When are you going to pop the question—or announce your decision?"

"Christmas. That'll give her another two weeks to realize how much she loves me."

"Well, good luck, buddy."

He handed Stephen the box and Stephen put it back in his drawer.

Just then Marina walked in. "Oh, I'm sorry. Am I interrupting a meeting?"

Marty replied dryly, "No, Stephen was just letting me in on his plans for expansion. Well, it's late, I'd better be going. 'Night, guys."

"Good night, Marty," Marina replied warmly.

"Let's take off, too," Stephen said, pushing back his chair and standing up. "We've got to stop and buy a Christmas tree on the way home."

"A tree? Somehow, you didn't strike me as the type to really get into the Christmas spirit."

"Are you kidding? I'm into tinsel and glitter, remember?"

She grinned ruefully. "You're never going to let me forget that, are you?"

"Nope." He put his arm around her and led her out the door. "Never."

In Santa Monica they stopped at a Christmas tree lot and bought a thick, tall tree, which was then tied to the top of the jeep. An hour later they had set it in a corner of the huge, empty living room.

"Well, there's plenty of room for it," Marina quipped.

"Now all we need are ornaments," Stephen said, standing back and surveying it. "How about a star for the top? Or would you prefer an angel?"

"You mean you don't have ornaments?"

"Nope. This is the first year I've bought a tree."

The expression in her gray eyes was thoughtful. "Why?"

He met her look. "Christmas trees belong in a home. Until this year, I didn't feel there was anything homey about where I was living."

"Why is it different this year?" Marina asked softly.

"Because you're here."

She felt her heart turn over with a bittersweet mixture of sadness and joy. Every year of her life she'd had a Christmas tree, both in her own home and at her mother's house, and at Rosie's, as well. She'd enjoyed the bright lights, the gay ornaments, the shimmering stars and exquisite angels, but she'd never fully appreciated how much that simple joy meant. She'd simply taken it all for granted.

Stephen had missed that. Along with everything else he'd missed in his life, he'd missed the wonder of sitting in a darkened room, looking at a brightly lit tree, feeling the mystery of Christmas.

She had to fight to keep her voice under control as she said, "In that case, let's go down to the drugstore in the village and buy some ornaments."

"You wouldn't rather wait and buy some nice, expensive ones?" he asked slowly.

She shook her head. "No. It doesn't matter what they cost. Even the cheapest ones look shiny and beautiful on the tree."

In two long strides, Stephen was beside her, enfolding her in his arms. He didn't say anything, but Marina sensed tremendous emotion coursing through him. When he finally pulled back, he said in a slightly unsteady voice, "Let's go buy every ornament in the store."

A half hour later they returned with boxes and boxes of every imaginable type of ornament: shiny balls of red, blue, silver and gold; wooden rocking horses with straw tails; felt reindeer; red-and-white-striped candy canes; garlands of gold; and tinsel—hundreds of silver strands, shining like a pirate's treasure.

Marina's cheeks were pink from being out in the brisk cold night, and her eyes were bright with excitement. She laughed as she and Stephen wound the garlands around and around the tree. Then, feeling as silly as children, they started throwing strands of tinsel at each other. They didn't stop until they fell down on the floor together, both covered with tinsel.

Finally, Stephen held Marina up so that she could place the white satin angel on the top of the tree.

"There," she said triumphantly, "it's done."

As he set her on her feet again, he pulled her against him and kissed her deeply. She felt as if she were drowning in his kiss and wanted it to go on forever. When it finally ended, she felt a twinge of regret that it had to end.

But there was one thing left to do. Pulling back, she said, "Now comes the best part."

She turned out the overhead light, then plugged in the Christmas tree lights. In an instant the tiny, multicolored lights were twinkling brightly. And on the very top of the tree, the white angel shone in the soft glow.

Stephen and Marina stood together, their arms around each other, silently admiring the tree.

He whispered, "It's like a miracle."

"The miracle is how something so simple can make us feel the spirit of Christmas so deeply."

He looked at her and on his face was an expression she had never seen before—an expression of utter peace. "The miracle is *you*."

The naked emotion in his voice left her speechless. She could only return his look, her lips parted slightly, her eyes warm with a feeling she didn't entirely understand.

Later, after dinner, when they finally went to bed, Stephen made love to her with a tenderness that was unlike anything Marina had experienced with him before. As she lay in his arms afterward, she thought of how tumultuous their relationship had been. And she knew that on this cold December night, they'd reached a new level of intimacy.

Chapter Thirteen

On Christmas Eve day, Stephen closed the office early. When he and Marina got home, he said, "Marty and Amy have invited us to drop by tomorrow. Would you like to do that?"

When Marina didn't answer at once, he said, "Hey, Earth calling Marina."

She glanced over at him and smiled. "Sorry. I was lost in thought. What did you say?"

"Marty and Amy have invited us to come over tomorrow. Would you like to do that?"

She'd been thinking about her mother's earnest appeal for her to come home on Christmas. She'd been thinking about it for two weeks now, and she knew she really should do it, no matter how uncomfortable it would be for her. There was no longer any time to put off making a decision—tomorrow was Christmas. Instead of spending the day with Stephen, as she would prefer, and dropping by to visit Marty and Amy, she decided to go home.

"I'm afraid, much as I would like to, that I can't. You see, I have to go home."

She understood his look of surprise. She hadn't said a thing to him about this.

Hurriedly, she continued. "I'm sorry, I know this is unexpected."

"Yeah," he replied dryly.

"Look, I didn't decide until just now. I don't particularly want to go home, but my mother would like me to come."

He looked at her curiously. "Why don't you want to go, Marina?"

She hesitated. Then she said vaguely, "It will be the first Christmas with my... my stepfather, and I feel awkward, that's all. It's no big deal. And besides, I hate to take time off from the script just when the first draft's almost finished."

"Don't worry about that now. It's coming along very quickly, faster than I expected, in fact. Of course you should go home. I understand."

She could tell that he was hurt, and was trying very hard not to show it.

Cupping his face in her hands, she said simply, "I want to be with you. But it means a lot to my mother that I come."

The taut line of his mouth softened. "It's all right. Honest. When will you leave?"

"I think I'll drive up first thing in the morning, then come back tomorrow night."

"You don't have to do that. You can stay over for a while."

"No, I want to make it a quick trip. It's only about a four-hour drive up to Clovis. It's not fun to do it in a day, but it's not all that hard."

"Why not fly?"

"I doubt that I can get a flight this late."

"Let's call the airlines and see."

There were only two airlines flying in and out of Fresno, the big town next to Clovis, and both were completely booked, with long waiting lists of standby passengers.

"Well, so much for that idea." Stephen sighed. Then he gave Marina a thoughtful look. "Listen...how about if I drive you up there?"

At her look of surprise, he went on quickly, "I don't want to horn in on a family gathering, but—"

"Oh, Stephen, you wouldn't be horning in! Would you really not mind going with me?"

He smiled tenderly. "No, I wouldn't mind. In fact, I would like it very much."

"It won't be much fun for you, spending Christmas driving up to Clovis and back, to be with people you don't even know."

"I'll be with you. That's all that matters."

She threw her arms around him. "Oh, Stephen, you're definitely too good to be true."

"Now that's something that isn't said about me very often," he said with a laugh.

He kissed her lightly, then said, "All right, woman, let's get down to serious business here. What are we going to do about dinner tonight?"

"Not to worry. I'll cook something wonderful, since you are hopeless in the kitchen."

"I can't even argue with that, it's true. All right, let's go shopping."

They joined a crowd of other last-minute grocery shoppers raiding the depleted shelves of the nearby supermarket. Then they returned home and Marina began cooking a big dinner of roast, scalloped potatoes, asparagus with hollandaise sauce, and chocolate mousse for dessert. While dinner was cooking, she and Stephen went for a long walk on the beach. By the time they returned, it was ready. The meal was delicious, and when they finished they sat in the living room, in front of a roaring fire, talking softly.

It was a lovely evening. But when they went to sleep, Marina felt her glow of happiness fade. In less than a day she would have to face her father again. That would be difficult. At least, she thought with relief, Stephen would be with her. She was so grateful for that.

As he laid an arm across her breasts possessively before dropping off to sleep, she snuggled close to him.

They awoke early on Christmas morning. It was a habit from childhood that Marina had never gotten over, and Stephen was just naturally an early riser. After slipping on robes, they went into the living room.

"Shall we open our presents before or after breakfast?" Stephen teased.

"Before, of course. I've done all the waiting I'm going to do. You open yours first."

"Okay."

He picked up the large, square box that Marina herself had wrapped in shiny red foil with a red-and-green-striped bow.

As he unwrapped it, he admitted, "I haven't been able to figure out what it is. I even sneaked in the other night and shook it, but it didn't rattle."

Then the box was open and he was parting the tissue paper inside. For an instant, his expression was one of complete surprise. Then it turned to pleasure as he slowly lifted the quilt that Marina had made.

"Sweetheart." The word was full of affection and appreciation.

"Do you like it?" she asked, though she knew the answer.

"Yes. I like it. It's the nicest gift I've ever received."

Leaning toward her, he kissed her deeply. Inside she felt a stirring of desire, and knew that in a moment she would be in his arms, and then in his bed. Sensing the same thing, he pulled back reluctantly. His voice was hoarse as he said, "If we didn't have to leave in a few minutes..."

"I know," she whispered.

"But we do. So..." He let her go. Then, bending down, he picked up his gift to her and handed it to her. "They say good things come in small packages. I hope you agree."

She knew it was probably jewelry—earrings, perhaps, or a ring, judging by the shape and size of the box. But when she unwrapped it and opened the lid of the black velvet box, she was rendered speechless. She hadn't expected this kind of a ring.

It was dazzling. A diamond solitaire set on a platinum band. Marina was no judge of diamonds, but she knew this one must be several carats.

"In case there's any doubt, it's meant to be an engagement ring," Stephen said, a hint of amusement in his voice.

She looked up at him. Something in her expression made his amusement fade. "What is it, sweetheart? Is the ring too big? I was afraid it might not be your style. But we can take it back and you can pick out another...."

"The ring's beautiful," she said quickly. "But...I really wasn't expecting it," she finished lamely.

His smile returned. "I see. I suppose it would have helped if I'd said I love you. I guess I thought it was obvious."

When she looked away, still holding the open box in her hands, and didn't speak, he went on, "I love you, Marina. I knew it almost from the beginning. I only waited this long because I wanted to make sure you loved me. I'm sure of it now."

Finally, she forced herself to look at him. "How can you be so sure, Stephen?" she asked.

"Because it's apparent in everything we do together—in the way you comfort me, the way you touch me, the way you give yourself to me when we make love."

"How can you be sure that's not chemistry instead of love?"

He smiled. "I've been around the block a few times, Marina. I know the difference. I've been attracted to women. I even thought I was in love once. This is the first time I've been absolutely certain of how I feel."

Watching her unhappy, guarded expression, the truth began to dawn on him. "But you're not sure, are you?"

"I . . . I'm not looking for love. And definitely not marriage."

Her tone was miserable but firm.

Placing his hands on her shoulders, he looked directly at her and carefully said, "I want to spend the rest of my life with you. I want to have children with you. This isn't a commitment I take lightly."

"I know that, Stephen. But . . ." She took refuge in evasion. "Everything's happened so fast. We've only known each other a couple of months. Our life-styles are totally different."

"I'll have any life-style you want. Marina, I don't give a damn where or how I live, as long as it's with you. We'll make our home in Big Sur if you want, and I'll fly down here whenever I have to for business. George Lucas works out of Marin County, Francis Ford Coppola works out of San Francisco. There's no reason why I have to stay in L.A."

"It isn't that, Stephen. I don't particularly care about living in Big Sur."

"Then what is it?"

She countered, "Things have been wonderful. Why can't they go on as they are? Why do they have to change?"

"Because I want more. I want you to be my wife. I want you to belong to me legally and forever. And I want to belong to you in the same way. I'm too old to play house, Marina."

Legally and forever. A pretty thought, Marina told herself. But it didn't always work out that way. In asking her to marry him, Stephen was making a promise to her—a promise of commitment and love. But she'd seen how easily that kind of promise could be broken.

She wished he hadn't said any of this to her. It touched too many unhappy places deep inside her. Now, as she held the ring and he watched her hopefully, she felt trapped and scared.

"I don't know," she whispered helplessly.

"Do you need time? If I'm rushing you, I'm sorry."

Gratefully, she latched on to the temporary reprieve. "Yes, I need time."

He sighed heavily. "All right. Patience isn't one of my virtues, but I'll try to be patient for as long as I can."

"Just . . . just let me get through the final draft of the script. Please."

The pleading note in her voice tore at him. Gathering her to him, he whispered against her cheek, "Oh, Marina, I'm such a fool. When I want something I think I should have it immediately. And I've never wanted anything as I want you."

She buried her face in his chest, feeling the softness of his velour robe.

He went on tenderly, "All right, sweetheart. I'll wait until the script's finished. But I warn you, I'll hound you to get it done even faster now. And in the meantime I want you to keep that ring."

She looked up at him. "Stephen, I can't."

He placed a fingertip against her lips. "Hush, now. You don't have to wear it. Just keep it until we talk about this again."

Before she could argue further, he continued. "And now we'd better get going. It's a long drive up to Clovis. We can grab some breakfast on the way."

As they went into the bedroom to dress, Marina's mind was whirling. She honestly had not expected a proposal. She knew that Stephen cared for her, and she had to admit to herself she cared for him—more than was safe. But marriage...

Neither spoke very much on the trip north. They drove for four hours through the barren Tehachapi Mountains and into the San Joaquin Valley. Usually the valley was covered by a dense layer of fog at that time of year. Fortunately, this was a sunny day. The valley stretched for hundreds of miles northward, as far as the eye could see. The richest agricultural area in the world, it was a patchwork quilt of fields, orchards and vineyards. To the east, the towering Sierra Nevada were snowcapped. To the west, the lower coast range was dry and brown.

When they arrived in Clovis, Marina directed Stephen to her mother's house. This was a new home and Marina had never been there before. But Clovis was so small, she had no trouble finding the address.

"Nice house," Stephen commented as they pulled into the curved front drive. A two-story brick colonial, the house was warm and inviting, with lacy curtains and white shutters at the windows.

As soon as he turned off the engine, the front door opened and Marina's mother, Caroline, came out onto the front steps to greet them. She looked wonderful, Marina thought, younger and happier than she had looked in quite a while. Though Marina was reluctant to admit it, it was obvious that her mother was very happy in her new marriage.

When she got out of the car, Marina stepped into her warm embrace. But in the background she noticed Rafe, standing a few feet behind Caroline, watching her intently.

When Stephen came around the car, Marina introduced him to her mother.

"So pleased to meet you," Caroline said happily. "When Marina called yesterday and said you were coming up with her, I was so glad. It's a long trip to make by herself."

"It was my pleasure, Mrs. Marin."

"Caroline, please. And this is my husband, Rafe."

Rafe stepped forward to take Stephen's outstretched hand. Watching them, Marina caught a startled look on Stephen's face as he looked from Rafe to her and back again. He had seen the strong resemblance and was puzzled by it, though he was careful not to comment on it.

Rafe turned to Marina. "I'm glad you could come. Why don't we go inside where it's warm."

Despite her hostility toward him, she was grateful that he was being reserved. If he'd expected her to hug him, or even shake his hand, he didn't show it. But that reserve didn't extend to his eyes. Those gray eyes that were a mirror image of her own watched her with a deep, compelling sadness.

Inside, in a comfortable den where a brightly burning fire crackled cheerfully, Caroline had laid out hors d'oeuvres and drinks. There was hot mulled wine, coffee and tea. Both Stephen and Marina accepted coffee. After serving them, Caroline did the same for her and Rafe.

"This is a lovely home," Stephen commented politely. "It looks new."

"It is," Caroline responded proudly. "My wedding present from Rafe." Giving Marina a meaningful look, she finished, "I'm glad you're finally getting a chance to see it, darling."

For a while Rafe and Stephen talked about their respective work. Both Caroline and Rafe were fascinated by Stephen's filmmaking and asked a lot of questions about the business.

Marina leaned back in a corner of the sofa, sipping her coffee and occasionally answering questions from her mother. After about an hour, Caroline said, "Well, I'd better get the ham on the table. It should be done by now."

As she rose, Marina stood up also. "I'll help you."

"You don't have to, sweetheart. Why don't you stay and visit with the men?"

"No, I'd like to help," Marina insisted. She knew her mother wanted her to talk to Rafe, but she wasn't about to.

Caroline gave in gracefully. "All right, dear. The kitchen's this way."

In the kitchen Marina helped her mother finish the last minute preparations for the elaborate meal.

"I like your Stephen Kramer," Caroline said.

"He isn't mine," Marina insisted.

"Oh?" Caroline looked surprised. "But I thought—that is, the way he looks at you I thought you might be involved."

"We're involved in making a movie together. That's all. I'm not interested in any other kind of involvement."

"Still, it was awfully nice of him to drive you up here today."

"Well, we're friends," Marina admitted reluctantly.

Caroline gave her a knowing look. "He's quite attractive, isn't he? And surprisingly nice. So often really handsome men aren't nice. They don't have to be."

Marina didn't rise to the bait. Instead, she asked, "How's the shop?"

"Just great. Marcia and I are thinking of expanding. The market for our copies of antique porcelain dolls is growing."

"Good. I knew you'd do well. I've always loved your dolls. By the way, how's Marcia?"

"She's very happy in her new marriage." Giving Marina a meaningful look, Caroline added, "And so am I."

When Marina didn't respond, Caroline went on, "Your father's very good to me, darling. He's made me happier than I ever dreamed I could be."

"I'm glad for you, Mom. Really. But that doesn't mean that I must have anything to do with him."

"He's your father, Marina."

"No, he's the man who is biologically responsible for me. He has never been my father."

Tears came to Caroline's eyes. Seeing them, Marina felt horribly guilty. Perversely, she blamed it all on Rafe. Somehow it was all his fault.

"Mom, let's drop the subject, okay? I don't want to argue about it."

Caroline wiped the corners of her eyes. "I don't, either. I'm just so glad you're here. All right, I won't mention it any more today."

"Good. That will be easier on both of us."

They carried the food into the dining room, where the table was formally set with pristine white linen, silver and crystal. Caroline called for the men to join them.

All in all, it wasn't as difficult a meal as Marina had feared it might be. She concentrated on talking to her mother and said very little to her father. Stephen and Rafe talked easily and seemed to be getting along famously.

Afterward, Rafe invited Stephen to join him in a walk around the neighborhood, while Marina went to Caroline's workroom to see some new dolls she was making.

Outside the day was crisp and bright. Rafe and Stephen had put on their jackets over their sweaters and slacks, and they shoved their hands deep into the pockets to keep them warm. The more they talked, the more Stephen liked Rafe. He couldn't understand why Marina disliked her stepfather so much. Rafe seemed decent and sensitive. He and Stephen had a lot in common—both were self-made men whose ambition had propelled them from the bottom of society to the top. And both adored Turner women.

As Rafe talked about Caroline, it was apparent how much he loved her. Though he didn't say so, somehow Stephen sensed there was a special drama to their relationship.

At one point Rafe said to Stephen, "It was good of you to drive Marina up here. I've made that trip a lot of times and I know how miserable it is. There's nothing between here and Los Angeles but uninteresting country. Especially once you reach the mountains. They're downright barren."

"I didn't mind. To be honest, I was glad to have an excuse to meet Marina's parents."

Rafe gave Stephen a shrewd look. "You're more than just her boss, I take it."

Stephen nodded. "Yes. I've asked her to marry me. I hope that's okay with you and Caroline."

Rafe smiled warmly. "It's okay with me. And if you promise to make Marina happy, it'll be okay with Caroline."

"I'm definitely going to make her happy. Or try, anyway. The problem is getting her to agree to the idea."

Rafe stopped and shot a startled look at Stephen. "You mean she said no?"

"Not exactly. She's not too hot on marriage at the moment. But I intend to change her mind."

They continued walking, and Rafe was silent for a few minutes. Stephen sensed he was trying to make a decision about something that was very difficult. Finally Rafe said slowly, "There's something I think you should know."

They stopped walking, and Stephen turned to face Rafe.

Rafe went on, "I wouldn't tell you this if you weren't in love with Marina. But since you are, and since you're having a hard time because of her feelings about marriage, I think you should know where those feelings come from."

"She told me about her parents' divorce," Stephen said. "I get the feeling she's pretty bitter about it."

"Yes, she is. Caroline's husband didn't handle the situation with a great deal of sensitivity. One day he announced he was leaving, and that was that. He was completely involved with his new girlfriend, to the exclusion of everyone else, including Marina."

"So he not only divorced Caroline, he divorced Marina, too."

Rafe nodded. "I wasn't around then, but from what Caroline has told me, Marina was devastated. Her feelings toward men became less trusting."

"I can certainly understand why," Stephen commented with feeling.

"Yes, and you'll understand even more when I tell you what else happened."

"There was more?"

"Yes." Rafe hesitated. Clearly, what was to come was difficult for him to say. He forced himself to go on. "You see, even though Caroline and I were only married a few months ago, we actually met for the first time in high school. We fell deeply in love then, but our parents opposed the match. Her father was a banker, socially prominent, very conservative. He didn't want his daughter involved with a poor Mexican-American gardener's son."

"Why did your parents oppose it?"

"My father was frightened of the power someone like Mr. Cummings could wield. He thought I would be hurt. As it turned out he was right. Caroline and I were both hurt."

As Stephen's eyes met Rafe's clear gray ones, a vague idea began to take shape. Earlier he had noticed the black hair, so like Marina's . . . and the stubborn tilt to the chin . . . and suddenly he knew.

"You're Marina's father," he whispered.

Rafe met his look without flinching. "Yes. But I saw her for the first time only this summer."

"What happened?"

"It's a complicated, unhappy story. Our parents managed to make each of us believe the other didn't care. Caroline's parents moved out of town and took her with them.

She had Marina and eventually married someone else. Marina grew up thinking that man was her father.''

"But now she knows the truth?"

"Oh, yes. I met Caroline again at our twenty-fifth high school reunion. Eventually we unraveled the truth about the past. It was terrible and wonderful—we had found each other again, after all those lost, lonely years. And I had found the daughter I didn't even know I had. But . . .''

"But Marina wouldn't accept you as her father," Stephen finished for him.

Rafe nodded. "Caroline and I both talked to her, tried to explain. But she's so hurt and confused. She doesn't want to trust me. And I can't blame her."

"She doesn't want to trust me, either," Stephen said soberly.

Rafe's expression grew concerned. "That's why I'm telling you all this. I don't want to see Marina miss her chance for happiness, the way Caroline and I did for so long, because she's afraid to love."

For a moment both men were silent. Then Stephen said slowly, "I'm very grateful to you for telling me this. It explains a lot."

"What will you do now?"

"Make her understand that she's got to learn to trust again. She can't live the rest of her life in a shell. She has too much to give. My own feelings aside, it wouldn't be good for her."

"No. I want my daughter to have all the happiness she can."

"Well, I'm going to try to give it to her."

Rafe smiled. "Good luck."

"Thanks. I'll need it. That's one stubborn, headstrong young woman. But she's the woman I love. And I won't lose her."

"I hope not," Rafe replied, his smile fading. "Well, we'd better be getting back. You've got a long drive ahead of you."

As they walked back to the house, Stephen absorbed the information Rafe had just given him. As he'd said, it explained so much that was puzzling about Marina—her struggle between being giving and holding back, and her moments of insecurity and lack of self-confidence. He realized, in a flash of insight, that she must be confused about who she really was.

He could certainly understand why her view of male-female relationships, especially marriage, was so jaded. But he was determined to change her feelings about that. He needed her trust and commitment. He wasn't willing to settle for anything less.

Back at the house he and Marina said a quick goodbye, and were on their way back down to L.A. by five o'clock. It had been a short stay in Clovis, but an informative one.

Stephen didn't tell Marina that he knew the truth of her background. He realized that she would probably be furious Rafe had said anything. If she wanted Stephen to know, she would tell him. And if she did so, it would mean she'd come a long way in opening up to him.

All it will take is time, he told himself confidently. He loved her and she loved him. There was no way they wouldn't be together.

And then he remembered what Rafe had said—how much he and Caroline had loved each other. And they had lost each other, nearly for good.

Chapter Fourteen

On January thirtieth Marina typed FADE OUT on the final draft of *Casey*. She and Stephen and Carla had gone over each draft carefully. Now they all agreed this was the final shooting script. It would be turned over to Marty, who would decide the most economical order for the scenes to be shot.

That night Marina and Stephen went out to dinner at a charming little restaurant on the Malibu Pier. The atmosphere was warm and inviting—red-checked tablecloths, candles, fresh flowers—and the food was delicious. They talked about the script and the way the shooting schedule was shaping up. Stephen and Carla had finally cast the picture, and Marina was happy with their choices.

It was an absolutely perfect evening. As they drove home afterward, Marina leaned her head against Stephen's shoulder and fantasized about what it would be like when they made love, as they surely would.

But when they got home, Stephen didn't lead Marina directly to the bedroom. Instead, he turned on the light in the living room, lit a fire, then motioned to her to join him on the sofa.

As she sat down next to him, he began easily, "The question is: What next?"

Marina was confused. "What do you mean?"

"I mean, what next? The screenplay's done, Carla will be leaving for location shortly. What happens with you and me now?"

"Oh."

"Yes. *Oh.* I told you I didn't want you to leave when the script was finished. I told you I want to marry you. You know what I want. I need to know what you want."

"It sounds stupid, but I haven't given it any thought. I was so preoccupied with the screenplay...."

Her words trailed off helplessly. She'd purposefully put Stephen's proposal at the back of her mind. The ring—that fabulous ring—was carefully stowed in her suitcase.

"The screenplay's finished," Stephen repeated firmly. "I did as you asked and waited until now to ask you again. Will you marry me?"

Marina felt intensely uncomfortable. She knew that Stephen had been more than patient. She knew he had every right to bring up the subject of marriage again. But, perversely, she wished he hadn't. Everything had been so nice and simple before this, she thought irritably.

"Marina, it takes two to have a dialogue. I seem to be talking to myself."

"I'm sorry. I was thinking."

"There's not a great deal to think about. I love you. I want to marry you and have children with you, and maybe even make more movies with you. Either you want the same thing or you don't."

"Stephen, that's not fair. I want to be with you—"

His control snapped. "Damn it, Marina, do you realize that you never say *I love you*. You say everything else—you want me, you need me, you adore me. But never *that*."

"Why does it matter? It's only words."

"It's a lot more than words. And you know it." As she turned her face away, he ordered, "Look at me. Where do we go from here?"

"Why can't we go on as we are? Things are perfect...."

"Almost perfect. I'm not willing to settle for almost."

She had a hair-trigger temper, and now it snapped. "Why does it have to be marriage? Because you want to own me, to control me as long as it's convenient for you?"

"I can't own you any more than you can own me! And if I wanted control, I would have married some empty-headed starlet who would let me call the shots in return for supporting her well."

"I don't want to be married," Marina insisted. "I don't want to give everything to you, then have you turn your back on me when someone else comes along."

Stephen exploded. "Damn it, listen to yourself! Do you realize what you're saying? Just because it happened to your mother, doesn't mean it's bound to happen to you."

"No? Can you guarantee that?"

"There are no guarantees, and you know it. All I can tell you is that I've never loved another woman as I love you. I don't expect I will ever love anyone else as I love you. I'm offering you commitment, and I need the same thing from you."

Marina's voice was small and helpless. "Well, I can't give it. I'll live with you, as long as it's what we both want. But I won't marry you."

The silence between them was so highly charged it was as if a live wire was swinging in an arc through the room.

Then Stephen said slowly, "I know that Rafe is your father."

For a moment Marina just sat there, stunned. Then she whispered, "What?"

"I know. Everything. I wasn't going to tell you, because I knew you'd probably get mad that he told me the truth. But now I think we have to talk about it. Because that's what's really at the bottom of your refusal to get married."

"How dare he! He had no right to talk to you about something so personal...."

"Damn it, that's what marriage is! It's personal. It's being open with each other, sharing all the secrets, the good ones and the bad."

"And what if I don't want to share my secrets?"

"If you don't, it's because you don't trust me. And if you don't trust me, our relationship can't work, on any level."

"Maybe it can't."

As soon as she'd spoken the words, she regretted them. She wanted to reach out and pull them back, to pretend she'd never said them. But once spoken, they couldn't be recalled.

Stephen's angry expression was tinged with sadness now. He said nothing for a long moment, then he replied slowly, "If it can't work, it's because you won't let it. Because you won't let go of the past."

"What do you mean let go of the past? I don't want to think about the past, I don't want it to be part of my life in any way."

"Well, you can't let go of it until you face it and resolve it. Your parents made mistakes. Well, welcome to the club. We all do. I think they suffered for it more than you have, despite what you think."

"What do you know about it?" Marina was shaking with anger, and it was all she could do to fight back tears of outrage and pain.

"I know your father loves you. You would probably love him if you'd give yourself a chance. He's a decent man."

"I don't care!" she shouted.

"No, you don't care. You don't really care about any-one. You're an emotional cripple who can give only so much and no more. And you'll always be that way until you come to terms with your father."

Marina was icy with shock and anger. Standing up, she glared at Stephen as she backed away from him. Her breath came quickly and her voice was laden with emotion. He rose and made a move to step toward her but she pushed him away.

"I don't need your amateur analysis, thank you! I'm leaving. *Now.* I'd appreciate it if you'd send my things to me."

He stared at her, his face pale, his eyes blazing with pain and anger. "Damn you, Marina, will you listen to me?"

"No, I've listened to too much already. All I want is to get away from here and never see you again!"

She grabbed her jacket and purse and ran out of the room, slamming the front door behind her.

For a moment Stephen simply stood there, unable to be-lieve what had just happened between them. *She won't really leave,* he told himself. *She'll realize she's being a damned little fool and come back.*

Then he heard the sound of her Volkswagen starting up. Hurrying outside, he was just in time to see her driving up Gull Drive, away from his house—and from him.

Sometime after midnight, Marina stopped at a motel near the freeway and spent a terrible night. Exhausted, yet un-able to sleep, she tossed and turned until dawn. Stephen's words rang in her ears, haunting her.

At dawn, she got up and drove the rest of the way to Big Sur. By the time she pulled up in front of Rosie's house, it was nearly noon. She looked wretched and felt worse. It was all she could do to drag herself up the steps to knock at Ro-sie's front door.

There was an excited yapping as Homer got to the door first, then Rosie herself was there.

"Marina! For heaven's sakes, child, what's happened to you? Come in here."

She sat Marina on a chair in the kitchen, then poured her a cup of black coffee. After Marina had drunk it, and started on a second, she finally said in a tired voice that sounded oddly unlike her own, "I left Stephen."

"You did what? Why?"

Briefly, Marina told her of their argument, leaving out the more painful portions. But Rosie was good at reading between the lines, and by the time Marina's brief recital was over, she knew exactly what had happened.

"Oh, child, my heart goes out to you. I can see how miserable you are. And this is probably no time to say it, but I'm going to anyway. You're wrong. You're terribly wrong."

"I hate him," Marina insisted in a broken voice.

"No, you don't hate Stephen. You hate your father. You're just taking it out on Stephen."

"Rosie, I don't want to hear this. I'm going back to my place."

But as she started to get up, Rosie put a hand on her shoulder and gently pushed her down again.

"I know you don't want to hear it. But you've got to. I can't sit back and watch you make the same mistake I made."

"What are you talking about?"

Rosie sighed heavily. Then she went on slowly, picking her words carefully. "It was a long time ago. More than twenty years now. I don't ever talk about it and most people don't know about it. It was after I was divorced."

Marina was stunned. "I didn't know you were divorced. I didn't even know you were married."

Rosie smiled sadly. "Like I said, I don't talk about it. It's in the past, and I don't like to dwell on that. It's better to live for today. But I learned something then that you need to learn now, before you lose the man who truly loves you."

"I don't love him. I don't ever want to see him again."

"Maybe you feel that way now. But you won't always. Someday you'll have regrets—bitter regrets. Just like I do. It took me a long time to put that bitterness behind me. And even now sometimes it'll sneak up on me and start eating away at me again."

Despite herself, Marina was fascinated. She'd never heard Rosie talk this way before. "What... what happened?"

Rosie leaned back in her chair. Absently, one hand stroked Homer's ear. But her eyes were on Marina.

"My marriage was terrible," she began bluntly. "He drank, beat me, ran around. My parents told me divorce was a scandal and I'd better try to make my marriage work. But there was no way I could. Finally, when I couldn't take any more, I divorced him."

"But you did the right thing," Marina insisted.

"Course I did. I should've walked out right away. But I didn't. Anyway, at first I was just so happy not to be miserable anymore, I didn't think about the possibility of ever getting married again. Then I met a man...."

Marina smiled wryly. "Famous last words."

"Yes. He was a good man. I never knew a man could be as gentle as he was. He loved me and wanted to marry me. But I wouldn't do it. I liked being single, and from what I knew about marriage, I didn't want to try that again."

"What happened?"

"After a while, he gave up trying to get through to me. He married someone else, someone who had the sense to realize what a prize he was. They've been married for twenty years now, and that woman still looks like the happiest woman in the county."

"Oh, Rosie, I'm so sorry."

"I don't want your pity, Marina. That's not why I told you the story. I want you to learn from my mistake. I've got a good life. But it could have been so much better if I'd put the past behind me and not let it destroy my future with that man."

"I understand what you're saying to me, Rosie. But I don't want to get married. I don't think I'll ever marry. Stephen was right about one thing. I can't trust. And as long as I feel that way, our relationship wouldn't work."

"Marina, I know you. I know that beneath that tough, independent facade, you're vulnerable. You just try to hide it to protect your gentle heart. But I also know that you're stronger than you think. You can handle whatever life hands you no matter how bad it is. If things didn't work with you and Stephen, you'd survive. But you'll never know if they will or not if you don't take a chance."

Slowly, Marina shook her head.

Rosie looked intensely disappointed. "Think it over, child. There's still time. The man loves you. He's not gonna stop loving you overnight."

Marina leaned over and gave Rosie a big hug. "Thank you," she whispered. "For the coffee."

"What about the advice?"

"I'm afraid I can't use it."

She stood, gave Rosie one last grateful smile, then left.

The days passed with almost unbearable slowness. Marina tried to bury herself in her writing, but it didn't work. The words wouldn't come. Finally, she gave up and put her second novel aside. She threw herself into physical labor—making another quilt, cooking, cleaning, chopping wood.

Every day she borrowed one of Rosie's horses and went for a long ride alone back into the hills and canyons. But no matter how busy she tried to stay, it didn't keep her from thinking about Stephen. It was better this way, she told herself. He wanted more than she could give. It wouldn't have worked between them. After he calmed down from their argument, he probably saw it the same way.

He didn't call or write. For that she was grateful. It would have been too painful to hear from him again, even in a letter.

Still, when her suitcase arrived with all her things in it, she was surprised and hurt. He'd only done exactly as she'd asked him to do. But somehow she wished he hadn't done it.

In Los Angeles, Stephen drove himself and the people who worked with him unmercifully. One day his secretary came out of his office, after being yelled at for a minor mistake. Running into Marty, she asked, "What's wrong with him lately, anyway? He was really mellowing out there for a while. Now, he's worse than ever."

Marty, who knew about Stephen's argument with Marina, merely shook his head. Silently he wished there was something he could do. But Stephen had made it clear he didn't want Marty to try to fix things. This was between him and Marina. And one of them would have to fix it—if it was fixable.

Stephen stayed late at the office every night because he couldn't bear to go back to that lonely, empty house. When he did go back, he lay in bed, wide awake, till long past midnight. With every ounce of his being, he wanted to go to Marina, to persuade her, to force her if necessary, to come back to him.

But he knew that wouldn't work. She had to come to him. If she couldn't, then there was no hope for them. So he didn't call and didn't write, though it was agony not to pick up the phone. He packed her belongings and shipped them to her, without so much as a note.

But as the days stretched into weeks, he began to feel that there was no hope for them anyway.

On a sunny, warm March morning when the hills were carpeted with wildflowers and the trees were green, Marina heard a strange car drive up outside her door. For an instant, her heart leaped. But when she anxiously looked out the window, she saw that it was a Jaguar, not a jeep.

Beating back intense disappointment, she opened the door. And found her father standing there.

He was alone. Caroline wasn't with him.

Marina felt one emotion after another take hold of her—surprise, confusion, irritation, resentment.

"May I come in, Marina?" he asked politely.

She didn't want him in her home, but she didn't feel she could refuse to let him enter. Without speaking, she stepped aside, holding the door open for him.

He came in and looked around approvingly. "Nice little place. I can see you've done a lot with it."

She murmured a barely polite thank-you, then waited for him to explain this unannounced, unwanted visit.

Seeing her impatience, he came straight to the point.

"Until now, your mother has run interference for me. She's been a go-between, trying to smooth things out between you and me. But I realized that I was going to have to approach you on my own."

"And if I don't want to be approached?"

"I'm sure you don't. Even though you didn't grow up around me, you are still my daughter. You're more like me than you probably like to think. I understand some things about you, including your temper. Because it's just like mine."

"I don't want to talk to you, Rafe. You're wasting your time."

She could see that he noticed her use of his name, instead of calling him Father. A pained look crossed his face, then he went on stubbornly, "Well, you don't have any choice. You're going to listen to me whether you like it or not."

Realizing that this confrontation was unavoidable, Marina said tightly, "All right, get it over with. Then leave."

"You think I abandoned you and your mother."

"Yes."

"She tried to tell you what happened, but you wouldn't believe her."

"If she chooses to believe your story, that's her business. I don't believe it."

"It's the truth." He said the words so simply that Marina was taken aback. She'd expected vehemence, not a quiet statement like that.

"Prove it," she shot back.

"I can't prove it. Some things you have to take on faith."

Marina's smile was utterly without humor. "That's a convenient argument, but I don't buy it."

"Do you remember the first time we met, accidentally, outside your mother's old house?"

"Yes, what about it?"

"As soon as you told me your name, I realized you were my daughter. Didn't you wonder why I stared at you as if you were a ghost?"

She had wondered, but she wouldn't admit so now.

When she refused to answer, he went on, "I stared at you because I realized that Caroline didn't give you up for adoption as her father had told me. I realized that she kept our child, even though I'd been told she'd given it up because she wanted nothing to do with it. And I realized if that was the case, then maybe she had really loved me after all."

"Whether that's true or not, it has nothing to do with my feelings about you," Marina insisted.

Rafe answered angrily, "It's time you stopped thinking about your own feelings and started thinking about other people's. Do you have any idea what I went through, thinking that the girl I loved hated me for getting her pregnant? Thinking that somewhere out there I had a child—I didn't know if it was a girl or a boy—and I would never see it? Some other man would love that child. I wouldn't have the chance."

He stopped and his voice was hoarse as he continued slowly, "Every single day of my life I wondered where you were, if you were happy, if you were even alive. I had nightmares about you needing me and me not being there. It was hell. And it lasted for twenty-five years."

Marina was shaken by the naked emotion in his voice. And though she didn't want to be, she was touched. But she fought that feeling. She didn't want to feel sorry for him.

"Well, there were times when I needed you," she shot back furiously. "My father—the man I thought was my father—was too busy for me. I knew he didn't really love me. Children sense these things. And I wondered what I'd done to make him not love me. I thought if I could just be a perfect little girl, maybe he would love me."

Her voice broke and she couldn't go on. She'd never admitted these feelings to anyone, not even her mother. Facing them now was terrible.

"Oh, my God," Rafe whispered. "Marina, I'm so sorry I wasn't there for you. I wanted to be. Please believe that I wanted to be."

Marina dried her eyes on her sleeve. "Well, it doesn't matter now, does it? I mean, it's a little late."

"I couldn't be there for you when you fell off a bike or when a boy you liked didn't call. But I can be there for you now. I am your father. I love you more than my own life. I can still help you, if you'll let me."

She stood there, rigid, not responding. Within her, years of unhappiness were jumbled up with anger and resentment and a childish wish that somehow everything could magically be made all right.

Rafe finished in a whisper, "I need you. I want you to need me."

He stood there for a long moment, waiting for her to say something, do something, in some way respond to him. When she made no move at all and maintained an immobile expression, he shook his head sadly.

Then he turned and walked toward the door.

Watching him, Marina realized that for the second time in her life she was losing her father. Only this time, it didn't have to happen, she could stop it. If only she had the courage to cast off the chains of unhappiness from the past.

As he opened the door and started to walk outside, she said in a choked whisper. "Dad."

He stopped, unsure he'd heard what he hoped he'd heard.

She repeated in a slightly louder voice, "Daddy."

He whirled around and saw her standing there in the center of the small room. She wanted to go to him, but her feet seemed rooted to the spot. And so he came to her, crossing the room in three long strides and taking her in his arms.

And as he held her, she cried like a baby, and the years of unhappiness were shed.

Later, they sat at the table, drinking strong, hot tea and smiling at each other. Then Rafe said, "Your mother's up at Rosie's. Why don't we go up there? Rosie said something about baking some cookies."

Marina laughed. Not because it was funny, but because suddenly she was very, very happy and the slightest thing seemed amusing. "There'll be cookies if Homer doesn't get to them first."

"Homer?"

She smiled. "I'll introduce you."

As they rose, her father said, "There's just one more thing." He took a small box from his pocket and handed it to her. As soon as she saw it, she knew what it was. She'd seen that black velvet box before.

As she looked at it in surprise, her father explained. "I talked to Stephen. He told me what happened between you two. That's what really prompted me to come up here now. I couldn't let you two lose each other the way your mother and I lost each other for so long."

Marina opened the lid of the box, and stared at the ring. It was just as dazzling as the first time she'd seen it.

Her father continued, "Stephen gave this to me to give to you. If you want it."

"Gave it to you?"

"Yes. He's here, you know. In Big Sur. But he's only here for today to check on the movie."

Marina stood staring down at the ring...remembering how Stephen had felt lying next to her after they'd made love, remembering how vulnerable he'd been when he'd told her about Beth, remembering how strong and fierce and passionate he was.

She looked up at her father. "I'm afraid the cookies will have to wait."

He smiled and his gray eyes met hers in perfect understanding. "They're shooting at the West Wind," he explained. "Your mother and I will wait here for you."

Standing on tiptoe, she kissed his cheek. Then she ran out to her car and disappeared down the road in a cloud of dust.

The West Wind Restaurant was surrounded by all the paraphernalia of moviemaking: a crew of fifty people, trucks with wardrobes, electrical equipment, catering supplies and portable dressing rooms. It was organized chaos, as Stephen had once said.

As she parked, then walked toward the restaurant, Marina saw Carla sitting in the director's chair, going over something with Marty. When she drew closer, Carla saw her and beamed in surprise. "Marina! Where have you been? It's about time you dropped by the set. I've got a little break now, want to have coffee?"

Just then Marina saw Stephen standing a few yards away. Watching her, Marty smiled broadly. Then he said to Carla, "Look, why don't you and I finish going over this, then you can visit with Marina. I think she wants to talk to Stephen right now, anyway."

Catching the look that passed between Marina and Stephen, Carla said slowly, "Sure...whatever..."

He looks wonderful, Marina thought, her eyes on Stephen. Just the same. And wonderful.

His expression was guarded, but hopeful. Suddenly she realized he wouldn't come to her. She would have to go to him. There were only a few yards separating them now, but she would have to cross them.

Slowly, she walked toward him. And when she was standing directly in front of him, she held up her left hand. On her ring finger, the diamond solitaire glinted brilliantly in the bright spring sunshine.

The guarded look left his face. In those deep, cobalt-blue eyes there was only intense happiness.

Behind her, Marina heard Carla exclaim, "Would you look at that rock. Marina, where'd you get it?"

But she didn't turn around to answer. Just now all her attention was on Stephen. And she knew that was right where it would remain.

Silhouette Special Edition

COMING NEXT MONTH

AN UNEXPECTED PLEASURE—Lucy Hamilton
Cate and Jesse had been childhood friends, but hadn't seen each other for years. Chance brought them together again, seemingly forever. Then betrayal threatened to tear them apart.

HEART OF THE EAGLE—Lindsay McKenna
To ornithologist Dahlia Kincaid, Jim Tremain was like an eagle—dangerous and powerful. But he wasn't the predator he'd first seemed. Could she risk her heart for such a man?

MOMENTS OF GLORY—Jennifer West
Maggie Rand was a proud, wild, mean-tempered woman. Chance Harris knew better than to become involved. But somewhere in those velvet eyes was his future—and he couldn't turn away.

DREAM LOVER—Paula Hamilton
Her script had a message and there was no way Susan McCarthy would let some Hollywood wheeler-dealer twist it into a comedic vehicle for Bruce Powers's massive ego. But Susan had forgotten that Bruce was every woman's fantasy—including hers.

CATCH THE WIND—Caitlin Cross
It was Terminator's last chance—as well as trainer Allegra Brannigan's. Then Scott Charyn returned home to make peace with his father, and Allegra began to feel that she had another chance—this time at love.

TUCKERVILLE REVIVAL—Monique Holden
Tuckerville was a perfect example of a sleepy little town. But the town was fading, and Mayor Rhetta Tucker knew she had to save it. Then Bates McCabe buzzed into town—with a plan that could save them all.

AVAILABLE NOW: